PAWNS OF JUSTICE

PAWNS OF JUSTICE

A Novel

By the Author of *Broken Gavel*
Nicholas A. Clemente

iUniverse, Inc.
New York Lincoln Shanghai

PAWNS OF JUSTICE

iUniverse books may be ordered through booksellers or by contacting:

iUniverse
2021 Pine Lake Road, Suite 100
Lincoln, NE 68512
www.iuniverse.com
1-800-Authors (1-800-288-4677)

This is a work of fiction. All of the characters, names, incidents, organizations and dialogue in this novel are either the products of the author's imagination or are used fictitiously.

ISBN-13: 978-0-595-39636-8 (pbk)
ISBN-13: 978-0-595-84039-7 (ebk)
ISBN-10: 0-595-39636-4 (pbk)
ISBN-10: 0-595-84039-6 (ebk)

Printed in the United States of America

For Ann Marie
…This sweet wee wife o' mine.

CHAPTER 1

▼

Although they were attacking by sea, they were not Vikings storming ashore. Their weapon was neither axe nor sword, but stealth. Pete and Eugene were assassins.

Their target was a home on National Drive, a street that wended through upper middle class homes in Bergen Beach, Brooklyn, New York. An inlet ran along the rear of the homes, and small boats were tied at most of the backyard docks.

It was well past midnight and no notice was taken of two men in a john boat, with its electric motor, as it traversed the inlet. Eugene cut the engine and the boat silently glided to a dock. Pete pushed aside the sleek Chris Craft that was moored there. The dock swayed slightly under their weight as they alighted.

"Don't splash, damn it!" Pete said. The cool night air made Pete shiver slightly.

"How do you expect me to get out of this rowboat without getting wet?" Eugene said.

"By being careful."

"You sure this is the house?"

"Shut up, Eugene! What if it ain't? We kill the wrong guy?" He chuckled and rubbed his neck where his black turtleneck sweater itched him.

"I need a smoke," Eugene said.

"We're breaking into a house, idiot. I don't need your cough waking up the whole goddamned neighborhood."

"I don't have a cough."

"Yeah, and you don't have wet sneakers. Get off the grass, you'll leave footprints."

"What if they got a back-up security system, Pete?"

"You're always worrying. You saw what we did. It'll work, trust me." Pete had already, by the simplest of means, neutralized the burglar alarm.

Earlier, at around eight p.m., he had thrown a brick through Dr. DiTucci's front picture window. This had set off the alarm. Inside there had been no activity.

Then they had waited. First the Security Patrol had arrived, followed by the Police, who then checked the house. They would notify Dr. DiTucci, who would either return home to reactivate the alarm, or ask the Security firm to board up the front window and shunt the zone in the living room. DiTucci had not returned and Pete, from his car well down the street, had watched the security men patch the window and leave.

Now Pete and Eugene went around to the front of the home. They pried open the sheet of plywood and slipped into the living room.

When they entered the home, they donned night vision glasses.

"In the old days, all we needed was a small crow bar," Eugene said. "Now look at us."

"State of the art. Got to keep up."

Pete surveyed the center hallway and spotted the alarm control panel. With his small set of tools he quickly disabled the system.

"You hit the nail on the head, Pete. I never seen motion detectors in a front hallway."

"The trick ain't in disabling the alarm," Pete said. "The trick is putting it back so it don't look tampered with."

"Why do they want it to look like an accident?"

"Beats me," Pete said. "Who the hell cares?"

"Well, it bothers me," Eugene said. Shouldn't we check upstairs?"

"Nah, the wife and kid are on vacation. Why you think the Doc ain't home yet?" Pete said. He was heavier than Eugene but just as quick in his movements.

"Ain't anybody faithful, anymore?" Eugene said.

"Maybe he's doing a heart transplant at midnight."

"He's transplanting something." Eugene laughed and rasped his smoker's cough.

They wandered through the well furnished home.

"Drexel dining room suite," Eugene said. He ran his fingers along the table. He wiped away the mark he made in a sweeping motion and then realized that he did not have to be concerned about fingerprints. Both were wearing latex gloves.

"Drexel, my ass. It's Ethan Allen. The chandelier is Waterford, though." Pete was proud of his keen eye, especially for other people's valuables.

"Too bad we're not here to rob the place. My mother loves Lladros." Even in the eerie reddish light, Eugene was able to accurately appraise a porcelain figurine.

"Put it down. You might drop it!" Pete's voice was harsh.

"So what if I drop it?"

"The noise, you dummy! Some nosy neighbor might be walking a dog."

They stopped in the living room to check the photographs on the mantle.

"That's him. Dr. Gabriel DiTucci." Pete pointed.

"He looks like a smart man," Eugene said. He picked up a photograph of a slim man with a walrus moustache, wearing a cap and gown.

"I think I'm going to grow a moustache."

"A moustache won't make you smarter."

"No, but I'll look smarter," Eugene said. He touched his imaginary moustache.

"He's no smarter than you. You never made it past seventh grade but you got a lot in common and don't even know it."

"What's that?"

"You're both killers." Pete laughed. "Doctors get away with it, that's all."

They walked through the foyer and opened the side door that led to the garage. It was neat and empty.

The two men returned to the living room and sat down on the sofa.

"What time he usually come home?" Eugene said.

"You're the one that checked him out, didn't you?"

"He's late tonight. He's never been later than half-past one," Eugene said.

"He's not late yet." Pete looked at the mantle clock. It had just struck One.

As if talking about it made it happen, a blue Mercedes pulled into the driveway. The sound of the garage door opening in the late night quiet, seemed louder than clanking chains. Pete motioned to Eugene. They moved to the interior garage door. When they heard the car pull into the garage, and the door grinding close, they entered the garage.

Dr. DiTucci was half way out of his car when he saw them. He was a slightly overweight man. His bushy moustache was now salt and pepper gray.

"What? What do you want?"

"Get back in the car," Pete said. His pistol was in his hand.

The Doctor returned to his car and sat down. He clutched the steering wheel with both hands.

Pete opened the rear door and sat directly behind the Doctor. For a brief moment, Pete thought he might have the wrong man. DiTucci was heavier than the picture on the mantle.

"Had anything to drink, Doc?"

"A little. Look I have a watch and cash. About eight hundred dollars. Take it." He pushed his arm forward to show the Rolex. "Just leave me the credit cards, O.K.?"

"Start the car," Pete said.

DiTucci turned on the ignition and moved to hit the remote garage door opener. Pete, however, grabbed his hair and pulled his head back.

"Put your hands back on the wheel."

Eugene reached in and pressed a chloroform saturated cloth over DiTucci's mouth. Dr. DiTucci struggled only briefly.

Pete then closed the car windows. He checked the gas gauge.

"Plenty of gas. By the time this guy wakes up, he'll be dead."

"Not bad. Liquor in his blood and carbon monoxide in his lungs." Eugene cast down the ends of his lips and nodded in satisfaction.

"Let's get out of here. Accident or suicide. Let them figure it out," Pete said.

"Nobody should die with eight hundred dollars in his pocket." Eugene started to grope the inert figure.

"I'm going to kick your ass, Eugene. We're here to kill DiTucci, not rob him."

Pete pushed Eugene through the door into the foyer.

"Shouldn't we at least take the Rolex?"

They departed as they had arrived, carefully reattaching the plywood to the front window. The only thing that went wrong was that Eugene had not charged the marine battery and the electric motor quit. Pete, however, was prepared for even that contingency. He made Eugene row.

CHAPTER 2

▼

The newly built Marriott Hotel, with its typical glass and polished steel, was just across the street from the New York State Supreme Court. That evening, it was the site of the Trial Counsel Association's annual dinner.

Justice Ronald Goodman looked more like a soccer player than a Judge. He was sturdily built, and although he seldom mentioned it, had, in fact, been an outstanding center forward, both in college and in a semi-professional league. His nose, over the years, at war and in play, had been broken several times. That, with his deep set eyes, encased in a boney brow, gave him a craggy look. His wide smile, however, produced pleasing folds of dimples that softened his rugged appearance. But it was his long purposeful walk, almost sideways, like John Wayne that marked him as a person who would not be inclined to give way to anyone. Thus, it seemed incongruous when he tripped as he stepped off the double-story escalator that led to the ballroom.

He fell forward and twisted to the side to avoid bumping into Christine Fisher, the lawyer who had preceded him on the escalator. His right knee struck the floor, but the sharp pain centered in his wrists, as his hands broke his fall.

Ron rose quickly, more embarrassed by his clumsiness than concerned about any injury. He checked his trouser and brushed away a slight smudge on his clothing. No tear. No damage. Perhaps, a scrape on his knee. No matter, he wiped his hands with his handkerchief. Miss Fisher was smiling. Commiserating? Or, was she mocking his age? Justice Goodman passed his hand along the side of his head as if to insure that the fall had not mussed his graying hair.

The grenade fragments still lodged in his leg, made him more susceptible to falling. He did not walk with a limp, but was nevertheless, prone to stumbling.

"Every time I get off an escalator, I feel like I'm jumping out of a plane," she said.

"Parachuting is much safer," Ron said.

"Have you ever sky-dived, Judge?"

Ron just smiled in reply.

"Yes, I heard you were some kind of war hero," she said.

"No one's a hero in war. Miss Fisher. There are only the wounded and the dead."

"Aren't trials like war? Aren't we in constant vicarious combat?"

"The losers in my court only walk away poorer..." Ron paused. "...but they walk away."

Ron gazed at her. She had tried several cases before him and, although she had the reputation of being a pugnacious adversary, she had always been courteous in Court. Nevertheless, this type of social banter from her was unexpected.

She wore a deep cut mauve cocktail dress, he a tuxedo.

"Whenever I see you, you're dressed in black. Whether it's robes or a tux." Her smile was fixed and steady, like a model posing.

Christine Fisher was in her early thirties, and although her red lipstick was a shade too bright, it went unpunished by her white, perfect teeth. Her raven hair, which was usually swept back when she appeared in Court, now flowed about her face.

Ron stiffened slightly. It was as if her unchanging smile was a signal of insincerity. It made him cautious and reminded him of the gulf between lawyer and judge. The danger of favoritism was omnipresent and rival lawyers, justified or not, always suspected partiality when the judge was too "chummy" with the adversaries. So, when the conversation extended beyond the fragile line of innocuous repartee, it was time to move on. Already, several lawyers had glanced sidelong at them as they passed by.

"Bar Association dinners are hardly the highlight of my day." He bowed slightly to Christine Fisher. Ron was slightly over six feet tall and was momentarily surprised by Christine Fisher's height. He remembered her to be comparatively tiny and now, she was almost at his eye level.

She caught his quick glance down to her spiked heels.

"I wear flats in Court. It's more comfortable."

"Yes, comfort is very important," he said. She was quick. Notices everything. Yes, she was like that at trial, too. Have to be more careful of facial expressions. No tipoffs. Didn't juries pick up on a judge's non-verbal messages? Hadn't he always known that a good judge cultivated a "poker face"?

Ron extended his hand to hers and shook it lightly. "It's a pleasure to see you, Miss Fisher. I hope you have an enjoyable evening." Ron gave his cordial, half-smile and watched her walk off. He was sure that she accentuated the movement of her hips, purposely.

The cocktail hour with its orgy of appetizers, was held in the large anteroom to the ballroom. In the center were food islands laden with shrimp, oysters, cheeses, baby lamb chops, chicken, several types of pastas and sliced melon, cantaloupe, grapes and various fruits.

Positioned about the room were mini-bars, where liquor, wine, beer and soda were served.

Ron waited in line for his martini and turned only when Justice Donovan tapped his shoulder.

"Long time, no see," Ron said.

"Not since lunch." Justice Donovan was a florid-faced Irishman. He was tall, well over six feet and weighed almost three hundred pounds. His face seemed to roll in time with his stomach as he laughed. Neither advanced age, he was nearly 75, nor his weight, had taken a toll on him.

The bartender delivered the martinis and the two judges clicked glasses.

"*Salute.*"

"Why do we come to these affairs?" Ron said and downed half his martini.

"For the free meal?" Bill Donovan said.

"Nothing is, Bill."

"Maybe, but I bought my last drink when I went on the bench," Donovan said.

"Jokes like that can get you into trouble."

"Hell, I wasn't joking," Donovan said. He laughed. What was meant to be an affectionate hug made Ron wince as he felt crushed by Donovan's huge hands.

"I keep promising myself that I've attended my last dinner and here I am again," Ron said.

"Why are you in your sour puss mode? The company's good, the drinks are free and you have lawyers tripping over themselves to be recognized. Besides, you have something better to do?"

"I could go home and surf the net."

"It's pretty lonely at home since you lost Alice, isn't it?"

"It wasn't so difficult when the kids were at home. It's gotten to the point where I can't wait to go to work in the morning and dread going home at night."

"I'm just the opposite. I have a wife to go home to."

"That's not funny, Bill." Ron shook his head sadly.

It was almost time for dinner and the room was jammed with people juggling their drinks and their appetizers.

Ron and Donovan, arm in arm, walked into the banquet hall.

The not so subtle price paid for being a guest of the Bar Association was the seating arrangement. The various judges were distributed about the room so that one or two judges were seated at tables with the paying lawyers.

A long table with white tablecloths had been erected on an elevated platform in the main room. About thirty distinguished guests, Bar Leaders and the Honoree, would march to the dais.

Light from giant chandeliers danced off the cutlery, plates and the three different types of glasses that were set on the hundred odd tables that crowded the spacious ballroom.

"What table are you at?" Donovan said.

"Table Six," Ron said.

"I'm at Thirty four."

"You're sitting with me." Ron took Donovan's arm and led him. They weaved about the room until they reached Table Six. No one was going to contest where a judge sat.

"Your Honor. It's good to see you." Manny Lentino rose from the table. He was about forty years old and thin. Lentino's most prominent feature was his deep set beady eyes and his lacquered hair that probably required daily ministrations by his barber.

"Judge Donovan is joining us," Ron said. "Is that all right?"

"Of course."

"I know Mr. Olivo," Donovan said. He pointed to the lawyer who, like the others, had risen when Ron approached the table. "That was a tough case you lost last week. Maybe next time, you'll listen to me when I tell you to settle."

Olivo reached over and shook Donovan's hand. He was dark with enormous white teeth. He was young enough so that his skin still glistened. Olivo. An appropriate name.

"It wasn't me, Judge. The insurance carrier didn't want to offer any money on the case."

The only woman at the table remained seated and when no one introduced her, she thrust out her hand to Ron.

"I'm Sarah Baruch." She wore a silver sequined gown that reflected the light at dazzling angles. The empire style of her gown, bound tightly about her bosom, showed her figure to great advantage. Her black as pitch hair was cut short and business like. It was her piercing eyes, sky-blue and framed in black make-up, much like Nefertiti, that seemed to mesmerize him.

Ron sat down and she moved to the seat next to him. Damn she smelled good. Ron caught himself staring at her. Although she looked away several times in the conversation, her gaze left no doubt of her interest.

"How long have you been on the bench?" Sarah asked Ron.

"Ten years."

"Do you enjoy it?" Her voice, low and cultivated, had a tinge of expectancy to it as if his answers would be important to her.

"It's my life's work."

"My, that's so passionate," Sarah said.

"I have been accused of that. Judge Donovan here, says that I'm much too serious." He pointed to Bill and then regretted it. He did not want to include anyone, even his friend in the conversation.

"I guess justice is a serious business." She smiled and touched his arm. It was light and almost a caress.

He stared at her as if to memorize her. High cheekbones, and perfect teeth seemed to enhance her happy smile. Maybe thirty three or thirty four. Slender body. Must have long legs. Her swan-like neck was accentuated by a pearl choker. Great clavicles. Great clavicles? Come on, Ron, he thought.

"Sarah, do I have to be a judge before you pay any attention to me?" Manny Lentino tried to sound jocular.

As if inflamed by the remark, Sarah reached over and slapped Lentino's arm. It was not a love tap.

"I hate jealousy in a man," she said.

Ron was momentarily startled by her sudden anger. There would be no amber warning light with this woman, he thought. She utilized her beauty the way a surgeon used a scalpel. Quick and neat. Beautiful women did not need an excuse for their impetuosity, did they?

She picked up a wine glass and held it toward Ron.

"Red, please," Sarah said as if she had not chastised anyone.

Ron reached over and filled her glass. It was white wine.

Sarah sipped it.

"She said red wine, stupid," Donovan said.

"Wine is wine," Sarah said and took another sip.

"I'm sorry. You caught me not listening," Ron said.

"Does that happen when you're on the bench?"

"It's very easy to tune out lawyers."

"Well, don't tune me out…" She smiled. "I'm not a lawyer."

Her perfume wafted over him. Shalimar. Ron thought of his wife. But wasn't she too young for him?

"I'm a widower. My wife died two years ago. Ovarian cancer." What in the world made me say that? What was this? True confession time? This woman was having an untoward effect—or was it the third martini?

"I know."

"You do?"

"Manny told me all about you. He thinks you're the best medical malpractice judge in Brooklyn."

"Well, I respect him, too. He's a very competent trial lawyer."

"What I don't understand is, if you're a Supreme Court Justice, how is it that you preside at trials?"

"In New York, the Supreme Court is a trial court. Our highest appellate court is the Court of Appeals.

Ron caught her blank look as though she had asked the question without really being curious and her mind, elsewhere.

"You're not too old for me," she said, as if reading his mind. His surprised look confirmed her assessment. "I'm thirty eight. What are you, fifty—fifty two? At our ages, age doesn't really matter anymore."

"You're very direct, aren't you, Miss Baruch?"

"When you see what you like, you have to seize it."

"*Carpe diem*, eh."

"Anybody can seize the day. I'm more interested in seizing what I need," Sarah said.

"And what do you need?"

"Whatever it takes to survive."

It had started out as harmless repartee but the hard look on her face made him ask, "At any cost?"

"It's a rough world," she said.

"You don't take what doesn't belong to you," Ron said.

"You know, this is all very sophomoric." Her eyes were unblinking and there was no smile on her lips. "Next, you'll be asking if the end justifies the means."

"It was nice meeting you." Ron half-rose from his seat.

"Sit down," Sarah said. "I don't believe it! You can dish it out, but you can't take it."

"You're much too pugnacious for me, Miss Baruch. All I asked you was, 'what it was that you needed'?"

"And I said, whatever it takes to survive. Do I really have to spell it out for you? I need love. I need understanding. I need companionship. And just incidentally, I need money. Lots of money that I earn. I'm not a *housfrau* who waits for some man to give me money."

"That's fair enough. You didn't have to come across like some calloused, hard-nosed neanderthal. We all have those kinds of needs."

"Is this a private fight or can anyone join in?" Bill Donovan said. He smiled, looked around the table and raised his hands in a boxer's pose.

Lentino and Olivo chuckled as if that would break the tension.

Sarah paused, then, as if deciding that the remark was not worth the interruption, ignored it.

"Can we at least agree that we have mutual needs?" Sarah said. The smile returned.

"I'm afraid you can't satisfy my most pressing need."

"And what is that?" She reached out and rested her hand on his arm.

"I'm looking for an apartment in Manhattan." Ron smiled.

"That's not a problem. I'm a real estate broker," she said.

CHAPTER 3

▼

"The wife called us," the uniformed police officer said. He pointed to the distraught light haired woman who sat on her living room sofa. "Mrs. DiTucci."

John Zangara motioned to his partner, Tom Scott, and pulled the officer out of earshot of the widow.

"Anybody touch anything?"

"Not that I know of. A neighbor said that she came home and then ran out of the house screaming."

"That car must have been running in the garage for a full day before it conked out." Zangara sniffed the air.

"I opened all of the windows. The fumes seeped into the house. The Mercedes was a diesel and stunk to high heaven."

"There was no note," Scott said. "Guy comes home drunk and falls asleep with the motor running."

"What makes you think he was drunk?"

"It's a classic case. I bet you a steak dinner that the autopsy shows alcohol."

Scott slicked back his straight blonde hair as if to call attention to Zangara's baldness. Scott was a little more than thirty five years old. His six foot frame was already a chunky 250 pounds. The weight seemed to center onto puffy cheeks and a prominent double chin. Scott was at least thirteen years younger than Zangara. He had been promoted to Detective on the spot for heroism in a highly publicized hostage rescue.

Zangara's rise was not spectacular. Eight years a cop, it took him nearly twenty years to make first grade Detective in Homicide, not counting the brief purgatory period in auto theft.

"Maybe you're right, Tommy, but let's look around a little before we jump to conclusions."

"Like interviewing the widow? She looks like some piece." He nudged Zangara.

"Let's just look around." He placed a pill under his tongue. "I got enough problems."

"You take those things, without water?" Tom Scott said.

Zangara did not reply. His bulging eyes indicated an over-active thyroid. Then there was the atrial fibrillation and the high blood pressure—forty eight and popping pills. It had to be the job. Wasn't it curious that he should love the job that made him ill? Better lose some weight before the next Departmental physical.

They walked around the exterior of the house and then into the garage. Before the Emergency Medical Service men zippered up the body bag, Zangara took another look at the body.

Dr. DiTucci's walrus moustache was caked with his dried spittle. Otherwise, he was neatly dressed.

"Any visible injuries?"

"No," said the EMS officer.

"Look, Tom? The guy's tie is still fastened up to the collar."

"So what?"

"I don't know," Zangara said. "A guy comes home drunk, the first thing he does is loosen his tie. Take a look at his neck. He probably bought the shirt when his neck size was smaller."

"Maybe the shirt shrank. Or maybe he was so drunk, he didn't care about choking."

"It's always the little things, Tom."

"Sure. Sure. Make a homicide out of this. We'll call it the case of the 'choking' collar." Scott laughed.

Zangara turned to the EMS officer.

"Can you give me an estimate as to the time of death?" Zangara said.

"Date of death would be more accurate. This guy's been dead for at least two days. If his wife hadn't come home, he'd still be here," the officer said.

"Strange that no one reported him missing," Zangara said.

"Going to make another federal case of this? He dies on Friday night. Today's Monday. Nobody looks for him over the weekend. Simple." Scott smiled triumphantly.

"What about the broken front window? I hate coincidences. And did you notice how the nails in the plywood didn't match up? Simple? I think this thing stinks—and not from car fumes," Zangara said.

"All right, so you do the arithmetic, what do you think it adds up to?"

"I don't know. Usually it's money. Was there an insurance policy? Does it pay off double indemnity on accidental death? What about suicide? What about murder?"

"You're really reaching, Jack!"

"That's the point, Tommy. You might be right but you'll never know for sure when you jump to conclusions."

"I'll still bet you the T-Bone, it was the booze."

Zangara shook his head in resignation. "Let's go talk with the wife."

The brick that had smashed through the picture window, still lay on the Persian rug. The larger pieces of broken glass had been removed and, although it was daytime, the table lamps were lit. The light cast long shadows against the boarded up window.

"Mrs. DiTucci, I'm Detective Zangara. I have to ask you some questions." His voice was gentle.

Barbara DiTucci was attractive. Deep blue eyes. Slim but not skinny. She was tan and her hair was bleached by the sun. Lithe, Zangara thought. That was the word to describe her.

She looked up at him. Her eyes were red and swollen from tears. She nodded.

"Did you know about the vandalism?"

She shook her head.

"Any recent burglary?"

"No."

"I'm terribly sorry, ma'am, but I have to ask you. Was Dr. DiTucci depressed or...?"

"Detective..." She looked up at him. She clenched her fist as if she was going to pound it on the coffee table for emphasis.

"Zangara..."

"Whatever your name is. My husband did not kill himself. He never drank, except for an occasional glass of wine. He was not drunk and he did not kill himself."

"Can you tell me when you last spoke with your husband?"

"It was Friday. Friday afternoon."

"You had no contact with him before…?"

"My husband was supposed to attend a seminar this weekend. At the Hilton, in Manhattan."

"But you didn't call?"

"I tried to reach him on his cell phone. I left a message. I expected him to call me." She wiped the tears from her cheek with a small handkerchief. "I was in the mountains with our son and he was at a convention. I was concerned when I didn't hear from him, but I wasn't really worried." Barbara DiTucci squeezed her wet handkerchief as if it would wring out her sorrow.

Beauty was indeed truth and Zangara, despite his preaching to Scott, came to the immediate conclusion that her grief was real. This woman was not faking!

"There's nothing missing and he had a substantial sum of money on him when he…died." Jack checked his notes. "It could have been an accident."

"It wasn't an accident. I just know it. My husband had enemies."

CHAPTER 4

▼

"All rise," the Court Clerk said. "The Supreme Court of the State of New York, Part 8, is now in session. Draw near, give your attention, and you shall be heard, the Honorable Ronald C. Goodman, presiding."

"Good morning, everyone," Ron said and sat down. He motioned for everyone to resume their seats.

The courtroom was an interior one. There were no windows. The florescent lights embedded in the twenty foot ceiling supplied the only light. The oak walls with their panels sections distinctly rounded, easily identified it as a structure built in the 1950's. The overhead ducts, grimy with soot, were now barely able to regulate the temperature.

The Judge's bench was elevated and centered in the rear with the witness box slightly lower to the right. Off to the same side was the jury box. On the opposite side was the Clerk's desk and the Court Reporter's chair. Two large tables for the lawyers were in the well and beyond the rail were spectator benches.

There was no doubt that in a courtroom, height was a tool of power. God might look down on man, but so did a judge in his courtroom.

The Clerk, Bob McCann, a heavy set man, had a deep authoritative voice consistent with his size. He leaned over the bench.

"Your Honor, we're still missing one juror on the case on trial, but we have lawyers here on an Order to Show Cause. They claim it's an emergency." He handed the judge a sheaf of legal papers.

Ron took a quick look at the papers, and to show his annoyance, he haphazardly tossed them down. The title to the lawsuit was unremarkable. A medical malpractice case. *"Ruth Santo and Victor Santo against Gabriel DiTucci, M.D., Aaron Spender, M.D., and Beth Torah Hospital."*

He looked up and nodded for the lawyers to approach the bench. There were three of them. Roger Firestone for the plaintiff and two defense lawyers. Christine Fisher was one of the lawyers. Manny Lentino, the other.

"What's so special about this case? Why didn't you just make a motion on notice?" Ron's voice was testy.

Ordinarily, a motion required notice to the adversary with liberal time limits, often two to four weeks before the return date. When immediate relief was necessary, then a litigant might present to the Court an Order to Show Cause. Too often, it was a lawyer's trick to have a case brought before a Judge, quickly—and out of turn. As the application for the order was *ex parte*, that is, by one side only, the case could be heard within a few days. The Order to Show Cause required a good reason for its issuance.

"Mr. Firestone has persistently violated your preliminary order for discovery. I've sent him a dozen letters but he still hasn't given me the hospital or medical authorizations," Christine Fisher said.

"And that makes it an emergency?"

Her head just about reached to the top of the bench. It occurred to him that Christine Fisher was wearing flats.

"You all know that I hate these motions. To proceed by Order to Show Cause instead of by Notice of Motion, makes me even more upset. You're all aware of your obligations as to disclosure, why can't you do it without the intervention of the Court?"

"My client is ready to be deposed at any time," said Roger Firestone. He was a large portly man with a sallow face. His forehead glistened with a thin sheen of perspiration.

"How are we supposed to examine Mrs. Santo when we can't be sure of her injuries until we have copies of all the records," Fisher said. "I represent Dr. Spender and I represented Dr. DiTucci."

"Represented?" said Ron.

"That's such a stall, Judge. It's their hospital. They have the original hospital chart," Firestone said. "Besides, I've sent them authorizations three times. Their office keeps losing them."

"Represented?" Ron repeated. He shook his head and gave a side-long glance at Firestone for ignoring his question.

"That's not the emergency, your Honor," Manny Lentino said. "Dr. DiTucci is dead! That abates the action. I think that, under the circumstances, you can't even hear this motion."

"That's true, Mr. Lentino," Ron said. "Do you want a continuance until a representative of the deceased is appointed?"

"I don't represent the deceased. I represent Beth Torah Hospital," Lentino said.

"I'll need at least two months to make the substitution," Christine Fisher said.

"Judge, I'm not interested in holding things up," Firestone said. "Dr. DiTucci was the referring doctor but he and Dr. Spender are insured by the same company."

"So…?" Fisher said.

"So, I'm willing to discontinue my action against Dr. DiTucci," Firestone said. "I'm sure Dr. DiTucci's estate will have no objection."

"With prejudice?" Christine Fisher said.

"We're not looking for any money from his widow," Firestone said. He took a Kleenex from his pocket and wiped his brow.

Ron gazed at Firestone. He couldn't be more than thirty-nine years old. His navy blue, double-breasted suit was expensively cut and fit him perfectly. His tie was jagged like a Picasso painting with vivid reds and blues. It seemed an unwritten rule. Plaintiffs' lawyers often wore flamboyant ties, while defense lawyers, as if protecting the insurance companies money, wore conservative monochromatic ties.

"I don't have any objection," Lentino said, "provided I get copies of the plaintiff's personal medical records."

"I only have to give you authorizations for them." Firestone reached down and took papers from his briefcase. "Here. Now you have them for the fourth time."

"Look," Ron said and put on his stern face. "I'm supervising disclosure in seven hundred cases. All medical or dental malpractice cases. You all know the drill. When discovery is complete, you file a Note of Issue and then I give you a date for trial." He rubbed the two inch long scar where a Viet Cong bullet had once creased his forehead. Odd, he thought. Why was he aware of the wound when he was irritated by lawyers? Or did the wound throb because it was a rainy day.

"This Order to Show Cause has delayed my present trial and caused other lawyers and litigants to wait around. It's not fair to them. Now, I want you lawyers to straighten out all your other disclosure matters—on your own. Is that understood?"

"Understood," said Lentino.

Firestone nodded.

"Let's put the discontinuance on the record," Ron said. "Let's not be purists about abated actions." He motioned to the Court Reporter, who then recorded the agreement that was dictated by Christine Fisher.

"Since there is no longer a lawsuit against Dr. DiTucci, there is no abatement. Now, counselors, can I get back to my case on trial?"

"Judge, my client is dying and I'm going to need an immediate trial," Firestone said. "That's why I consented to the discontinuance."

"When disclosure is complete and you file your Note of Issue, you can make a motion for a special preference."

"Can I do it by Order to Show Cause?" Firestone said.

Ron looked at him. Ron closed his eyes and shook his head in disbelief.

The case on trial was a small case, as malpractice cases go. The claimed injury involved an improperly inserted shunt in the right arm, preparatory to a heplock for routine dialysis.

There had been an interrupted flow of blood. Gangrene had then set in. Several fingers had been amputated and there was now, a loss of use of the arm. Then, a fasciotomy—the peeling away of the arm muscle had been performed.

The monetary value of a case was often calculated by the circumstances surrounding the injury and its permanence. Cold-blooded, as it was, since the plaintiff, Martha Johnson, was seventy eight years old, she would be awarded less that a younger person because, in effect, she would suffer for a lesser period of time.

The opening statements were lengthy and the plaintiff's lawyer, in conventional strategy, called the defendant, Dr. Peter Bellamy, as his first witness. Although it was technically direct examination, the witness was obviously hostile, and leading questions were permitted.

Dr. Bellamy, sought to justify his actions, and droned on about the difficulty of inserting a needle into the wrist in order to obtain arterial blood gases.

"Yes. I've performed this procedure many times. No…I was not successful the first time…yes, Mrs. Johnson did complain about the pain…No, I tried twice in the same arm…Yes, but she kept moving her arm."

"Dr. Bellamy, are you saying that it was Mrs. Johnson's fault?" the plaintiff's lawyer said.

"She didn't help. Mrs. Johnson is old and it's very difficult to get blood from an artery."

"Did you try the femoral artery?"

"I didn't have to," Bellamy snapped. "I got it from her radial artery!"

"How many times did you say you punctured her wrist, Dr. Bellamy?" The plaintiff's lawyer asked.

Ron looked at the clock on the far wall. Why did time always seem to drag when you're in a hurry? Why was he so anxious?

Ron looked at the clock again. It was almost 1 p.m. "Come on counselor. The witness has already answered the question…at least three times."

"I don't think he has, Judge," the lawyer said. "But if you think he has, then I have no further questions."

"Is there any cross examination?" Ron said.

"Not at this time, but I'm reserving the right to call Dr. Bellamy on my case," the defense lawyer said.

At 1:00 Ron quickly left the courtroom. He would not be late, after all, for his luncheon date with Sarah Baruch.

When Ron arrived in his chambers, he found Sarah chatting amiably with his secretary, Joan King, a plump, rosy cheeked woman of fifty. Sarah wore a white hat. It was a small, pancake thing—almost a beret that seemed to sit precariously on her head. Her hair seemed lighter than he remembered it and, in the daylight, seemed to have a halo about it. Unlike the evening dress she had worn at the Bar Dinner, Sarah wore a navy blue business suit. A wide white belt accentuated her waist.

"Your Honor, Ms. Baruch is absolutely charming," Joan said.

"I'm glad you approve," Ron said. He smiled but it was evident from his tone that he was not pleased.

"The Judge thinks I'm too outspoken," Joan said.

"He thinks the same about me," Sarah said.

"Wait until he hears what we were discussing," Joan said.

"Which is?"

"I was explaining to Joan the volunteer work we do at the Domestic Violence Hotline. She's perfect for the job. Joan has a nice, even disposition. We need people who don't lose their heads when victims call," Sarah said.

"Do you really think I can help? My husband always says I should be more involved in community work."

"It is important work," Ron said. "Many people think that it's only for spouses, but the children need protection, too."

"That's exactly what we're focusing on," Sarah said.

"But I bowl on Wednesdays," Joan said.

"It's only for a few hours. You pick your night."

"How often do you go?" Ron said to Sarah. He said it nonchalantly as if he were not seeking important information.

"Two, sometimes three nights. I'm also available for emergencies."

"What would I say when someone calls?" Joan said.

"We have an extensive training program." Sarah reached into her purse. "Here's my card. Call me and we'll get you started."

CHAPTER 5

▼

When Ron and Sarah entered Orlando's, a restaurant on Montague Street in downtown Brooklyn, the owner and Maitre D', menu in hand, greeted them.

"Good afternoon, your Honor. It's so good to see you."

"And you, too, Orlando."

Orlando smiled and led them to Ron's favorite table in the far corner of the room.

"What are you having?"

"A diet coke. No drinking on the job."

"It's the exact opposite with me. My clients expect me to drink with them. I'll have a Stoli martini, extra dry."

"The truth is Sarah…," Ron gazed at her. It was the first time he had called her by her first name. "The truth is Sarah, that I'm trying to lose weight."

"You're funny, Ron…" She had never called him by his first name, either. "If you lost any more weight you'd be considered malnourished."

"You sure you're not a lawyer?" Ron smiled and patted his stomach. "Usually the only compliments I receive are from lawyers."

"I say what I think. Many people think I'm too pushy. Do you think that?"

"Not at all. Some people confuse forthrightness with aggression." Ron then added, "I'm not attracted to passive women."

"So you think I'm your type?" Her voice was saucy.

"I loved the way you enlisted Joan in your Domestic Violence Program."

"We need all the help we can get," Sarah said.

"I know that. But I was amazed at how quickly you converted her. You made a friend there, and she's not easy, let me tell you."

When the waiter brought the drinks, he also brought a plate of *bruscetta*. The garlic bread was soaked in olive oil and covered with diced tomatoes.

"Not exactly diet food, but it's a house specialty," Ron said. "Try it if you're not planning to kiss anyone for a week."

He watched as her tongue tentatively touched the food. "Hmm. That's good," she said and bit into the garlic bread.

"So. You're not planning to kiss anyone this week," Ron said.

"Can't tell. Perhaps I'm looking for someone to take my breath away."

"Or someone with the same breath?" Ron smiled.

"You're a devious man, your Honor," Sarah said. "All this talk about garlic and kissing doesn't fool me one bit. Why don't you ask me what you really want to know."

"And what is that?"

"What's my relationship with Manny Lentino."

"That's none of my business."

"We're not talking about business. We're talking about what's on your mind."

"So? What is your relationship?"

"Friends. Just friends. He'd like to sleep with me, of course, but he knows that it's not in the cards."

"He appeared before me today on an Order to Show Cause."

"Did he?" She said it as if it had little significance. "Doesn't he appear before you regularly?"

"I thought it was quite a coincidence." Ron looked at her searching for some hint of artifice.

"My, but you are the suspicious one."

"It's an occupational affliction," Ron said.

"I'm a real estate broker. Manny is a friend. He asked me to the dinner."

Sarah picked up the menu and studied it.

"How's the *frutti di mare*?"

"It has plenty of garlic," he said. His laugh was easy as if he were apologizing for his suspicions.

"Maybe I'll try the *calamari*. Is that fried?"

"Yes," he said.

She reached out and touched his hand.

"Should I be afraid of heartburn?" she said.

"I'm on constant guard against it," Ron said.

"So I've noticed. Perhaps we can do something about that."

CHAPTER 6

▼

Ruth Santo struggled to inject herself with the insulin, but fumbled with the syringe.

"You got your goddamned wish. You started off as a hypochondriac and finally found doctors who really screwed you up," her husband said.

"You have to help me with this, Victor. I can't do it by myself."

"You're going to have to learn. I can't be with you every time you have to take a shot."

Ruth put down the syringe and began to sob. She was 35 years old but looked almost 55. There were dark rings about her eyes and her housecoat hung loosely about her. The veins and cords in her neck were unduly prominent and underscored her emaciated condition. Her once thick hair was now stringy and all vestige of youthful beauty was gone.

"Here, for Christ sake, I'll do it." Victor picked up the syringe and with one sweeping motion, lifted her housecoat and jabbed the needle into her stomach.

"I have to go to work. I can't be at your beck and call every minute."

"You find time for your girlfriend," Ruth said. She put her hand to her mouth in a vain gesture to recall her words. What had she achieved? Force him to tell another lie?

"What girlfriend? You're sick in the head, too!" He shook his head vigorously and with his hand, made a circular motion by his temple. "Really nuts. You should worry about taking care of the kids before you worry about me having a girlfriend."

Victor was a tall man and he bent over Ruth as if to slap her. He was muscular but at forty two, starting to spread out. He raised his hand over her and then stopped. "Nah, you're not worth it."

"My sister saw you the other day in Manhattan."

"That's a good trick since I was at Aqueduct. Your sister is a trouble-making bitch!"

"Oh Victor, you're not gambling again?"

"What else do I have to do?"

"The doctor told you. It's the diabetes and the medication. I'm just no good in bed. You have to give me a chance to recover, Victor." She wrapped the housecoat tightly around herself.

"You've been complaining for ten years!" Victor said.

"I'm sick, you son of a bitch and you can't wait to run out every night!" Her dead eyes came to life. It seemed that marital conflict was much more restorative than marital bliss. "You're a womanizing gambler. I'm the one who has to face the landlord. He called three times about the rent."

"Well, how about this?" Victor took out a wad of bills and waved it so that it rippled. "Now, you can pay the rent."

"You won at the track?"

Victor flung the money at her. Ruth quickly gathered up the strewn bills.

"You really won?" She counted the money. It was a thousand dollars.

"No, I had to go to the loan sharks." He shrugged as if it didn't matter how the money was obtained. "We're going to be all right once we get the money in the lawsuit. Firestone said he's not going to talk with the insurance company for anything less than a million."

"A million dollars?" She winced.

"What's the matter? You going to be greedy?"

"I don't know, Victor. All I've been through, and what we're facing for the rest of my life, it doesn't seem a lot after the lawyer gets paid and we pay our debts. I was hoping that we'd have enough to get out of this apartment. We could buy a house. Some place with a good school district. Ross is already playing hooky and he's only eleven years old! Amelia goes around with her hand covering her mouth because her teeth are crooked."

"For once in your life Ruth, I want you to shut up! I'm taking care of things."

"I have to think of the kids, too. They're not in a good environment, Victor. Who's going to take care of them if I can't? The doctor said that my pancreas is gone. No insulin. The glaucoma will make me blind, eventually. I'm 35 years old! What kind of life can I have?"

"We have to win the case first, baby." His voice was soothing and he moved toward her. Instinctively, she put the hand that held the money behind her back.

"I need some of that money."

"No!"

"Come on, sweetheart. I need six hundred. The landlord at the store is hounding me, too."

"You're not sweet talking me, Victor." She counted out two hundred dollars and handed it to him.

He grabbed for her other hand but she thrust it behind her back again.

"Take it or leave it," she said. "You have to pay for throwing the money at me." She smiled and for that fleeting moment, they were young lovers again.

"Come on, Ruth. Just another two hundred. I need five hundred."

"You can't bargain with me."

"What are you talking about, who do you think taught me?" Victor touched the Star of David that she wore on her necklace. He laughed at his half-joking prejudice and then hugged her. But Ruth still kept the money out of his reach.

CHAPTER 7

▼

"Come in Detective Zangara," Barbara DiTucci said. "I'm glad you called. I was beginning to wonder what happened to you."

"It's only been two weeks," Jack said. She seemed less tan than he remembered her. Was it the pallor or the make-up? Maybe it was the contrast with the black dress. Her cheekbones were pleasingly high, but not full. They sloped flatly down, angularly, making her mouth seem smaller than it was. But her wide smile contradicted that estimate. Was she too attractive or too wealthy for him? Just do your job and admire the view, Jack.

She led him to the living room and motioned for him to sit on the sofa opposite the window. Instead, he sat in a wing chair. The picture window was now repaired and the sunlight filled the room.

"Can I get you some coffee?"

"No, thank you."

"Today's the first day of school and it's been hectic." She sat on the sofa and crossed her legs. She pulled down on the dress that seemed suddenly to be too short.

She did have great legs. Smooth. Muscular. His glance at them was quick but not quick enough. She tugged at her dress and seemed to blush. Or was it he who was blushing? Stick to business, Jack!

Zangara reached into his breast pocket and took out several papers.

"The autopsy report?"

She extended her hand but he held on to the papers.

"You really don't want to read it. The details. It's too graphic."

"A sensitive detective?" She hazarded a small smile.

"Are you telling me that there was something about my husband that I didn't know about? A secret?"

"No. Nothing like that. Quite the opposite. Death was by asphyxiation, but his blood alcohol was 0.04."

"Which means?"

"That when he died, he was not intoxicated."

"Which means?"

"It was unlikely that he fell asleep in your garage."

The phone rang and Mrs. DiTucci rose to answer it. Her dress was tight and clung to her.

Detective Zangara's eyes followed her across the room.

"Yes, he's here now...no...I'll have to get back to you." She hung up and turned to him. "That was my insurance agent. I have to be frank with you. My husband recently took out a million dollar life insurance policy and the two year incontestability clause does not apply. My agent tells me that if my husband's death was an accident, then I'm entitled to double indemnity. If he committed suicide, then the insurance company will pay me nothing. Have you ruled out death by natural causes?"

"His death was not from natural causes," Zangara said. "The autopsy report makes that pretty clear."

"And if he was killed, would I be entitled to the million alone?"

"You'll have to discuss that with your insurance agent." Oops, Zangara thought. It was the second time that she had given that as an alternative. Was this an unconscious confession on her part? Or was she angling for more money?

"Then your official report will be crucial," Mrs. DiTucci said.

"What are you suggesting?" Zangara said.

"Damn it! I'm not suggesting anything. You have the autopsy report. It tells me that my husband is dead. I want to know how and why he died. I have a child. He's young and I will need money. If I'm entitled to it, then I want it!"

"I can understand that," Zangara said. A million. Two million. Wives have had their husbands killed for a lot less. "I will need your help, though." He took out his pad as if to make notes.

"I just know that my Gabe would not commit suicide."

So that's what she called him. Not Gabriel. That was something in her favor.

"You said that Dr. DiTucci had enemies," Zangara said.

"He specialized in Family Medicine, not Psychiatry, but there's not much difference when you consider the mental state of some of his patients. Several of them believed that he mistreated them. There were threats."

"Do you think that your husband was murdered, Mrs. DiTucci?"

There it was. The question came out, casually, as if it was the only logical explanation. Suicide would be out. A million or two would be in.

"Isn't that your job, Detective Zangara? What do you think?"

"I don't like coincidences," Zangara said.

"What does that mean?"

"Vandalism. A brick thrown through a window, the same night as a death? We did find that the nail holes on the front window didn't line up, like they were pried open and then re-attached but that might have been done by the workers. If there was a break-in, nothing was stolen, right?"

"I can't find my husband's Rolex. He always wore it."

"It wasn't in the personal effects returned to you?"

"No."

"I'll check on it," Zangara said. Son of a bitch! It must have been a cop who glommed it. A $5,000.00 watch was quite a temptation. Or was it something to throw him off the track?

"If my husband was murdered, that would make me a suspect, wouldn't it?"

"No," he said. "If I thought that, I wouldn't be telling you my suspicions. It could be suicide. I don't know. It could be an accident. Maybe he came home late that night and he was tired. I don't know...or it could have been..."

"I want you to find out, Detective Zangara. I want Gabe to rest in peace. More importantly, I want the truth. I want my child to know that his father did not kill himself!" She walked over to the chair and stood in front of him. "Please."

She was so close to him that he could not rise. He looked up at her. If this was an act, it was one hell of a performance.

"I'll need the names of his patients."

"I'm closing down his office. I didn't know where to put his records so I'm having them stored in my basement." She stepped back. "Is that all right?"

"Yes," Zangara said. Was that all right? It was wonderful!

It was a perfect excuse to see Barbara DiTucci again.

CHAPTER 8

▼

Sarah Baruch's apartment was on 78th Street off Third Avenue in Manhattan. The Concierge wore a tuxedo as his uniform and spoke with a British accent. He raised the phone to his ear and punched in the numbers. He waited and then softly announced Ron's presence.

"Miss Baruch will be down momentarily."

Ron sank into one of the sofas in the waiting area. He marveled at the ingenuity of the building owner in orchestrating elegance. This glorified doorman, instead of opening doors, sat behind a desk and pushed a buzzer. How much did they jack up the rent for that? And rent was on his mind because this Saturday, Sarah was going to show him an available apartment on Park Avenue South.

Ron wore a blue sport jacket and cream trousers. His red striped shirt was casually open.

When the elevator door opened, Sarah stepped out. She wore a beige two piece pants suit. Her aqua-marine blouse was flared and open at the neck.

"You look very beautiful," he said. Her sky blue eyes seemed to be the same color as her blouse and her full lips lightly touched with raspberry lipstick, made her smile even more appealing.

"Why thank you, Ron." Sarah took him by the arm and paraded him out onto the street. "Where's the car?"

Ron pointed to the black Cadillac that was parked by a traffic sign that read, "No Parking Except Trucks Loading and Unloading."

"With no traffic ticket?" Sarah said.

"With my placard in the windshield, I can park here. It's one of the few percs judges have these days."

Sarah looked at the big car as he held the door open for her.

"A person can tell a lot from the color one chooses for his car," Sarah said.

"Don't tell me that it is because I have a conservative bent." Ron laughed. "It was one of those 'Dealer's Specials', with a large discount."

"Nevertheless, I'm impressed," she said.

"It's ten years old. Ready to fall apart."

"No. I'm impressed because you can park right by my apartment at any time, without fear of towing. My Mercedes has been towed twice this year."

"Fasten your seat belt and tell me where we're going." He started the engine.

"I have you for the day and I'm not going to waste it. I'll show you the apartment later. Why don't we go to a museum?"

"Which one?"

"Surprise me," she said.

He headed north on Third Avenue and west on 90th Street. He weaved through the traffic.

"You drive like a taxi driver," she said.

"I drove a hack when I was going to law school," he said. "Along with the G.I. Bill, it helped pay for my tuition."

"You certainly haven't lost any of your driving skills."

"And that brings me to the business at hand. Sarah, I can't afford a high rent."

"Don't judges make the big bucks?"

"You're a tease, aren't you, lady? The lawyers who try cases in my court, make the money."

"That shouldn't upset you. Doesn't the star player make more than the umpire?"

"You know the answer to that," Ron said.

"But in your game, the umpire can quit and become a star, can't he? Plenty of judges leave the bench and make tons of money."

"Money is important but it's secondary with me," Ron said. "I like being a judge. I have very specific needs and a very tight budget. I don't want to cry poverty, but you'll have to take my word for it."

"Your credit is impeccable. I've already checked it with TransUnion."

"What else have you checked?" he said. There was a tinge of annoyance in his voice.

"Manny kind of filled me in on your life history."

"Kind of? Am I that open a book to lawyers?"

"Not really, but given a few facts, people can make a lot of deductions."

Ron had made a left turn onto Fifth Avenue heading South.

They drove slowly by Frank Lloyd Wright's cylindrical masterpiece, with its progressively larger layers set on top of each other.

"Oh, we're going to the Guggenheim?" she said. "It's a magnificent structure, but it's built in the wrong place." She nodded at the adjacent buildings that squeezed in the Museum.

Although there was a parking space to the side, Ron double—parked the car.

"What facts? What deductions?" he said.

"You're going to lose that parking space," she said.

Ron did not respond.

"Why are you so upset? We have to check the credit of a potential tenant."

"What facts did you learn and what deductions have you made?" Why couldn't she just answer the question? Damn! This woman was infuriating.

"I must admit, I went a little further than with an ordinary renter." Sarah patted his hand that rigidly gripped the steering wheel. "I don't see it as such a crime. So I pumped Manny for a little information. When you're attracted to someone, you ask questions."

Ron backed into the parking space. "And what did you learn?"

"Well, we know you're a widower."

"I told you that."

"You have twins that are not identical."

"That would be hard since one is male and the other is female."

"Do you want to hear or not," Sarah said. "First you look at me like you want to tear my head off and now, you won't let me finish."

"I'm sorry," he said, although clearly he was not.

"OK. Facts: You own a house in Brooklyn with equity in it of about $800,000.00. Your wife was a homemaker. Apparently she never worked. Your daughter attends Boston College and your son is at the University of Chicago. Combined tuition, with living allowances—approximately $120,000.00. Your salary as a judge is $136,700.00. You don't have to be Sherlock Holmes to deduce that you were probably never able to accumulate much money. Since you worked your way through law school, your parents weren't rich and you're not going to inherit much. You're the kind of parent who would rather suffer than burden his children with student loans. Therefore, you have to sell your house and move into an apartment—that I'm going to get for you," Sarah said triumphantly.

"My wife had a two hundred thousand dollar insurance policy and I've been able to save a few dollars."

"Most of that was probably eaten up with first year tuition and paying medical expenses."

"Almost all of Alice's medical expenses were covered."

"It must have been terrible," Sarah said.

"Death doesn't end pain...except for Alice."

They sat together in the car for a long time before Ron spoke again.

"What about you," he said finally.

"There's not much to know."

"I do know one thing," Ron smiled. "Getting a straight answer from you is like pulling teeth."

"Vassar rebel. My parents are dead. My father made and lost several fortunes. He was a gambler. Big gambler. When he was riding high, we lived on Park Avenue. Most of the time, though, we lived in Brooklyn. Thank God for my cagey mother. She squirreled money away for me and my sister to go to college. A lot of good it did my sister. She's married to a brute of a man. A carbon copy of my father. She's sticking it out although he'll probably kill her in the end. She's the only person in this world, at least up till now, that I truly love. I tried marriage but it didn't work. In a way, I guess, I married my father, too, except my ex is a lawyer. You lawyers are shifty people. Maybe that's where I learned to evade questions."

"You seem to be doing fine, now—at least financially," Ron said. He ignored the lawyer bashing.

"Not from any divorce settlement, my dear. My former husband is a two bit shyster. Come to think of it, I prefer a widower to a divorced man. It's like divorce shows failure—by either party. Death is an unpleasant consequence of life but at least you know that whether the marriage was good or bad, the widowed person showed commitment."

"You have an interesting way of changing the conversation."

"I didn't change the conversation." Sarah leaned over and kissed his cheek. "Now you know everything about me."

"I don't think I know anything about you," he said. "What's your former husband's name?"

"You wouldn't know him. He's not a trial lawyer."

CHAPTER 9

▼

Birdie's Tavern on Eighty Sixth Street in Brooklyn was dark, although it was day-time. Joe "Pencils" Penna and Victor Santo were at one end of the bar. Several patrons and the bartender discreetly moved away at a glance from Penna.

"Six Fingers Sal wants to lean on you, Victor. You ain't even paid him the vig this week," Joe Penna said. He made a chopping motion with his hand. "You know there are some things I can't help you with."

"I'm not asking you to pay my debts."

"I didn't mean that," Penna said. He was a squat man. His bulk filled the bar stool. He turned sideways and looked up at the six foot tall Victor Santo. "The Falcon don't like loose ends."

"Sal's a leech," Victor said. "He's never satisfied."

"I heard you did all right at the track the other day."

"Christ. You have some grapevine, Joe."

"It's part of my business. I don't know, Vic. You got the world by the tail and you throw it all away. You neglect your business. The money you do make, you piss away on the broads and the ponies."

"Give me a break…Pencils."

"You know I hate that nickname," Joe Penna said.

"Then don't talk to me about pissing away my life. You were the one who got all the 'As' in school. You should have been a doctor or something. Look at you. Now you keep the accounts for the Falcon—and you ain't even an accountant! I should have called you 'Scribbles' because now all your writing is on little pieces of paper."

"I don't owe bookies and loan sharks and I don't have somebody out to break my legs, Vic. I'm, telling you, there are limits to our protection."

"I'm not worried Joe. I'm going to deal directly with the Falcon. He's not going to let anyone bother me. At least not while my wife's case is going on." Victor brushed imagined lint from his cashmere jacket.

"You're playing with fire," Penna said. "You know that? And your track record, you'll pardon the expression, ain't so hot. Look at you. You had two gas stations but you had to have a third one…and you lost them all. Your drop cloth factory made money and then you expanded to plastics. You screwed that one up. Now you're running your dry cleaning store into the ground because you're not paying attention to business. What else? Oh yeah, the candy store. Everything you've ever touched has turned to shit, so I wouldn't be that sure of making a score."

"So, I've had some bad luck. But this is a sure thing."

"A sure thing? Now, I'm really worried," Penna said.

"Firestone says the case is worth a million but he's low balling me. If it's a jury verdict, it can go to fifteen million."

"A lot of these cases are settled so you may have to take less."

"Firestone says that they've refused to make any settlement offer."

"People have been known to change their minds," Penna said.

Victor rose to his full height and placed his hand on Penna's shoulder. "Now that's the Joe, I like. You're beginning to talk like the Falcon, too."

Penna looked crossly at Victor. To accept such a comparison with the boss was as deadly as an assassination attempt.

"You know, flattery can shorten a guy's life span, too," Joe Pencils said.

"For Chrissake, Joe, lighten up. All I meant was that you're going to make Firestone look like the smartest lawyer of all time."

"Cut the crap, Victor. Just make sure you see Six Fingers."

CHAPTER 10

▼

Sarah directed Ron to a pre-war apartment building on Park Avenue South. That meant high ceilings and ornate detailing.

"I was thinking in terms of the Upper East Side," Ron said.

"Those are all new buildings and there are no bargains there, darling." Sarah had assumed her professional real estate broker tone. "This is Murray Hill. Gramercy Park is a few blocks away and the area is much more desirable. Besides, just wait and see what I have for you."

The elevator was creaky but there was a doorman. Ron noted that he neither wore a uniform nor spoke with a British accent.

The apartment consisted of four and half to six rooms—depending upon how one counted. It was a corner apartment with huge windows in each room. The windows, framed with wide, old style molding, matched the cornices.

"The landlord will paint, of course, and they'll scrape the floors. That's real oak!"

"Is there only one bathroom?"

"There's a sink in a small area off the master bedroom."

"I have a big old house in Midwood. I've lived in Brooklyn for my entire life. It's going to be difficult in an apartment," Ron said.

"Perhaps you should stay there and have the children get student loans." Sarah sounded testy.

"I'm not saddling them with debts if I can help it."

"Ron. I can imagine how difficult this must be for you but you'll have to make up your mind."

They were alone in the large living room and Ron went to the window. It was a city view—no trees, no lawn, just buildings across the streets and cars humming along.

"No student loans. Maybe for law school or graduate school, but I'm not going to saddle them with that kind of debt just for college. Their scores in the SATs were almost perfect. I could just as well have sent them to a State University. They're fine schools but the kids deserve the best, and I'm willing to sacrifice for them."

"My mother was like that," Sarah said.

"The funny thing is that Colleen will be the one that will protest the most. Children hate change. It's like their universe is altered. They can leave, but they require us to keep things the way they are."

"Colleen Goodman?"

"My wife was Irish."

"And your son's name?"

"Alan. But don't ask how we came up with that name."

"I'm sure your children will love it here. Manhattan is the place to be. If they remain in New York after they complete school, they'll probably want to live in Manhattan."

"It would be kind of cramped in this apartment, wouldn't it?" Ron said. He was hesitant and it bothered him.

"What makes you so sure that they'll want to live with you? Kids today are pretty independent."

"That doesn't matter. I just want them to know that there's always a home for them."

"There are all sorts of arrangements you can make. You can put a sofa bed in the living room, or you can put a day bed in one room and make it your study. These rooms are immense." Sarah checked her notes. "The apartment is over twenty one hundred square feet."

"And the rent?"

"That's the best part of it. The rent is $1,875.00 a month!"

"What? There must be some mistake."

"There's no mistake. This apartment was occupied by a woman for thirty-five years. When she died, her daughter then occupied the place. This apartment has been rent controlled for over fifty years! The owner has been fighting with the Rent Stabilization Board and they finally fixed the rent. It's yours for $1,875.00 with a two year lease."

"Isn't there some sort of waiting list?"

"Don't look a gift horse in the mouth. You have to understand, the old tenant was paying $635.00 a month. So the landlord is making triple his money. Besides, it's prestigious for a judge to live in his building."

"I have to sell my house," Ron said. Things were moving too fast.

"You live in the Midwood section of Brooklyn? You'll sell your house in a week."

"It's very nice, but I'd like to think about it."

"You'll do nothing of the sort! Comparable space goes for $5,500.00 to $7,000.00 a month. There are apartments in this building, smaller than this, that rent for $6,000.00 a month."

"You're not going to give me time to think it over?"

"Absolutely not! We might lose the deal if you hesitate," Sarah said. "Besides, I'm waiving my commissions on both the apartment and the sale of your house. That's a savings of more than $50,000.00."

"I can't let you do that!"

"Of course you can," Sarah said. She embraced him and puckered up her lips and gave him a noisy kiss on the mouth that echoed in the empty room.

Ron was startled by the sudden movement toward him but rejected neither the embrace—nor the smooch.

"Do you think you can sell my house by Christmas? The kids will be home for the holiday."

"Piece of cake," she said and chucked him playfully on the chin.

Chapter 11

▼

Sal Montana was called "Six Fingers" because he was born with vestigial fingers—little knobs that the surgeon had neglected to amputate at birth. Six fingers claimed that it never bothered him physically although, there were those who believed that the genetic defect extended to the operation of his brain. He gave the impression of having a jovial manner, but that could change in an instant, especially when he suspected deception, which was most of the time.

"Hey, my man," Six Fingers said. His voice was nasal, as if it were being filtered through his long, thin nose. "Now, that's what I like. A man who doesn't try to avoid me just because he owes me money."

Victor had walked into the rear room of a garage on Third Avenue off Douglas Street in Brooklyn—the "office" of Sal Six Fingers. The room was barren except for a desk, telephone and several chairs. Peeling green paint and uncovered pipes signaled that there was no need to bother with amenities.

Just outside the door, several men lingered in the doorway. Their casual manner announced to the discerning that they were Montana's bodyguards.

Victor moved to embrace Six Fingers but was held off by Six Fingers' extended hand.

"You've been seeing too many movies, Sal," Victor said. He pushed aside the hand and hugged Six Fingers anyway. He leaned his weight on the man. "We're all friends and we all have mutual friends. I'm really hurt that you complained about me to Joe Pencils."

"It wasn't really a complaint. I just happened to mention it to the Falcon."

"You mentioned me to Andrew Peregrino? To the Falcon? And here I was blaming Joe! You Fuck! Have I ever stiffed you?" Victor stared at Six Fingers.

"What's this? The best defense is a good offense? Sit down and have a drink. Don't get so excited." Sal reached into a desk drawer and took out two plastic cups. He filled them with DeWars Scotch. He raised his cup but Victor shook his head.

"What? You're not going to drink with me?" Sal glared at him, daring Victor to insult him.

Victor relented.

"*Salute.*"

"*Per cent anni*," Victor said.

"Ah, we'd all like to live for a hundred years, but some of us ain't going to make it, Vic." Six Fingers leaned back in his swivel chair.

"What's your beef? So I'm a little late."

"That's a nice tan you have. I wish I had more time to get the sun."

"Stop being so clever." Victor looked toward the door. The bodyguards were peering at him.

"The weather was gorgeous at the track, eh?"

"And I won, too. Seems the whole world knows that."

"I heard. I thought sure that you'd at least call me."

"I had other obligations."

"That's what I mean, Vic. You're not fair. You borrow from me and then bet somewhere else. It don't take a genius to figure out why. You're into me for twenty large. If you bet with me and win, I deduct it from your tab. You go someplace else and win, then I have to chase you. It's not fair."

"I'm good for it and you know that, Sal."

"It's just not fair. Your tab is getting so big, that not only don't I get paid, but I lose a customer." Six Fingers drummed his fingers on the desk. "I have obligations, too!"

"That's what I am? A customer? You really know how to piss me off. Tomorrow I wipe the slate clean!"

"Hey Vic, why are you so angry? You make it sound like I owe you the money."

"You made me look bad with the Falcon. From now on, Andrew Peregrino will talk for me."

"If the Falcon says you have no tab with me, then the slate is clean."

"That's what the Falcon is going to say."

Victor turned to leave but the doorway was filled by two men.

The bodyguards stepped aside, but not before the men raised their arms to show that they carried no weapons.

"Say hello to Pete and Eugene," Six Fingers said.

Victor looked at them.

Pete was burly like a weight lifter who had ceased lifting and was almost as tall as Victor.

"It's a pleasure," Victor said and extended his hand.

Eugene, smaller, thin and quick in his movements merely nodded.

"That job I had in mind for you didn't pan out," Six Fingers said. "I tried to call you but there was no answer."

"That's show biz, I guess," Eugene said. He looked at Victor and appraised him. Big, but soft and fat. He wouldn't be too hard to take.

"What's that expression they have in the theater?" Pete looked at Victor so that there would be no mistake.

"Break a leg," Eugene said. There was no humor in his voice.

CHAPTER 12

▼

"Sissy, I'm at my rope's end, I'm…" Ruth held on to the kitchen table as long as she could before she dropped the phone and collapsed.

When Emergency Medical Services responded to the 911 call, no one answered the doorbell.

"Break the door down," one EMS officer said.

A crowd began to gather around the house. On both sides of the street were semi-detached, two-family brick homes, separated by common driveways. A youngster scaled a sycamore tree and tried to gain access by climbing onto the pitched roof.

"The second floor window looks open," the youngster said.

"Stupido," said an old man. "That's a separate apartment. Even if he gets in, they're going to have to break the door down."

"Break the door down, Dave," the EMS officer said.

"Is this the right address?" Dave said.

"We're always sued anyway. Too late, or wrong house, what's the difference?"

The old man moved close to him and bent down to read the officer's name tag. "Laramie. That's Itallian, ain't it?"

"What, you a comedian?" the African American said.

"Does anyone know what's going on around here?" Dave said.

"That's the right house," the old man said. Saliva dribbled from the corner of his mouth. The lady in there, she's always sick. She's home. I saw the kids leave for school this morning. The ambulance took her away three times last month."

"Her husband owns a dry cleaning store on Eighteenth Avenue. Call him."

"What's the name?" Dave said.

"Santo."

"So, now we have a name," Laramie said. "Now, will you break the door down?"

The found Ruth Santo laying on the kitchen floor amidst shattered glass and crockery. She bled profusely from a gash on her forehead.

"That's a nasty cut," Dave said.

"Needs a few stitches. Looks worse than it is," Laramie said. He cleaned away the blood and applied pressure to the wound.

Ruth's housecoat had parted, exposing her shrunken breasts. Laramie checked her carotid artery for a pulse and delicately drew her lapels together.

When Dave lifted her arm, he saw the ID bracelet fastened to her wrist.

"She's a diabetic. Insulin shock."

"Yeah, clammy and unresponsive," Laramie said. "I can butterfly the cut. That'll hold for a while."

Dave nodded and moved as if nothing more had to be said. He attached a blood pressure cuff to her arm and donned his stethoscope.

"Her pressure's very low."

"I'll check her blood sugar, Dave. You want to insert the IV lock?"

They worked together. Quickly and surely. Laramie pricked Ruth's finger and put the blood on a tab. He ran it through the little portable machine and waited for the read-out.

Meanwhile, Dave inserted the IV line in her forearm—and they were ready.

"Her blood sugar is so low it doesn't even register," Laramie said.

"I've got the D-50. Here goes!" Dave took the large syringe and injected the 50 ccs of glucose into the vein.

Laramie propped her up and held her gently in his arms.

"This is a pretty sick lady. She's all skin and bones."

They lifted her onto a gurney and covered her with a blanket.

On the way to the hospital, siren blaring, Ruth awoke. The butterfly bandage had stopped the bleeding and the glucose had restored her.

"Where are you taking me?" Ruth said.

"Coney Island Hospital," Laramie said.

"Over my dead body. You're not taking me to any City hospital."

"We can't take you any place else, Ma'am."

"Then take me back home," Ruth said. She tried to sit up.

"You're going to need stitches."

"Please take me home." Her forehead was beginning to throb.

"Please. My children will be coming home from school."

"We can call your husband."

"Why can't you just take me back? I'll sign any kind of release you want."

"We're taking you to the hospital, Mrs. Santo."

"Like this?" She clutched her bloodied housecoat.

"You're not going on television," Laramie said. "You're going to a hospital."

CHAPTER 13

▼

Andrew Peregrino was a man of respect. Not burdened with the civilized covenants of society, he had the power of life and death. No trial. No appeal. In short, the Falcon, a name that everyone called him—except to his face—was a mobster. Not a soldier, but a made man. A capo.

His patina of graciousness was like a soft glove that concealed a callused hand. Those who knew him were neither deceived nor comforted by his courteous manner. He rarely smiled but when he did, it was not necessarily a good sign. A glare was often preferred to a smile because a glare would be informative, but not fatal. Unlike a smile, it was used to indicate displeasure not duplicity.

Perregrino was not yet fifty years old. Gray tinged the sides of his otherwise black hair. His deep set brown eyes seemed to hide behind his tinted, rimless, eyeglasses. He was not a tall man but he held himself erect and this added to his imposing presence.

A person who came to him, whether for favors or for tribute, accepted his *gravitas* in the same manner as a subject humbling himself before a prince. He never wore casual clothes. His suits were stylish and expensive. His white shirts were always starched and he rarely wore the same tie twice. His only affectation was a large diamond pinky ring that he wore as if it were an insignia of rank.

The people enjoyed certain advantages by his presence. He neither extorted money from the local store owners nor allowed the sale of drugs. It could be done- and profitably. But not on his streets. Prostitution was rampant, but relatively discreet. No street-walkers. "We don't need complaints. Let people be glad we're here. Let them be afraid of the cops, not us."

Much of his energy was reserved to battle encroachment on his turf. No illegal enterprise or scheme was allowed in his territory without his consent.

"When you hijack a truck, I get my cut. That's the taxes you're paying," he had said. He was benign when given his due, but otherwise merciless.

"Committing a crime without permission is like doing business without paying taxes. Where would this country be if it couldn't collect taxes? But we're at a disadvantage," Peregrino had told a burglar who had stolen on his own. "There's no jail to put you in."

"Gee, I'm sorry Mr. Peregrino. I only cleared a thousand on the job." The man had reached into his pocket and held out the money. The presence of the two hefty bodyguards had made the gesture understandable. "It won't happen again, I promise you."

"I know that young fellow." The Falcon had then smiled, the smile that could end all smiles and took *all* the money.

The Falcon did not charge any rent for the clubhouse on Eighteenth Avenue. "La Societa di Oliveto" was written in large letters across the storefront. He made a point of keeping the window plain and the interior well lighted. In the evenings, the street was filled with people, relaxing after a day's work. Most were post World War II immigrants, who congregated by the numerous coffee shops on the Avenue. They spoke mostly in Italian, but sometimes in English.

When the weather permitted, the Falcon held court at a table set up in front of the store. He would nod to those smiling persons who pretended to be merely passing by, rather than passing in review. "See," he was telling the world. "We operate in the open."

Andrew Peregrino had little fear of assassination. "If it's going to happen, it'll happen," he had often said. His fatalistic view of life, however, was not so fool-hardy. His bodyguards were always at his side. His henchmen, never less than two, worked the crowd no less faithfully or professionally as secret service men who guarded the President of the United States.

In bad weather, a table was set inside, but in a far corner, away from the other tables that were occupied by card players. Only people who were not connected with him were allowed to hang out or play cards. Whether it was the thrill of being close to the powerful, or merely the desire for companionship, there were always plenty of card players. One who could say, "I play cards at Oliveto" thus, transformed himself from innocuous to ominous.

No wine was permitted. No beer. No fights. No trouble with the cops. Arguments between patrons were considered irrelevant and settled by a glance toward them.

It was eight p.m. when Victor Santo arrived. The late summer air was brisk, but it was not yet cold. The Falcon sat at the outdoor table. His back was to the window and there were several empty chairs around it. No one sat down without permission.

"Hello Mr. Peregrino," Victor said.

There was no response for some time. Several men who had been huddling close to the Falcon moved away from Victor as if he were a leper.

"The ambulance took your wife to the hospital?"

"I went there as soon as I heard." Christ. What a grapevine. What else did the Falcon know?

"I'm having a hard time respecting you, Victor." The Falcon adjusted his tie. His fingers were long. The colorless nail polish seemed to glisten as much as his diamond pinky ring.

"Some people have been bad mouthing me, Mr. Peregrino."

"You have a good friend in Joe Pencils."

"I know." Some friend, Victor thought. Pencils was tripping over himself to rat him out to the Falcon.

"What more can I do for you?"

"Six Fingers..." Victor fidgeted. The Falcon had kept him standing.

"That's done already."

"I can't tell you how much I appreciate..."

"We have our understanding," the Falcon said.

"But you will do exactly as I say. No foul ups. No harebrained schemes. Contact Tony Vecchio. He's your lawyer, not Firestone."

"But Tony's not a malpractice lawyer."

"Don't be stupid, Victor. I'm directing Vecchio. He'll direct Firestone. Then I'll decide what's to be done...and when it's to be done. Do you understand?" So that there would be no mistake, he glared at Victor.

"I'm not sure. Firestone is still the lawyer on the case?"

"He'll prepare the case and be the trial lawyer. All negotiations will be through Vecchio."

"Now I understand."

The Falcon nodded to a bodyguard who had been waiting by the door. The man placed two cups and an espresso pot on the table.

"Joe Pencils tells me that you think the case is worth ten mill."

"With your help Andrew."

"You listen Victor. Your future is in your own hands. Any problems. Any questions. You see Joe Pencils."

The Falcon turned away and beckoned to another man who had been waiting at a respectful distance.

"Giovanni, come. Sit down." The Falcon picked up the coffee pot and filled the two cups. "Have some espresso, *Compare*."

As Victor Santo walked away, the Falcon called after him. "Victor. Victor! You take care of that beautiful wife of yours. She's a valuable asset."

Victor noted the smile of the Falcon's face. He much preferred the glare.

CHAPTER 14

▼

Sarah had been correct in more ways than one. Ron's house was put up for sale and within a week, it was sold for $925,000.00, the price he had asked for. No bargaining. It was the perfect time. The perfect market. It seemed that only death or flight to the suburbs made one of these three story Victorian houses, with their nine to ten rooms, available for sale.

After satisfying the mortgage, Ron would clear $675,000.00. His money problems were solved. Colleen and Alan's future tuition was secure.

Sarah had also been correct in her analysis of the trauma that the transactions would have upon him. "Ron, I understand change, all change is difficult. Your house was not only a financial investment, but it was also an emotional one. You have to shuck off the old the way a snake sheds its skin."

"That's a hell of an analogy," he had said.

"What I'm talking about is pain and growth. The best thing that could happen to you is selling your house. Even if you had never met me." She had smiled. "But then that was your lucky day. You leave everything to me and you won't regret it."

Ron was grateful that Sarah had insisted upon speed. She seemed to know, intuitively, what to do. When to move. What to store. What to throw out. What new furniture to purchase.

They had gone shopping at Macy*s and at her insistence, purchased all new kitchen utensils; pots, pans, cutlery, earthenware.

"New things for a new apartment," she had said and he did not complain.

There was a joy in shopping with Sarah. Her face would beam as she contemplated the most innocuous item, whether it was a toaster or a blender.

The occasions, however, were tempered by the memories of his prior days with his wife, Alice. He had never liked shopping with her and to enjoy it now, with another woman seemed somehow a betrayal of her memory.

Sarah had been marvelous. She seemed to sense his ambivalence and had been gentle in handling his guilt. "To paraphrase Descarte," she had said, "I shop, therefore I am."

His last visit, before the closing, was particularly traumatic. They had been wandering through the rooms in his Midwood home when Sarah stopped at the door to the master bedroom. It was large and furnished with a full bedroom suite. Sarah's look was quizzical.

"I'm keeping my bedroom set," Ron said.

"It's too bulky. Too many pieces. You don't need a vanity."

"I can put the vanity in Colleen's room."

"I think you should throw out the entire bedroom set," Sarah said. She picked up a small purse that was laying on the dresser. Inside was fifteen dollars. "I'll bet this was your wife's purse."

"I never needed the money," Ron said.

"So you just left it there? What is this? Some Egyptian fetish? Money for the next world?"

"It was there for an emergency. I just never needed it."

"Like the hair brush?" Sarah pointed toward the master bedroom's toilet. "There are long hairs on the brush. Probably from your wife."

"I never use a hair brush."

"Face it Ron, you haven't gotten over Alice's death."

"You're wrong Sarah. These are just little things. Don't give me any of your two dollar psychology. The bed stays! I like the mistress...I mean the mattress." Ron's face flushed.

Sarah pushed Ron onto the bed and they laughed, hysterically.

"I like the mattress, too," she said. Sarah picked up a pillow and struck Ron. He grabbed the pillow from her and pulled her onto the bed. He took her face in his hands and pressed her down with his body.

"Oh no you don't." Sarah broke away from him and sprang off the bed. "The first time we make love is not going to be in the bed of your dead wife!"

"That's a pretty crude way to put it, isn't it?"

"It would be crude to make love here. I'm really attracted to you. But I want you and I want you with the least possible baggage. I'm not saying that you have to forget your wife...or the past, but I don't want it to interfere with our future."

"Sarah, I didn't think it was possible but I really believe that I can love you. I might already. But I have been concerned about Colleen and Alan. They're going to love you, I'm sure of that, but they have needs, too. They have to have connections with the past."

"Colleen can have the vanity. Everything else should go."

"The dresser is in excellent condition," Ron said.

"How would you like me to give you a framed portrait of my former husband? We can keep it on the dresser."

"Ouch!" Ron said.

CHAPTER 15

▼

"An insurance company is not going to pay you out of the goodness of its heart," Roger Firestone said. "We have to prove your pain and suffering. And we can do that only by your testimony. No surprises. The law allows both sides to investigate the case. That's why you signed authorizations for medical and hospital records."

They were sitting in the conference room of his law office. Rather, Firestone was pacing about the long chrome and glass table. For a large man, he moved with surprising grace. Ruth and Victor sat up straight in their chairs in respectful attention. Tony Vecchio stood off to the side.

Vecchio was of medium height and was no more than 40 years old. His pencil moustache was almost as thin as the pin stripes of his suit. His dapper appearance was confirmed by the shine of his patent leather shoes. He, too, wore a diamond pinky ring.

He nodded as Firestone spoke.

"That's why I had to allow the insurance company doctor to physically examine you, Mrs. Santo."

"You got a copy of his report, Roger?" Vecchio said.

"Certainly. And it was positive. They're probably not going to contest that Ruth has pancreatitis. The fight will be on what caused it and the extent this has injured her."

"I understand," Ruth said. She clutched her handbag.

"Today we're going to take your depositions. It's an examination before trial. Both of you will testify. The other lawyers will ask you questions and a stenographer will record it. This EBT is very important. It can be used against you at the trial. So you answer the questions. Don't volunteer any answers. If the question is improper, I'll object. If I object, then you don't answer unless I permit it. Do you understand?"

"Understand? Look at my wife and what they did to her," Victor said. "They destroyed my wife. They ruined our lives, Mr. Firestone. Somebody has to send them a message that they can't ride roughshod over people."

"Cut it out, Victor," Vecchio said. "You're over your head. These other lawyers are very smart people."

"Victor, you can't be the client and the lawyer," Firestone said.

"He's going to behave. Aren't you Victor?" Vecchio said. "Tell Mr. Firestone that you're only going to answer the questions they ask you." He spoke slowly as if to a child.

"Yeah. Yeah. I'm just upset with what they did to my wife."

The conference room intercom rang and Firestone picked up the phone.

"Is the stenographer from Diamond Reporting here yet? How about Mr. Lentino and Ms. Fisher? We're almost ready. Tell them to wait a few minutes."

Firestone hung up.

"Are you going to sit in on this, Tony?"

"No. Unless you want me."

"Could I see you in my office?"

Firestone led Vecchio into his inner office. It was opulently furnished and clearly designed to impress clients. The tan wallpaper had a rough hemp consistency and the Damask drapes with thin satin weave gave the effect of an inner sanctum. A mahogany desk and chairs attributed to be exact copies of furniture that once graced Napoleon's study, were set diagonally in a corner. An Aubusson rug covered the floor.

Vecchio went to the diplomas that were stacked on a wall.

"Brooklyn College?"

"Look at the other one," Firestone said.

"Harvard Law. I *am* impressed!" Vecchio said.

"That's not why I asked you in here. Tony, you're entitled to a fee as the forwarding attorney, but you obviously have more control over this idiot than I do."

"This guy screws up everything he touches."

"Then I think you had better sit in on the EBT."

"If this goes to trial, I think you better second seat me, too."

"Will Goodman allow that?"

"Yes. He's pretty liberal. It's two against one now. If you sit beside me, then in his mind, it will just level the playing field."

"I'm pretty busy. Why don't we just leave it that if you need me, I'll be there," Vecchio said. "DiTucci's death cut the odds even more, didn't it." He smiled. It was a half smile, barely showing his teeth. He clasped his hands and rubbed them together to show his satisfaction. His diamond pinky ring flashed in the light.

"It was, God forgive me, a lucky break," Firestone said. "DiTucci's testimony would have supported Spender's version. But I told you all this before, didn't I?"

"I'm a good listener," Vecchio said. "I want to be kept informed of every development. What I can take care of, I'll take care of."

"How about an advance on the disbursements? With expert witnesses, all the depositions and daily copy…you know we're going to need a transcript of each day of trial. I'm going to be laying out thirty to forty thousand dollars."

"Come on Roger. You worried?"

"No, but I already have eight thousand in disbursements. These experts won't wait for their money."

"I'm guaranteeing this one," Vecchio said. "It's ironclad."

"It's not so ironclad, Tony. We have other problems."

"Like what?"

"I'm examining Spender soon. He's going to be more dangerous than DiTucci. He's a cocky bastard but he's one of the more eminent gastroenterologists in the field."

"You know him?"

"Aaron Spender? I've used him as my expert witness a dozen times. Now, he's a defendant. I've seen him make and break cases. He's nasty, but juries respect him."

"That's the problem?"

"Not quite. Spender is in deep shit and we're in it with him."

"In what way?"

"Spender is going to claim that there was no malpractice. That's expected. But his insurance company went belly up last month—and it was a lousy off-shore carrier. That means that we can't collect on a money judgment. The hospital may still be liable. *Respondeat Superior*, remember? We're going to have to prove that Spender committed malpractice, and then prove that he was connected with the hospital."

"Can you do that?" Vecchio said.

"I'd better because if we don't, then even if the jury comes back with a multi-million dollar verdict, it would be uncollectible. Maybe I shouldn't have let DiTucci's estate out of the case."

"No, you did right. It would only have held up the case. Besides, wasn't his insurance the same as the hospital?

"Yes, but…"

"No buts, Roger. Even if you could settle the case it would all come out of the same pocket."

"It might have made the hospital more willing to settle," Firestone said. "Now we only have the hospital."

"How about Spender? Does he have any money?"

"I'm not going after him personally, Tony. He'd either hide his assets or go into personal bankruptcy."

"Maybe I can still help," Vecchio said. He cast his thin lips downward and nodded as if he were agreeing with himself.

"Sure, Tony. You can come up with the cash for disbursements. I'd like that better than an ironclad guarantee."

"I didn't go to Harvard Law, Roger, but I did do my undergraduate work at 'School of the Streets'. We've prepared for any contingency."

"We?"

"You and me," Vecchio said. "Let me ask you, Roger, you knew at the start that Spender only had a million insurance, right?"

Firestone nodded.

"Without your bullshit, this case is worth 9 or 10 mil?"

Firestone nodded again.

"Whether or not Spender's insurance is up, the only one with the deep pockets is the hospital. It was the target all along, wasn't it?"

"It's not as easy as all that, Tony."

"Sure it is Roger, I guarantee it." Vecchio patted Firestone's cheek.

CHAPTER 16

▼

Tom Scott staggered when he came in the squad room. His fingers checked his tie and then he straightened it, as if that would conceal his condition.

Jack Zangara sat in the chair at his desk reading a file and pretended not to notice the noisy entrance.

Scott went to a file cabinet. He slammed open a metal drawer and flipped through the folders.

"So, all of a sudden you're a lone wolf?" Tom Scott said.

"What are you looking for?" Zangara said. He tried to sound amused.

"The DiTucci file. The autopsy report," Scott said.

"You owe me a steak dinner. The doctor was not drunk…like you," Zangara said.

"You think I'm drunk? You've never seen me *really* drunk."

"You could have fooled me," Zangara said.

"I'm just pissed off, Jack."

"Why?"

"I thought we were partners," Scott said. "The best one you ever had—if I'm quoting you correctly."

"You're not. I said you had the *potential* to be the best. All you have to learn is how not to jump to conclusions so fast."

"Like now?"

"Why don't you ask for a transfer, Tommy. This job is starting to affect you."

"Maybe. Maybe the job is starting to affect you—not me," Scott said.

"You know something I don't know?"

"The DiTucci case. You've been investigating without me."

"You were on vacation," Zangara said.

"You bang her yet?" Scott sat on the desk. He pulled a cigarette from a pack. He lit it, took a deep drag and smiled. "Not that I blame you."

"It's not an open and shut case like you said. What was I supposed to do? Wait for the trail to get cold?" Zangara averted his eyes. Hadn't he timed his visits to Barbara DiTucci to coincide with Scott's absence?

"Jack, Jack. Why don't you just admit that you've been bitten by the love bug."

"Like I said, Tom, you have great potential as an investigator but you're too quick on the draw."

"Is that right? Then why are you blushing?"

"You're nuts," Zangara said. "Everything is open and above board."

"If you're not being devious, why are you hiding the DiTucci file from me?"

"What are you talking about. It's right here." Zangara pulled the file from a slim briefcase that lay at his feet. He threw it on the desk.

"Since when you carry files in a briefcase?"

"I always have. You never noticed."

Zangara watched Scott pick up the file and thumb through the papers.

"Yeah, yeah. So what kind of homework have you *been* doing?"

"There's a lot of work to be done. DiTucci's medical records are in her basement. She put them there to save money on office rent. Is there anything wrong with that?"

"Maybe. Nine times out of ten, the little lady is in on it. Wouldn't that be a kick in the ass!"

"Then help me prove it, Tom. The Rolodex alone has six hundred names in it. And for each name, there's a medical file."

"Now you're nuts!"

"Come on, Tommy. We can go through the files in shifts or together. Either way. I have a hunch about this case."

"We had seven homicides in the last month. Three of them with no suspects. You going to put all this time in for one lousy suicide?" Scott said.

"Four of the homicides were family related. Not much investigation are needed on those. We round up the suspects and jail them. They confess—end of case. The other two were gang related. We're never going to catch them until we get a tip. So what do we have left? Time for you to go out and get drunk?"

"I'm not doing your grunt work, Jack."

"I could really use you on this one. There may be something more to this than an accident or a suicide."

"Bullshit, Jack! I don't think you want my help at all—it might be too inconvenient." Scott threw the file back onto the desk.

"You're wrong. This case is no different than any other," Zangara said.

"Is that so, Jack? Come on, stop trying to kid me. If you come up with something, I'll follow it up for you. Meanwhile, give my regards to the widow." Scott blew smoke into the air.

CHAPTER 17

▼

There were only a few spectators in the courtroom when Sarah Baruch entered. The sound of the door opening was not loud but it, nevertheless, caught the attention of several jurors as their concentration was disrupted by the entrance of this comely woman. She was wearing a full length mink coat that was at odds with her large athletic bag.

Sarah sat in a rear row behind two court buffs who turned to look at her.

William Bellard, the defendant's lawyer, continued the cross examination of Dr. Whitmore, the plaintiff's expert witness in Ron's current trial.

"Isn't it a fact that all pregnancies take place in the fallopian tubes?"

"I have no quarrel with that," Dr. Whitmore said.

"And when the zygote, that is, the fertilized egg begins to grow in the tube and fails to descend into the uterus, it's called an ectopic pregnancy."

"Again, I have no quarrel with that if you're talking generally."

"This causes great pain, doesn't it?"

"There may be swelling and tenderness in the abdominal region, yes."

"And don't these symptoms mimic appendicitis?" Bellard said. His stare was steady and fixed on Whitmore as if he were daring the doctor to contradict him.

"Absolutely. It also mimics PID, Pelvic Inflammatory Disease. That's why an exploratory is urgent and necessary. The patient was 32 at the time and had already had a fallopian tube removed. The other one could have been saved. If Dr. Gambali had acted promptly, the ectopic pregnancy would have been resolved. Administering Mexthatrexate would have dissolved the fetus."

"I didn't ask you that, did I, doctor?" Bellard said. "Your Honor, I move to strike the answer."

"Strike it," Ron said. "The jury will disregard the answer."

"There was an 85% chance of a new pregnancy. Now she has no chance," Dr. Whitmore said.

Ron did not wait for an objection. "Dr. Whitmore, you know better than that!"

The whispered conversation of the court buff took on added volume, as much from excitement as to impress the lovely lady. "Watch this. Judge Goodman won't let Whitmore get away with it."

He turned to look at Sarah.

"Hush," Sarah said and tapped the man's shoulder.

"Quiet!" the court officer said. He glared at the court buffs.

"The jury will disregard the last statement by Dr. Whitmore." Ron then turned to Dr. Whitmore. "Doctor, you've testified before me many times."

Dr. Whitmore fidgeted in his seat and reflexively touched his brush moustache.

"I'm sorry your Honor. I was just trying to set the record straight."

"I'm sure you were," Ron said. He turned to the jury and smiled. They had surely gotten the message. Dr. Whitmore had not played fair and had been chastised.

"Speaking of setting the record straight, doctor, how much are you being paid for your *expert* testimony?" Bellard said.

"Ten thousand. That's provided I don't have to come back tomorrow," Dr. Whitmore said.

"You won't be coming back for me," Bellard said. He shook his head and smiled. "I could never afford your fees!"

CHAPTER 18

▼

When court recessed for the day, Ron took Sarah down the rear hallway, past the jury rooms. In her high heels, she was as tall as Ron.

"I see you're ready for action," Ron said. He looked at her athletic bag.

"Ron that was really exciting. The trial is like impromptu theater. What goes on! The nuances. The clash of minds. The tension must be tremendous. And the way you controlled the lawyer and the witness was masterful. I was really impressed."

"I'm glad you enjoyed it but you didn't see very much."

"I saw enough," Sarah said. "It's like watching someone swing a golf club. One swing and you know if he's a golfer. The same with you, Ron. Everything Manny Lentino said about you is true."

"Wait until you see me play racquetball," Ron said.

"There, you don't stand a chance," Sarah said.

"I'm a pretty good player. Don't be so confident," Ron said.

The racquetball court was regulation size with a twenty foot ceiling and a glass back wall.

Neither was above pushing the other to avoid being blocked. They played on, scarcely pausing between points.

Finally, Sarah smashed the ball low enough and to the side, forcing Ron to lunge for the ball. He missed it but she had hit the ball so hard, that it rebounded off the back wall of the racquetball court. Ron recovered and scooped it in an underhand motion. The ball hit the front wall and then the ceiling. When it hit the floor, the ball bounced high, driving Sarah back. This time she waited until the ball descended, almost hitting the floor. She crouched low, following the ball and then swung her racquet, "killing" the ball. Ron, with no chance of a return watched the ball roll to him.

"What a shot!" Ron said. He reached for a towel and wiped the perspiration from his face. He hunched over with his hands on his thighs out of breath.

"That was one hell of a volley. We went back and forth on the point for a least a minute." Sarah patted herself with her towel. She was hardly perspiring. Her white sweat band made her dark hair puff out around it. Her white pleated shorts fit her tightly, but not so fetchingly as her red tank top, which barely concealed her brassiere.

"You were toying with me, Sarah. You hit the ball from side to side and made me chase after it! You have no mercy, and me with shrapnel still in my leg."

"You get no handicap for a handicap, my sweet. You'll have to come up with a better excuse.

"I'm out of shape. That's what I am." Ron patted his stomach.

"I like what I see," Sarah said. She circled him in the manner of one assessing a thoroughbred horse.

"I'm not the greatest racquetball player but you made me look bad," Ron said.

"You'll do better next time. Especially if your eyes follow the ball instead of me." She playfully whipped her towel at him.

"You noticed, eh. I think you wore that outfit just to distract me. Some people will do anything to win." He touched her cheek and moved closer to her. He kissed her lightly on the mouth and they embraced.

He turned and noticed a group waiting to play racquetball. He stiffened and pulled away.

"Damn!"

"What's the matter?"

"The glass wall is for spectators not spectacles," Ron said.

"Are you afraid that those people are lawyers?"

"The one in the green shorts, is." Ron waved to him.

"This is a racquetball court, not a court of law," Sarah said.

"The legal community is a very small one."

"Let's give them something to really talk about." Sarah pushed her body against him and put her arms around his neck. She then, ostentatiously, soul kissed him.

When they walked off the court, the lawyer in green shorts stepped aside.

"You play a hell of a game, Judge," he said.

CHAPTER 19

▼

Time seemed to quicken in direct proportion to activity. The daily court work, the trials, one after another, the decisions, the research and his duties, were subsumed in the events that were taking hold in his life. The house was sold and the move into the Manhattan apartment was accomplished with less stress than he had imagined.

Sarah seemed to camp out at his doorstep, ready at a moment's notice to suggest ideas for the decor or the arrangement of furniture.

"Colleen will hate the pink curtains," Sarah said.

"That's my daughter's favorite color."

"She's been conditioned to pink but yellow is probably her favorite color. It's more intellectual."

"Her favorite color is pink!" Ron said.

"And Alan's favorite color is blue?"

"Sarah, you're such a smart ass."

"I can be a shrinking violet, too," she said and smiled like a coquette.

"And a tease, also. You have my tongue hanging out. Even pre-school teenagers today don't wait this long," Ron said.

"Anticipation is the spice of life. The kids don't know what they're missing."

"I know what I'm missing," he said.

Ron had visited Sarah in her apartment on four different occasions but she had never invited him into her bedroom.

Despite candlelight and wine, she always seemed to change the subject.

"Tell me about Vietnam, Ron." They completed dinner and moved to her sofa. She stroked the scar on his forehead.

"Another time. It was not pleasant."

"Then tell me about when you were an Assistant District Attorney. That wasn't painful was it?"

"I ultimately became Chief of Homicide with the District Attorney's Office."

"That's very impressive."

"I didn't start there. I ended up there," he said. "I tried seventy-three murder cases—personally."

"And that qualified you to be a judge in medical malpractice cases?"

"That's another story."

"How did you become a judge?"

"That's also another story." Ron laughed and shook his head.

"Are you really half Italian, Ron?"

"My mother's maiden name is Carioscia. Concetta Carioscia."

"And your father?"

"Believe it or not, he was a Mayflower descendant. He was killed in a car accident."

"Oh, I assumed he was Jewish."

"So do a lot of people," Sarah said.

"Well, you order people around like you're 100% Italian," Sarah said.

"You think you're a pussycat?" Ron said.

"I had a good teacher. My ex-husband is Italian."

"Sometimes you wonder whether its nature or nurture. My kids are such opposites."

"Tell me about your children Ron. I can't wait to meet them."

"It's like they were switched at birth. Not physically, but psychically. Colleen was the tomboy while Alan was the shy, sensitive one."

"My son from the earliest age, loved poetry. I encouraged him. He cut his baby teeth on Vachel Lindsey. By the time he was thirteen, he was reading Samuel Taylor Coleridge's Rhyme of the Ancient Mariner and Kubla Khan."

"The only conflict I had with Alice was concerning my son. Some sort of bell went off in her head about him. God forbid Alan would come home crying after a schoolyard fight! Suddenly it became my obligation to 'toughen him up' and take him for Karate lessons. So I told her that the only useful purpose of a black belt was to hold up Alan's pants. Believe me, you wanted to know about Vietnam? That was nothing compared to the fights we had over the kids."

"Sometimes husbands and wives fight as if they were siblings."

"That's so true, but I was at a disadvantage. I had no experience in that kind of combat. I was an only child."

Ron moved closer to her on the sofa.

"Spoiled and used to getting your way?" Sarah interposed a throw pillow between them.

"And what about you?" Ron asked.

"Me? My marriage was short but not sweet. I make a lot of money. Commissions on the rental of commercial space can be very lucrative. I specialize in the renting of offices. I just have to put together one deal for say, three or more floors of a building, like the Woolworth Building, and I've made my money for the year. And I put together a few deals in a year—enough to own a Mercedes instead of a Chevy."

"I've heard all these things before," Ron said. "What about your sister. You never talk about her. Your parents, they still alive? Brothers, uncles, cousins. Anything! I've told you the most intimate details of my life and you've told me nothing about yourself. I want to know everything about you, too. Was your life so terrible that you're so secretive?"

"Secret? It's no secret. I started making more money than my husband and he started to live off of me. How can you respect a man like that? So, I left him."

"I thought he was a lawyer?"

"The worst kind," Sarah said. "A lazy lawyer."

"What's his name?"

"You don't know him and I want to forget him!"

Ron looked at her curiously. Truly, she must have had a traumatic childhood. One thing was obvious. Her apartment, its furnishings, and the quality of her clothes left no doubt that she was financially secure. If the Louis the Fifteenth desk, along with the china closet filled with Pre-Columbian artifacts, were any indication of success, then Sarah's apartment reflected success. She had the eye of a decorator, or had she hired one?

"Success breeds failure." Ron looked around the living room.

"What does that mean?"

"You're so successful in business but you're an emotional cripple."

"You think I'm frigid?" Sarah said.

"That occurred to me."

"And if we make love?" Sarah said. "Then I would be normal?"

"I think you've been teasing me."

"Perhaps just enticing you."

"Or overplaying your hand." Ron rose. "Goodnight, Ms. Baruch."

Sarah remained seated on the sofa. She watched as he retrieved his coat. "Make sure you close the door on the way out," she said.

Ron stood for a moment gazing at her and then opened the door.

At the door, he tripped on the door saddle. He felt his bad leg give way and he stumbled forward. He crashed to the hallway floor.

Sarah ran to his side. She offered him her hand but he slapped it away.

"Maybe we can settle this out of court." Sarah smiled and clutched her breast.

"That's very funny," Ron said. "I just ruined my best suit."

"It's just a little dirty," she said. "Nothing is torn. Come on inside and we'll clean it."

She led him to the bedroom and insisted that he remove his jacket and his trousers.

"A little brushing and they'll be like new." She left the room.

When Sarah returned, she was in her bra and panties.

"You must think that I'm made of wood," Ron said. He felt foolish sitting on the edge of her bed without trousers.

"Not at all, my darling," she said, "wood doesn't drip blood on my satin sheets."

He rose from the bed. It was only then that he saw the blood flowing from his skinned knee.

"Don't worry about it," she said and pushed him back onto the bed. "Sit!"

She left the room again and returned with a first-aid kit.

"Used to be a Girl Scout," Sarah said. She dropped to her knees and separated his legs. She cleansed the scrape with a washcloth. She then applied bacitracin to the wound and covered it with a large band-aid.

"There," she said. "That ought to hold you."

He looked at her and then lifted her up. She allowed herself to fall to his side onto the bed. He kissed her and fumbled with her bra.

For a long time afterwards, they lay together. She seemed compliant in her passivity as he touched her face. Stroked her hair. Stroked her body. Kissed her. Ears, cheeks, breasts, shoulders. There was not a part of her body that he did not caress. She put her finger to his lips when he tried to speak.

"Do you still think I'm frigid?" she murmured.

CHAPTER 20

▼

Joe Pencils seemed genial enough when he called Victor Santo to meet him at Birdie's Tavern. This congeniality, however, was like a red flag to Santo

"Have a cigar," Pencils said. He took a case from his jacket and opened it.

"Come on, Joe. You know I don't smoke."

"That's one way to stay healthy." Pencils took a cigar and bit off the end. He turned and spit the tip to the floor. "But I know a better way."

"Joe, why are you always threatening me? I thought we were friends."

"If we weren't friends, do you think I would warn you?"

"Does the Falcon think I can't do anything right?" Victor said.

"You're a hot head. That's your problem. Blowing up is all right if you're doing it for a purpose. But you're like a volcano. The eruption is unpredictable. And that's what has the Falcon worried." He lit his cigar and puffed on it deeply. "Ah. Nothing like a good cigar."

Pencils blew the smoke toward the other patrons who were at the front of the bar as if it was a smoke screen.

"I thought the Examination Before Trial was all in our favor."

"Not according to Vecchio—and he was there. Your wife came across good. But you? The Falcon nearly went crazy when he heard how you acted. Screaming at lawyers?"

"I didn't scream at them. They just got my goat."

"Didn't Firestone tell you that they would try to provoke you? Make you say things in their favor."

"They were asking me personal questions. Like how many times I used to sleep with my wife before the operation."

"And you said?"

"Five times a week and sometimes twice in a day, and now, never. That last part is true."

"And the first part is unbelievable. Not for a man whose been married for thirteen years. Not for a man who has a girlfriend."

"They were hinting about that. In front of my wife, too!"

"So you decided to create a small diversion?" Pencils said.

"So I banged on the table a little. Big deal."

"Big deal is right, Victor. Andrew's laid out a lot of money on this one, and it's still not finished."

"Tell the Falcon not to be so nervous."

"Andrew's not nervous. That's his nature. He's not used to laying out money on spec."

"What money has he laid out?"

"Are you a moron, Victor?"

Joe Pencils smashed his cigar into the bar top. The mark took its place there, along with the other scars that testified to his frequent annoyance.

"Christ, you are touchy today, Joe."

Joe Pencils always sat on the last bar stool. He would lean on the bar occasionally but he kept the front entrance in his line of sight at all times. Victor was made to sit on a bar stool with his back to the front. Consequently, he was not aware of the two men who approached.

"Good to see you," Joe said to Pete and Eugene.

Victor turned in surprise.

"Say hello to my friend, Victor, here," Pencils said.

"We already met," Pete said.

"Really?" It was Pencils' turn to be surprised.

"Yeah, Six Fingers introduced us," Eugene said.

There was a long period of silence. It soon occurred to Victor that there would be no further conversation in his presence.

"I have to be going," Victor said. "Tell our friend not to worry. Everything's under control."

Before Victor left, he considered offering a handshake but Pete and Eugene stood with their arms folded.

The bartender, in response to a nod by Pencils, set an *espresso* on the bar and then quickly retreated.

Pencils handed a piece of paper to Pete who looked at it and then showed Eugene.

"Damn. I thought the job was to take care of the shit that just left," Eugene said. "That one, I do for free."

"This is a very heavy contract," Pete said. He took the paper from Eugene and handed it back to Pencils.

"No heavier than the last one."

"Why we hitting doctors?" Eugene said.

"You got a problem with this?" Pencils said.

"What the fuck is wrong with you?" Pete said. He punched Eugene's arm hard. "We either do the job or we don't. We don't ask 'why'."

"So I ain't perfect," Eugene said.

"You need this?" Pencils said and offered the paper to Pete.

"No. Eugene has a photographic memory. The only paper we need is what's in your pocket."

"The usual, half now and half on completion."

Pete nodded and Joe Pencils took a thick envelope from his pocket.

Pete weighed the envelope in his hand and then gave it to Eugene.

"Any special way you want the job done?" Eugene said.

"I don't care how it's done. But it has to be quick. By next week," Joe Pencils said.

"Rush jobs are extra," Eugene said.

"Not for the Falcon it ain't." Pencils turned his back on the two men and drank his *espresso*, holding the cup with his pinky finger straight out as if to avoid wetting his diamond ring.

CHAPTER 21

▼

Jack Zangara was so deep in concentration that he did not hear the creaking steps when Barbara DiTucci came down to the basement.

She stood behind Jack and watched him.

The basement was unfinished and a desk lamp was the only light. The filing cabinets that held the dead doctor's records flanked the desk and the dim light, cast eerie shadows along the floor.

Jack sat hunched down. He reached over and flipped through the Rolodex and then examined the several medical files that lay on the desk.

When she touched his shoulder, he jumped.

"I didn't mean to startle you," Barbara said.

Jack took off his reading glasses and rubbed his eyes. He looked at her. She was in his shadow. He slid his chair to the side and the desk light shone on her. She wore a white, starched, apron and seemed to him to be as an apparition in a spotlight.

"It seems like I've put you in a dungeon."

"No, it's fine. It's quiet and it gives me time to think."

"Do you know that you've been at it for five hours?" Barbara said.

"Five…?" He put on his eyeglasses and looked at his wristwatch. "The time flies when you're having fun."

"Some fun."

"It's my day off. Has your son come home from school?"

"David was here two hours ago. He came down here and you showed him your gun. Don't you remember?"

"Alzheimers," he said and slapped his temple. "I thought it was yesterday."

"David really likes you. You have a way with children."

"I have a secret weapon when it comes to kids. I pay attention to their questions and I give them direct answers."

"What kind of questions did he ask?"

"He wants to know about his father."

"And what did you tell him?"

"For a doctor, your husband had a pretty good handwriting." Zangara picked up a file as if it were a sample and pointed to a page.

"I thought you gave direct answers," Barbara said.

"Only to children," Jack said.

"Do you have any children?"

"No. And I probably would never be able to employ *that* secret weapon with my own. The job seems to always come first."

"Jack, I can't tell you how grateful I am." She touched his shoulder again.

"It's a case that has to be solved—one way or another."

"Just a case?" Barbara said.

"When I get a case that's a puzzle, I can't let it go. I guess it's the Sicilian in me."

"My husband was Sicilian."

"Was he? Now I have more reason to solve the case if it was more than an accident. Blood revenge!"

"You won't solve it for me because I'm Jewish?"

"You are? I thought you were Italian."

"Some detective you are!" She smiled. "But I cook great Italian."

"None of my ex-wives could ever cook."

"Ex-wives? How many times have you been married?"

"Twice. But it was my fault—both times. It's the job. They all complained that I loved it more than them."

"Did you?"

"Love never lasts." He passed his hand over his head as if to rearrange the few remaining hairs on his bald spot.

"My, the cynical policeman."

"As I said. It's the job."

"And you're doing a wonderful job. People would never believe the time you've put in here. The next time someone engages in cop-bashing, I'll set him straight."

"A letter of appreciation to the Police Commissioner will be fine."

Barbara took his chair and spun it around.

"Why can't you just accept a compliment?"

Zangara peered at her. Had he made her angry? The desk lamp did seem to cast a halo about her. Jack. Jack. Come to your senses! Was the prolonged investigation merely an excuse to be with her?

"I'd better be going." He looked again at his watch.

"You'll do no such thing. I cooked dinner for us. Why do you think I'm wearing an apron? David is at his friend's home for a sleep over. I thought this might be a good time for us to talk."

"Talk?"

"Yes. Don't you think I want to know what you've discovered? Or are you going to treat me like a suspect?"

Barbara, true to her word, did cook great Italian. The gravy had simmered for hours and would have passed any test given by his mother.

"Delicious," he said.

Although they sat at the kitchen table, the crystal was Waterford and the plates were Lennox.

"I thought that the dining room would be too formal," she said.

"Hey, I count myself lucky if I get a paper napkin," Zangara said.

He noticed that Barbara not only cooked but served Italian style. In that spirit, he tucked his cloth napkin in his shirt collar. The spaghetti as the *primo piatto* was followed by the meatballs, sausage and chicken, with the salad last.

There was little conversation during dinner as if she did not want to interfere with his enjoyment of the meal.

"Delicious," he repeated as the various courses were served.

She set up the coffee cups and dessert on the coffee table in the living room.

"Go. I'll clean up." Barbara swept the dishes off the kitchen table.

"Can't I help?"

"You're a guest," she said. "I'm just putting everything in the dishwasher. There's a humidor on the coffee table if you would like a cigar." When he sat on the living room sofa, he noted that the photograph of her dead husband was no longer on the mantel.

"I don't smoke," he said. He looked into the humidor. It was newly filled. He took a cigar and put it in his pocket.

"I'm taking one for my partner, Tom."

"Is he working on the case, too?" she called out.

"Off and on." It wasn't exactly a lie. Wouldn't Tom be working on the case when he brought his partner up-to-date?

Barbara still wore her apron when she entered the living room. She carried a tray with the coffee and desserts. She set them on the table and then sat next to him. She poured the *espresso* and handed him the *demi tasse* cup and saucer.

The tray was laden with miniature Italian pastries.

The cup rattled in the saucer as he reached for a canoli. He spilled his coffee.

Barbara whipped off her apron and bent over to clean the table.

"I'm sorry." His eyes were drawn to her cleavage. He was transfixed.

"No harm done. It didn't get on the rug." She sat back in the sofa but did move to the other end. She waited until he finished his coffee.

"Now tell me what you found out."

"It really is confidential," Zangara said. He wasn't going to be bribed by a dinner, was he?

"Jack, that's not fair. Please." She looked at him with eyes that seemed too innocent. Wasn't that a tipoff of guilt?

"My investigation is not complete. I'm really not comfortable talking to you about this."

"Jack, you're the closest person to me since my husband's death. My so-called friends have taken to the tall grass as if his death was my fault. You're not my last hope, you're my only hope. All those hours you put in, you must have uncovered something. What about the threats?"

"A dead end. I've been through all the records and checked out a few of the threats. I interviewed a patient by the name of Jones. He's 78 years old. Another person who threatened your husband was in Florida at the time. The other three people were cranks, not psychotic killers. Barbara, I'm just not sure anymore. I'm a homicide detective and my initial conclusion is always violence. But it's like somebody is playing with my mind. A thief could have by-passed the alarm, but then nothing was stolen. I hate to say this but your husband's watch could have been taken by a cop, or other personnel, on the scene. But I'm not going to assume that there was a crooked cop at work here.

So, if it wasn't for the patched window and the missing Rolex, I would have to say that it was suicide."

"Not an accident- or something else?"

"There was little alcohol in his blood. Tired people don't just fall asleep after they're safely home. Drunk, yes."

"There has to be something else. You're a detective. Some clue—something." Barbara's voice trailed off.

"There's nothing else."

"I'll never believe that Gabe killed himself. I knew him. He was too full of life. Somebody killed him!"

"I think I'd better go."

Barbara gazed at him and extended her hand as if to ask him to help her to her feet.

"What happens now?" she said.

"As I said, I haven't finished the investigation. But I don't expect to find any loose ends. I did see some legal papers in the file. Did your husband have many lawsuits against him?"

"Just one. It upset him. Gabe had never been sued before."

"I saw that there's a lawsuit by a woman named 'Santo'."

"Do you know her?"

"I knew very few of my husband's patients."

"So you don't know her?"

"What motive could this woman possibly have," Barbara said. Her tone was sharp and curt, as if she felt that she was being cross-examined.

"I hate when I can't get a straight answer from someone."

Zangara rose and walked to the door.

"You want a straight answer, Jack? I don't think you're angry, I think you're bashful.

"Could be," he said. When he walked toward his car, he walked—slowly. Now that was an invitation! Was he really being bashful? But then wasn't he always bold only when he didn't give a shit?

"Detective Zangara?" she called from the doorway.

He stopped. He saw her standing there expressionless, except for her eyes that were wide and open. Uncertainly, and then with more rapid steps, he returned to the house.

CHAPTER 22

▼

Christmas was happy time. Christmas was family time and Ron envisioned it as a gathering of his clan, such as it was. It seemed, however, that everyone else had different plans. His son, Alan, arrived from Chicago, took one look at his new room and announced that he was off to visit friends in Boston. The incongruity of it was that his daughter, who was studying at Boston College, came home and immediately left for Chicago.

"Daddy," Colleen had said, "my room is lovely and I like the decor but what ever possessed you to paint it yellow?"

Ron was sure that if he had not sold his house, that instead of running off, Colleen and Alan would have brought their friends home for the holidays.

"I'm losing my children," he had told Sarah. In that secret part of him, however, he was not that unhappy. It would afford him more time to be with Sarah.

The Christmas recess, including the holidays and weekends, rounded out to nine uninterrupted days. Museums would be his last option. Racquetball would keep him in shape. And, of course, there would be that delicious other. They had made love in his new apartment—on his new bed and at her place. They had joked about "home and home" engagements.

"Sarah. We are so perfect for each other. We're so attuned to each other that I can't imagine a day without you."

"Is this a proposal of marriage?" she had said without enthusiasm.

"Well…yes. I guess it is." Why had she been so surprised? She was more than his lover, she was his friend.

"It's too soon. Much too soon," she had said.

"So then we'll play it by ear." Ron had embraced her but she had remained stiff in his arms.

When Ron called her office on Christmas Eve, her secretary told him that Sarah was in Spain.

"You're joking."

"I never joke, your Honor. Mrs. Baruch left last night from JFK Airport and won't be back until after the holidays."

"Where in Spain?" Ron tried to conceal the disturbance in his voice. He had never heard her secretary call her "Mrs. Baruch."

"I'm not sure, it might be France or Italy," the secretary said.

Ron caught the evasion in her voice.

Ron considered flying to Europe. But where? Surprise her in Paris? Or worse, meet her in Rome, traveling with another man. Even that prospect occurred to him.

Why had he told her that he was losing his children? Had that made Sarah back off? Did she think that she was too disruptive an influence? Why couldn't she share his fears with her? What the hell was wrong with her?

On Christmas Day, Ron went to his mother's apartment on Shore Road in Bay Ridge.

He went there alone. No children, no fiancée, laden with excuses instead of presents.

His mother was 75 years old and garrulous. She had always been combative but it seemed that age had only intensified her worst qualities.

"Where's Colleen? How come she's not here?" Her voice was heavy with criticism.

"I told you, Mom. Colleen is in Chicago."

"And Alan?"

"Boston. The kids are adults. They're visiting friends."

"They should be home with their family for the holidays," Mrs. Goodman said.

"They'll be home for Easter."

"You're too soft," she said. "When are you going to learn that children need direction? Discipline!"

"The way you raised me?" he said.

"I didn't do so bad."

"Mom, I have enough problems. I came here to have dinner."

"I cooked for an army." She pointed to the kitchen stove that held several large pots.

"I wanted to take you to a restaurant. You didn't have to cook."

"Christmas, you should have a traditional Italian meal. You're not going to get my sauce at any restaurant." Mrs. Goodman lifted the cover from the pot that contained the tomato gravy.

"You're right about that, Mom." Ron smiled as he breathed the familiar aroma.

"How come you didn't bring the girl. What's her name, Sarah?"

"Her mother is sick. She had to go to California," Ron said.

"For a judge, you're not a very good liar."

"Judges don't lie."

"So the girl dumped you, eh?" Concetta Goodman said.

CHAPTER 23

▼

They sat in Eugene's old fashioned kitchen. The cabinets over the sink and stove were heavy with layers of paint that left them slightly ajar. The chipped Formica counter was edged in nineteen fifties chrome. Nevertheless, it was clean and functional, as if it was managed by a person who cared, but not too much.

"Everybody thinks that a hit is easy," Pete said. "Boom! Boom! And it's over." He pointed his finger at Eugene as if it were a gun. "It takes planning, knowledge and inform…"

Eugene chewed on a hero sandwich and shrugged as if Pete were restating the obvious.

Pete stopped speaking when Eugene's mother poked her head in the doorway.

"Hey Ma. We ain't finished yet. Go back and watch the TV." Eugene's voice was more loud than annoyed.

"You father's not gonna like it. I got to make his supper."

Eugene's mother was short as was Eugene but one had to look closely for any family resemblance. He was wiry where she was obese. His face was thin and consistent with his quirky nervous movement while her's was what her husband called a "fat face."

She stared at the two men who were ignoring her. Then she waddled back to her TV. Her shrug left no doubt that if there were any blame for the late supper, it would be on the shoulders of Eugene.

"I told you we can't talk here," Pete said. "We should have gone to my house."

"She's hard of hearing. Can't you hear the television blasting? With all the noise, you never have to be worried about any wire tap."

"Yeah, but you can't hear yourself think. What did you find out about this Dr. Spender?"

Eugene put down the sandwich and wiped his mouth. "It's going to be tough to make the hit."

"Christ, Eugene, let me do the planning. Just give me the details."

"Spender lives in Sea Gate. Elmwood Road. That's in Coney Island. Private community. Gate at entrance, twenty-four hours. Sea Gate Police. Dress like cops and have the same powers to arrest."

"What kind of a car does he drive?"

"An old shebang. A white, 1999 Lincoln Town Car. Guess he figures that it won't be stolen."

"Or he's cheap."

"Probably. Did you know that a white car doesn't show the dirt as much?"

"Now that's really intelligent, Eugene. Are there any other pearls of wisdom you want to share with me?"

"His wife drives a Jaguar," Eugene said. "But they're divorced." Eugene smiled as if dribbling out facts was the essence of wit.

"I don't have time for your shit, Eugene! What else did you find out."

"We can't pop Spender at his house. All visitors have to show ID at the gate—and the cops there keep a record. The fence around the place is like twenty feet high except for the houses that overlook the bay. We can't do it like we did the other doctor because he don't have a beach-front house."

"How did you get in?"

"I went to a real estate place and told them I was interested in buying a house there. They waltzed me right in." Eugene could plan things, too. Couldn't he? "I even wore a suit. Gave a phony name. It worked like a charm."

"O.K. So we can't do the job there," Pete said. "What about his office? What about his routine? Christ, you've been tailing this guy for four days."

"Yeah, and we had a snow storm the other day."

"He didn't see you, did he?"

"You kidding? I could tail a cop and he wouldn't know it."

"What about the office?"

"That has problems, too. He's on the eighteenth floor of the Williamsburg Bank Building. You know, the one with the big clock on top."

"Eugene!" His mother shouted from the living room. "I can't make your father's meal one, two, three!"

"We're still eating for chrissake." Eugene held up his plate as if his mother could see it. "We'll be out of here in a minute."

"Your father don't like to wait!"

"Let's go to my house," Pete said.

"You never have anything to eat there."

"Why don't you just tell me what else you found out." Pete shook his head in resignation.

"Spender has office hours from eleven to one, every day, Monday to Thursday. But he's in and out. Sees patients mostly by appointment. He's at the hospitals every morning from seven to ten and then again after two o'clock."

"Hospitals?"

"He's all over the place. Lutheran Hospital. Beth Torah, Sacred Heart, Victory Memorial, Maimonides. He's a specialist and gets called in by other doctors. It was a hell of a job tailing him. But I figured out his routine." Eugene smiled in self-approval.

"You did good, Eugene. But I haven't been exactly asleep. I checked him out on the Internet but they only showed him as being at Beth Torah Hospital. He's a gastroenterologist. Specializes in Endoscopic Retrograde Cholangelo Pancreatography," it was Pete's turn to smile.

"Shit. What's that?"

"He takes out gall stones by passing a tube down the throat."

"Why the fuck don't they just talk English."

"Fancy names, fancy prices."

"Yeah, up goes the medical insurance," Eugene said.

Pete shook his head. In their business it was the other people who had to worry about the cost of insurance.

"Where does he park his car when he goes to his office?"

"He parks it on the street."

"Not in a garage?"

"Nah, he's got M.D. plates. He parks right in front. There's a bank guard, too. He comes out every so often and checks the cars."

"So he moves around a lot but he's always at his home or in the office." Pete stroked his chin to indicate that he was evaluating the information. "You trailed him to all the different hospitals?"

"Yeah."

"What's the least time he spends traveling in the afternoon?"

"It depends on the hospital. But it's never less than half an hour. Daytime traffic is a killer."

"You always come up with the right word, Eugene." Pete patted Eugene on the cheek.

"But he doesn't get home the same time every night. I didn't tell you about the girlfriend. What a piece of ass. He's an ugly bastard but money gets you everything."

"Eugene. You'd need more than money."

"Thanks a lot, Pete. You ain't no prize package either."

"Forget about the girlfriend. You say that the one constant is his office?"

"Yeah. I guess I did say that. So that's the place where we pop him?" Eugene asked.

"We're going to kill him, Eugene, but we're not going to shoot him," Pete said.

CHAPTER 24

▼

Eugene watched anxiously as Pete bent over his workbench.

The basement was unfinished but all manner of tools and equipment, such as saws, sets of wrenches and screwdrivers were neatly arranged and hung on the wall above the workbench.

Pete and Eugene had known each other since kindergarten, and they had recognized each's propensities almost immediately. In a school yard fight, Pete had always seemed to hit a little harder than was necessary, and Eugene had always been at his side—to help him or goad him on. Neither could remember the exact moment when they had graduated into killers, although Pete conceded that he had had a head start—he had killed his father!

Sixteen at the time but already full grown, he blamed his alcoholic father for the death of his mother. She had died of breast cancer. No. His father had killed her by his neglect. He had been too cheap to take her to the doctor and when he did, it was too late.

He had pressed a pillow over his drunken father's face. A brief struggle. No signs of violence. A heart attack. Myocardial infarction listed as the cause on the death certificate.

Even for the Oedipal Act, he had been paid. He had inherited the house!

There had been no remorse. If he could kill his own father, he could murder anybody. The Army had completed his education of violence. Infantry. Jump School. Special Forces. "Pathologically asocial" was the psychiatric report that formed the basis of his Bad Conduct Discharge. He admitted rolling a grenade into an Officer's tent, but insisted that it was only a prank. If it wasn't, wouldn't he have removed the pin?

"Some day I'm going to write a book about different ways to make a hit," Pete said. He tightened the vise on his basement workbench. He leaned over and examined the bomb.

Eugene watched closely but warily.

"I'm not saying you're wrong, but I don't like this," Eugene said.

"Relax."

"That's easy for you to say but I have to put the bomb under Spender's car."

"Do it with your left hand. You don't need all those fingers."

"Very funny. Maybe you should plant the bomb since you're such an expert."

"I'm too big to fit under the car, dummy."

"Well I think there has to be a better way to make this hit."

The pipe bomb was a simple device with an igniter, a wristwatch for a timer, and a magnet. Pete used black electrical tape to fasten those items onto the pipe that he filled with gun powder.

"Why don't you use plastique?"

"It has to look homemade, Eugene. If I use C-4, the Feds will be all over the place thinking it's the work of terrorists. We don't need them on our backs."

"This ain't going to throw them off. They'll come in anyway. I don't like this!"

"Think of the publicity then, Eugene. You'll be famous."

"That's what I'm afraid of." Eugene squeezed his left hand as he visualized himself in the hospital with no arm.

"I don't like it in this basement. It's too creepy."

"It's better than your mother's kitchen." Pete held up the finished product and offered it to Eugene.

"Now, remember, you attach it to the tail pipe as close to the muffler as you can. We can't rely on the magnet alone. He might hit a bump while he's driving. Then, you press the winder on the watch..." Pete held the bomb still closer. "...for chrissake. Take the damned thing. It's not going to bite you."

"I'm really nervous about this. If this thing goes off at the wrong time, I'm dead—and so are a lot of innocent people."

"Since when you worried about innocent bystanders?"

"You put the bomb where I tell you, then nobody else is going to get hurt. Christ, I'm an expert!"

"I still don't like it. I got a bad feeling about this." Eugene shook his head.

"Unwind, will you. The watch is a 4G—shock. The best sports-watch they make."

"Unwind? I'm shitting in my pants and you're making jokes."

"Trust me. This is the best way. All the risks are up-front. Once the bomb is on the car, we're in the clear."

Pete tossed the device in the air and juggled it.

"Why don't we pop the doc and be done with it?" Eugene said.

"Where? We can't hit him at home, he travels around too much. The only place is the office. If we take him out in front of the office building, we can't control the number of witnesses. With your luck, Eugene, we'd get a flat tire when we made our getaway."

"Masks are no good? We could go up there and throw the bastard out the window."

"The secretary and the patients, too? Besides, you remember the dopey bastards who robbed an office and then took off their masks in front of the surveillance cameras."

"There's no cameras on the floors. I checked that."

"What about the lobby?"

"Yeah, I guess you're right but I'm still the one that has to get under the car."

"There are too many buttons to press," Eugene said, despite knowing that it was a losing argument. He much preferred guns—even knives.

"You are a dummy." Pete held up the quartz watch. "You press the top right button twice. Then press the lower button to activate the timer."

"See. I set it for 1:40 p.m. We plant it at 1, it goes off when he's driving."

"What if he's running behind schedule with his patients?"

"You told me he's always out by 1:15 at the latest."

"Yeah, but what if…"

"What if…what if? If he's not out of there by 1:15, we call up and tell him there's a bomb in the building. That will get him on his way."

"How we gonna know when the car explodes? You're not thinking of following him, are you?"

"Of course not! They videotape all the spectators. That's how they catch the weirdos," Pete said.

Pete had a variety of suits and uniforms in his closet. Sanitation worker, postal worker, firefighter, and most appropriately for this occasion, a police officer's uniform. That would enable him, if necessary, to wave off the inquisitive bank guard and allow Eugene to slip under Dr. Spender's car.

They saw Dr. Spender, right on schedule, leave the Willliamsburg Bank building at 1:15 p.m. He stopped to chat with the bank guard who had come out to greet him. Then he entered his automobile, removed "the Club" that he had affixed to the steering wheel and drove away.

"Goodbye Mr. Chips," Eugene said.

"Hello money," Pete said.

That day, however, Dr. Spender did not follow his usual routine.

CHAPTER 25

▼

Christmas time was lawyers' time, too. It was ideal to vacation in Florida or the Islands for a few days, but it was also a good time to conduct depositions—examinations before trial. It was an essential element of Disclosure that always seemed to be deferred because of other pressing matters.

For the convenience of everyone, Manny Lentino and Christine Fisher had agreed that the deposition of Dr. Spender would be conducted at Firestone's office on Court Street. It was the same office building across the street from the Courthouse where Ruth and Victor Santo had been deposed. The deposition was scheduled for 1:30 p.m. on December 28—the very day that the bomb was placed under Dr. Spender's automobile.

Dr. Spender drove the short distance to Court Street and parked his car at the corner taxi stand. Before leaving, he lowered the visor to display a placard that read "DOCTOR EMERGENCY."

Spender was a tall man and his legs spread awkwardly when he exited his car. The skin on his face was mask-like, the product of a plastic surgeon's attempt at rejuvenation, but the rest of his body showed that Dr. Spender had not succeeded with any particular diet or workout regimen.

He tried to button his jacket but it was too tight so he allowed it to hang loose. He walked purposefully, without an overcoat, bracing himself against the wind, as if to advertise that he was a busy man who was being needlessly delayed.

Technically, Christine Fisher was Dr. Spender's lawyer. She had been retained by his insurance company and, although it was for all practical purposes defunct, a fund had been set aside for the payment of her legal fees. She had agreed with Manny Lentino to present a united front against the plaintiffs, Ruth and Victor Santo. Sink or swim together. At some point, their interests might diverge, but for now, they would defend the lawsuit—as allies. At the deposition being conducted by Firestone, both she and Lentino could object to the questions and ask their own questions, afterwards.

Firestone provided the defense team with one of his office rooms, where they briefly conferred with Dr. Spender.

That office, unlike Firestone's room, was small and furnished with bare-bone furniture. An old desk, several chairs upholstered in button downed leather and a table that was laden with old briefs and transcripts.

"How much time you need?" Firestone said. "The court reporter is here already."

"Give us ten minutes," Lentino said.

"Maybe five minutes," Fisher said.

She had already discussed the case with Dr. Spender on the telephone.

Firestone nodded and left.

"Doctor, please. Please do not volunteer any answer. This deposition is not for your benefit. It can only hurt us," Fisher said.

"The truth never hurt anyone."

"Bull shit, Doctor! You're not testifying as an expert witness at a trial. You're testifying as a defendant! You answer 'yes' or 'no'. Firestone is not interested in your reasons. You know that there are very strict rules on the use of an Examination Before Trial during a trial. Firestone can read any part of it he chooses. But, we can't."

"That doesn't seem fair."

"Dr. Spender, this is a lawsuit not a philosophical debate. Anything you say will be used to contradict you," Manny Lentino said. "You know that!"

"Yes. Yes. I've been through this before."

"That's why I'm telling you again!" Christine raised her eyebrows as if in despair.

"Every question can't be answered 'yes' or 'no'."

"Then say that you can't answer it in the form that it's presented," Lentino said.

Firestone's conference room also served as his library. Between the windows and around the room, floor to ceiling shelves were filled with law books.

The long polished oak table was set on a chrome base. The over-stuffed brown leather chairs that circled the table also had chrome arms and legs.

Firestone took the position of power at the long end of the table.

Fisher interposed herself between Firestone and the witness.

"Can the Doctor sit closer to me?" Firestone said. "The Court Reporter won't be able to hear him."

"She'll be able to hear just fine," Fisher said.

After several preliminary questions, it became evident that this would not be a tranquil deposition.

"Doctor, isn't it a fact that you did not perform the operation on Mrs. Santo?" Firestone asked.

"That's a lie!"

"Didn't Dr. Gould, a second year resident, actually insert the endoscope?"

"Absolutely not!"

"But he was present, wasn't he?"

"You think I can remember everybody who was present at every one of my operations? I've done thousands of these procedures in every hospital in the City. They come to watch me so they can learn."

"Was Dr. Gould present?" Firestone persisted. "I move to strike the answer. It's not responsive."

"He answered the question," Lentino said.

"He did not!" Firestone said.

"Yes I did."

"Let the court reporter read it back."

"Read what back?" Fisher said.

"Whether Doctor Gould was present or not!"

The three lawyers were sitting across the conference table and were shouting at each other. Dr. Spender joined in the cacophony with his own comments on the questions. "Stupid." "You're trying to put words in my mouth." "Wrong." "And dead wrong!"

Jane Sackheim, the court reporter, threw up her hands in frustration.

"Everyone is talking at once! Please. This transcript is going to be a jumble."

"Jane, read it back!" Firestone said.

She reached into the stenotype receptacle and leafed quickly through the unfolding paper. "Was Dr. Gould present?"

"The question and answer before that," Lentino said. Jane then re-read it.

"All right. Let's start over." Firestone said. His voice showed the first sign of defeat. They were doing a number on him. Frustrating him. Challenging him.

Anything to confuse the issues. It was old stuff. He had encountered that before. He was still on the first page of the questions he intended to ask. Reimbursement for the transcript would have to wait until the conclusion of the case, but the court reporter would have to be paid immediately—by the page, and Lentino and Fisher were running up the cost.

"If I can't get straight answers, I'm going to ask the Judge to supervise the examination."

"I've directed my client to answer all proper questions," Fisher said.

"And I haven't heard a proper question yet," Lentino said.

"All my questions have been proper. It's been the objections that have been improper." Firestone regretted the comment. He was falling into the trap of arguing with them.

"You want the Judge to decide? Then mark the transcript for a ruling," Fisher said.

"Dr. Spender, was Dr. Gould present at the operation of Mrs. Santo?" Firestone stood up and leaned forward on the table. "Is that clear enough?"

"If the hospital chart says so."

"It does say so!"

"Then he was present. That's what I've been trying to tell you. I have no independent recollection of his presence."

The deposition was interrupted by a tremendous explosion. It shook the building and shattered windows. The flash of fire was followed by black smoke that seemed to engulf the street.

Dr. Spender ran to the window and looked down to where his car had been.

"My car. My car is down there."

The smoke obscured portions of the street. People, except for the unlucky few, were running in all directions. The roof of the automobile was blown off, and up, into twisted petals of metal. There was, surprisingly, little debris. Some glass littered the street, but the major damage was caused by imploding window panes. Already the wails of sirens further announced the disaster.

"My God," Christine Fisher said. "This whole building may collapse and you're worried about a car?"

"Can you see the Courthouse?" Lentino asked. "What's going on over there?"

"It's a terrorist attack!" Firestone's secretary screamed.

Firestone looked out the window and across the street to the courthouse. People streamed out of the building.

"The Court Officers are setting up a perimeter. Looks like they don't know what's happening, either." Lentino said.

"Jane. Let's get out of here!" Firestone took her hand but she resisted.

"No. I'm not leaving without my stenotype machine." Calmly, Jane placed all of her paraphernalia into her travel case and then swung her huge pocketbook over her shoulder. "Now we can leave. Diamond Reporting has never lost an EBT." She smiled at her small joke but betrayed her own nervousness by walking rapidly to the stairwell.

It was crowded with people rushing down the stairs.

CHAPTER 26

▼

Ron Goodman's chambers were on the eleventh floor of the Courthouse, overlooking and across the street from Firestone's office building.

The chambers consisted of an outer office for his secretary, a middle room where his law clerk worked, and the larger room set at a right angle to the others. It was a corner room and his old-style mahogany desk was flanked with the American and State flags. He had positioned his computer to his left within easy reach of his telephone.

Now that Sarah did not fill his days, Ron turned to the Courthouse during Christmas recess. It was an opportunity to catch up on the decisions that required research and written opinions.

He had arrived at the Courthouse at his usual time, but was dressed casually in dungarees, boots, plaid shirt and suede jacket. His litigation bag was crammed with untouched files he had taken home and was now returning. He had a newspaper tucked under his arm.

"The robes hide everything, Judge," said the Court Officer, who guarded the entrance. He was genial and smiling.

"I wish it did," Ron said.

The entrance was lined with the Magnetometers, each manned by a Court Officer. Ron side-stepped the Magnetometer so as to not set off the alarm.

"Crazy people make our lives crazy, Judge."

In his chambers, he booted up his computer and then methodically emptied the files onto his desk. He stacked them in the chronological order he was to consider them. He picked up a file, glanced at it and then put it down. He picked up another. Replaced it with still another. This went on for some time as he juggled in his hands, as well as his mind, the relative importance of each matter. He finally selected one case. He read several pages of a brief and scrolled through Lexis to check the principles of law. After a time, his mind wandered. He could not escape Sarah.

His eye spied the headline of the *New York Daily News*. "Rape in Snow." He opened the newspaper and, like a person thumbing through a dictionary for a word, his interest went from article to article. He came to the daily horoscope. It reminded him of his daughter, Colleen, and her fascination with astrology. It was absurd, wasn't it? His daughter the scientist? Finding signs in the stars was as scientific as the studying of bumps on the head. Nevertheless, he read on. From sign to sign. What was Sarah's birthday? March 15. The Ides of March. Now, wasn't that appropriate! Pisces. He was Aquarius. Weren't they incompatible? He shook his head at the stupidity of it all. Or was it? Whether or not it was stupid, all thought of research evaporated.

Ron was shaken from his reverie by the phone's ring.

"Ron?"

"I saw your car in the parking lot. I thought you were taking off this week?" Justice Donovan asked.

"I had a lot of catching up, Bill."

"You don't sound so good, Ron. What's wrong?"

"Nothing."

"Why didn't you call me? You knew I'd be working. I have Special Term."

"I forgot," Ron said.

"Bull shit. You've never forgotten a thing. Open the door, I'm coming up."

Before Donovan arrived, Ron tucked the newspaper away and spread several files across his desk. Bill did not have to know that his mind was wandering.

Donovan, without invitation, sat in the sofa across from the desk and leaned back. He passed his hand along his mane of white hair.

"You're sulking, Ron. You have a fight with Sarah?"

"You need a haircut, Bill."

"So you *did* have an argument!"

"What makes you think that?" Ron said.

"You're joking? You guys have been hot and heavy for the past few months. I'm surprised you still have the energy to come to work."

"It's been that obvious?" Ron frowned. He picked up a pen and toyed with it.

"Your friends have been happy for you and your enemies envious. Or is it the opposite?" Donovan laughed his Santa Claus laugh and his stomach jiggled.

"I think it's over, Bill. We were supposed to be together and she just disappeared. Went to Spain, her secretary said."

"I gave up a long time ago trying to figure women out. You know what I always said, We should put them on one mountain and we stay on another. When our needs become urgent we can meet them in the valley."

"Please Bill! I don't need any barroom misogynism." Ron switched off his computer.

"You're going to break that thing if you turn it off like that!" Donovan said. "Breaking your heart is one thing. Breaking Court property is another."

"Thank you Justice Donovan for your concern."

"I *am* concerned. I just don't know what to tell you."

"After Alice died, I went into a shell," Ron said. "I thought my emotional life was over. There were opportunities, plenty of them. Attractive women seemed to come out of the woodwork, like I was wearing a sign 'available'. But I wasn't interested in anyone. For two years I lived like a monk! Vulnerable? That would be an understatement. But when I met Sarah, I didn't think in those terms. Sarah was like the woman of my dreams. Not a reincarnation of Alice, but a different— mature kind of love."

"Come on Ron. You're just in a state of arrested development. Everything has its phases. Even DiMaggio got tired of Marilyn Monroe—as did Jack Kennedy. It's like ice cream. You can love it but if you had it every day, you'd dread eating it."

"Bill. I can't sleep. I have no appetite. I can't work. I can't do anything except think of Sarah. So don't talk to me about ice cream."

"I wasn't talking about ice cream. Maybe I'm preparing you for a case of unrequited love. That's the worst."

"The worst? The worst part is that I know she's willful, bold and calculating. The worst part is that I can't live without her."

"That's a start. Knowing her faults is a good start to recovery."

"Bill, stop with the jokes. I don't want to recover. I want her back!"

"Then talk to her."

"I don't even know where she is. Do you know what I was doing before you came? I was reading her horoscope as if there was some sign from God." Ron tore away the files and picked up the newspaper. It was still opened to his horoscope.

"Pisces, that's her sign. It says, your adventurous spirit takes you on a wild ride and a romantic fire burns brighter for you. Tonight finds you looking for love that remains elusive."

"That's not so good," Donovan said. "What's your sign say?"

"A romantic foray has led you into deep trouble. But you'll change your mind about a certain person, so don't bad-mouth anyone now."

"So there," Donovan said. "It will all work out. Sarah's a terrific person. I'm sure she has a good reason. Maybe she has a sick mother in Spain."

"Her mother is dead." Ron slammed his hand on the desk top.

The sound coincided with the sound of the explosion of Dr. Spender's automobile.

Chapter 27

▼

When the bomb exploded on Court Street, people rushed to help the injured. Those who were not seriously wounded assisted the several maimed persons who lay bleeding on the sidewalk. Two pedestrians were killed and many were injured from shattering glass.

Court officers charged across the street.

"Richie, Eddie, get blankets. Bring the first aid kits and bandages," said a Lieutenant to his Court Officers. "Tom, clear the area."

The sirens of police, fire engines and ambulances converged on Court and Montague Streets.

EMS officers gave first aid to the more seriously injured. Others were routed to the nearest hospital. The dead could wait.

Although the car was barely smoldering, firefighters attached a hose to a hydrant and doused the entire area.

"Hey, be careful. Don't put the full hose on it. You might wash away some evidence," a police sergeant said.

"You want this whole thing to explode again?" the firefighter said.

"It ain't going to explode."

"I'm putting out the fire, Sergeant!"

In no time at all, the different agencies seemed to be bumping into each other as they began the task of determining what had occurred. The police SWAT unit arrived and quickly surrounded the area. Then, came the bomb squad. Finally, the FBI and the Bureau of Alcohol and Tobacco.

The streets were cordoned off with police officers, who redirected traffic. Cars and fire trucks were maneuvered into position and a path cleared for the vehicles that came and went.

When Jack Zangara and Tom Scott arrived, they had difficulty in getting through to the crime scene.

"Screw it. Park the car on the sidewalk," Zangara said. "It's only three blocks away."

"But it's beginning to snow." Scott pulled his coat around his throat.

They walked up to the mangled automobile just as the fire fighters were disconnecting the hose.

"Goddamned terrorists!" Scott leaned over and partially unzipped a body bag. "Poor bastard. In the wrong place at the wrong time. Nobody's safe anymore."

Zangara walked around the automobile. He crouched down and then peered into its interior. He said nothing.

Several of the Feds gathered bits of debris.

"It's Al Qaeda," an FBI agent said. "No doubt about it."

"Bull shit." Zangara said. "It's either a hit or a nut. No way is this a terrorist attack."

The agent looked at Zangara. "You came to that conclusion pretty quick, didn't you?"

"The license plates. They're still on the car," Zangara said.

"So what? They're probably stolen," the agent said.

"Maybe. But that's not the point, is it?" Zangara said.

"No," the agent said. He was about 27 years old and his crew cut enhanced his athletic look. "The force of the explosion. The damage sustained and its location. That's important."

"Exactly," Zangara said. "This was a homemade device. Somebody with a grudge. Maybe somebody who just wanted to tear the balls off a driver."

"We'll do all the tests. Find out the composition of the bomb and all that," the agent said. He continued to bag bits of debris.

"You guys going to hog all the credit again?" Scott said.

"We follow routine. That's all," the agent said.

"Yeah, you routinely take credit," Scott said.

"Your partner has quite an attitude," the young agent said to Zangara.

"I wonder where he got it from?" Zangara said.

"They jump to conclusions, faster than me, don't they Jack?" Scott smiled and brushed the snow from Zangara's shoulders.

Zangara nodded. "Meanwhile, we'll follow up on the only clue we have right now," Zangara said. "The license plate."

The snow was heavier now, as Zangara and Scott trudged back to their car.

"Thanks for sticking up for me back there," Scott said.

"When you're right, you're right," Zangara said. "The Feds do have a habit of hogging all the credit."

CHAPTER 28

▼

Within minutes, they knew the name of the owner of the Lincoln Town Car. Scott called from the car phone and was patched into the Motor Vehicle Bureau in Albany.

"Hey, you're the third guy who's called me about that car in the last five minutes," said the Motor Vehicle employee. "What's going on in Brooklyn?"

"Just give me the name and address," Scott said. "Dr. Aaron Spender. S-P-E-N-D-E-R. Spender. 1014 Elmwood Road, Brooklyn...yeah, I know. It's in Sea Gate." Scott put down the car phone.

"Spender?" Zangara said. His surprise was evident.

"You know him?"

"Dr. Aaron Spender is a gastroenterologist."

"So?"

"He was a consultant on about fifteen or twenty of Dr. DiTucci's patients. His name is all over DiTucci's office records."

"Jack, you're starting to make me a believer."

"Let's go see Dr. Spender and find out if his car was stolen, or by what coincidence his car was parked in downtown Brooklyn right by the Courthouse."

"Damn. It's cold outside. Why don't we just call it a day? We can do that tomorrow."

"Did you get Spender's phone number?" Zangara said.

"It's unlisted."

"Since when is that a problem? That's what I mean about you drinking. You get careless."

"Hey Jack. I didn't get it yet, OK! That make you feel better?" Scott took the car phone and called in for the number.

"And get his office number, too." Zangara was annoyed but not for the reason he pretended. DiTucci! Was there a connection back to Barbara?

"Yes. Yes," Scott said and wrote down the numbers. He then dialed. After a moment he said, "there's no answer."

"How about his office?"

Scott dialed the other number. "All I'm getting is his voice mail."

"Maybe we ought to go over there. You know, strike while the iron is hot."

"What do we do if he's not home? Break down the door?"

"We can wait. We've done that before."

They did wait in front of Dr. Spender's house for almost two hours. It had grown dark and it was cold. The snow had turned into a wet, icy rain and Zangara rued his dedication.

"Strike while the iron is hot! Ha," Scott said. He had been turning the engine on and off to heat up the car and then opening the windows to dissipate the fumes.

Just as they were about to leave, a taxi pulled up.

"That must be him," Zangara said, as a figure hurried to the door. "Looks like he lost his overcoat."

Zangara and Scott alighted from their car at the same time.

When Dr. Spender saw them, he fumbled hurriedly with his keys. As the men approached, Dr. Spender became more agitated. When he realized that he would not be able to enter his house before they reached him, Spender dropped his keys and pressed himself against the door.

"What do you want!" His voice was frantic and his eyes darted back and forth as he searched for an avenue of escape.

"Police!" Zangara said. "Are you Dr. Aaron Spender?"

Dr. Spender nodded. The use of his full name seemed to lessen his fear.

"We just want to ask you a few questions, Doc." Scott said.

"Are you really the police?"

"Is someone after you?" Zangara said, and flashed his badge.

"You scared the living crap out of me!" Dr. Spender retrieved his keys and unlocked the door.

They followed the doctor into the house. They did not wait to be invited.

Dr. Spender flicked on the light switches. It lit up the center hallway and the living room. There was a small rug by the door laying on the marble floor. Spender turned and blocked their path. They could enter but this was as far as they could go.

"I'm Detective Zangara and this is my partner, Detective Scott."

"Wipe your feet," Dr. Spender said. He was again in command.

"What happened to your car today?" Scott asked.

"What happened? It was blown to smithereens."

"Then it wasn't stolen?"

"No. I parked it downtown. Someone put a bomb under it."

"You think they were trying to kill you?"

"Why do you think I'm shaking? Then, I come home and two strangers come out of a car after me."

"Hey Doc. We've been waiting a long time and it's cold out there. Where you been?"

"Why do you think that someone is trying to kill you?" Zangara said.

"Someone tried to kill me, Detective—let's get our tenses straight."

"Why?"

"I haven't the vaguest idea."

"Did you know Dr. DiTucci?"

"What does he have to do with it?"

"Why can't doctors answer simple questions?" Scott said.

"Of course I knew him. He referred patients to me. We were very good friends."

"What were you doing on Court Street today?" Zangara said. He really wanted to ask about Barbara. But he was afraid of the answer. Good friends?

"I was attending a deposition in a lawyer's office."

"You got a lot of malpractice suits against you, Doc?" Scott's smile was equal to the sarcasm in his voice.

"You're an impertinent young man, Detective. You can both get out right now!"

"What lawyer and what case?" Zangara said.

"Mr. Roger Firestone's office. The action is by a Ruth Santo."

"Thank you, doctor." Zangara said. "And that's the one with Dr. DiTucci?"

"Why yes. How did you know this?"

Zangara paused by the door and allowed Scott to precede him out the door. When they reached their car, Zangara got on the radio.

"I want a twenty-four hour watch on Dr. Aaron Spender," Zangara said.

"What's the connection?" Scott said.

"You owe me more than a steak dinner," Zangara said. "Dr. DiTucci was murdered. This was a mob hit!"

CHAPTER 29

▼

Ron arrived at his chambers early the day after the New Year's holiday, and as in all beginnings, he was anxious to get started.

Joan King shook her head when Ron asked for his voice mail messages.

"There's a slew of messages but they're mostly from lawyers looking for adjournments. I gave them to your law clerk," his secretary said.

"No call from Ms. Baruch?" Ron tried to sound casual.

"No."

"Call her office, will you. Find out when she's expected back from Europe."

"I've already done that three times," Joan said. She, too, felt betrayed by Sarah.

At this woman's suggestion, she had become absorbed in the Domestic Violence Hotline. She no longer bowled, and, instead of the few hours a week, she now found herself occupied with the program every evening.

She never mentioned to Ron that except for an occasional appearance, Sarah seemed to have abandoned the project.

When Ron asked her again, only moments later to place another call to Sarah, it was with undisguised hostility that Joan said, "You're making a mistake, your Honor. Women don't respect men who chase after them."

"Joan! When I want your advice, I'll ask you. Just mind your own business."

"If I didn't care, I wouldn't tell you."

"Thank you Joan, but please make the call."

"And Judge, Jack Zangara called and left a message."

"Jack?"

"Said he had to talk with you. He said that he'd call back this morning."

"OK. But don't forget to call Ms. Baruch."

Sarah had to be back from Europe by now. He had called her daily, hoping that she would access her phone messages. The messages had started off with his expressing concern (Is everything all right? Please call, Sarah. I'm getting very worried). As days passed and he still had not heard from her, the messages tended toward anger (I'm not used to this shabby treatment, Sarah. What the hell's the matter with you). Finally, there was surrender (Sarah. Honey. I don't know what's wrong, but I love you. Please call me. Please).

Each time the phone rang, he waited for the buzz from the intercom.

"The bald detective is on line one," Joan said.

Ron picked up the phone.

"Jack, what's up?"

"I have to see you, Ron."

"Anytime buddy. I'm going on the bench at 9:30. Where are you?"

"I'm downstairs but I'm going to need about an hour of your time."

"You're making this sound very mysterious."

"Well, it's official business and then again, it isn't."

"Is it urgent?"

"I would like to talk with you as soon as possible."

"Hold on then Jack." Ron pressed the hold button and hit the intercom. "Joan. Call the courtroom and tell them I'll start the trial at 10:30."

"Your Honor," Joan said. "I just reached, Ms. Baruch. She wants you to call her at the Waldorf, Suite 1120.

"Thanks a lot, Joan. You sure know your priorities." He looked at the phone as if she could see his annoyance.

"I'm sorry, Judge. It won't hurt for her to wait a while."

"Just return the call!"

Ron switched back to line one.

"Jack, come on up." He put down the phone and stared at it. His chest felt heavy. His neck muscles tensed as he waited for the intercom to signal that Sarah was on the phone.

"Darling," Sarah said. Her voice was high pitched. Was it delight or embarrassment? "I have the most wonderful news!"

"Christ, Sarah! Where have you been? Where are you."

"At the Waldorf. Didn't my secretary tell you?"

"Your secretary? Don't insult my intelligence! And guess what? This conversation is over!" Ron slammed down the phone.

He found himself shaking with anger and did not answer the intercom despite the urgent buzzing. What a joke! He had toured the circle of passion—from anger to despair and now back to anger, but it was no joking matter! Yet she had called him. Was there was a logical explanation that could open the door to forgiveness? On the other hand perhaps it was a good idea to end it all with Sarah. Wasn't she too upsetting in his life? Disrupting.

After a moment, Joan popped her head in the doorway.

"You have to answer the phone, Judge, I think she's crying."

Finally, he picked up the phone but did not speak for a long while. He would just listen, as if silence was punishment.

"Ron, please, don't be angry. I have so much to tell you."

"Where have you been?"

"Mexico. Cancun. I flew in last night."

"You didn't go to Europe?"

"Where did you get that idea?"

"From your damned secretary!"

"Oh, she must have misunderstood. Are we having dinner tonight?"

"Absolutely not! Get lost *Ms.* Baruch. Go find yourself another patsy." He put his hand over the mouthpiece to muffle his rising voice.

"What about your last message? 'Sarah. Honey, please call. Please'." She mimicked his tone.

"You're at the Waldorf?"

"Business, silly. I thought you would have figured that out by now."

"You can't do this to me, Sarah!"

"Ron, let's have dinner at Tavern on the Green, tonight."

"It's snowing out."

"Central Park will be like a Winter Wonderland. It's beautiful."

"From the Tropics to the Arctic. The world traveler who never heard of Alexander Graham Bell."

"Ron, don't be so sarcastic."

"Not sarcastic, just disappointed."

"Ron, please have dinner with me. You have to give me a chance to explain."

"Tavern on the Green at 7. You make the reservation." Ron hung up and waited for a long moment. What nerve! Shouldn't have succumbed so easily.

He was so deep in thought that the buzz of the intercom startled him.

"Jack is waiting," Joan said.

When Zangara entered the room, he closed the door behind him.

"That all right?"

"All right? Come here you old bear," Ron said and extended his arms to embrace Zangara.

"Damn, it's good to see you Jack!" Ron moved to the sofa and sat down.

"Take a load off your flat feet," Ron said.

Zangara sunk into the arm chair opposite to Ron and sighed to show that he was going beyond comfort.

"It's not fun anymore, Ron."

"Our work was never really fun."

"You always did catch me with the wrong word. I'm talking about the enjoyment, our camaraderie when we went out on a homicide investigation together," Zangara said.

"Christ, that seems like a lifetime ago. It was exciting. The crazy hours and the gory cases."

"Yeah, the young District Attorney who was going to make a name for himself."

"And the young detective who was messing up his many marriages."

"We messed up a couple of cases, too. Do you remember when a woman called 911 to report that a burglar had killed her husband—but it turned out that he wasn't dead," Ron said.

"Yes."

"There he was on the kitchen floor, blood all over. The wife crying and denying she was the killer, and then suddenly, he jumps up and starts to curse her for whacking him on the head with a frying pan." Ron smiled and then laughed as he related the incident that needed no recall, except to reconnect a friendship.

"But we learned something from that, didn't we?" Zangara said.

"We sure did. Always check the body."

"Well, you sure have risen. Me? I'm still checking the bodies."

"You love it, Jack. You're so smart you could have done anything or been anything you wanted. Besides, First Grade Detective is not so bad."

"Yeah, and I have to thank you for that, too. You got me out of Auto Theft Squad when my career was going nowhere."

Zangara looked melancholy. The bags under his eyes seemed to darken. "I'm working on this case. A homicide. But funny things are happening."

"Is that so unusual?" Ron said.

"I was all over the place on this one. First, I thought it might be a homicide. Then a suicide. Then it began to look like an accident. And now I'm back to homicide because somebody tries to knock off the dead guy's colleague. They're both doctors and defendants in a malpractice case."

"Yes," Ron said to show that he was listening.

"It turns out that the plaintiff in the malpractice case and her husband, may have ties to the mob."

"What was it we used to say? When there's more than one coincidence, it ain't no coincidence!" Ron said.

"Exactly. I understand that there are five judges who handle the malpractice cases in Brooklyn. If I give you the name of the case, can you access it on the computer and give me its history?"

"What's the name?"

"I'm not asking you to do anything wrong, am I?"

"It's a public record." Ron went to his desk and tapped the keyboard. He waited a moment, checked the screen and then looked at Zangara.

"Ruth and Victor Santo against Dr. Aaron Spender, and maybe a Dr. DiTucci," Zangara said.

"Hey. That's my case. The doctor was...dead. Of course. And Spender! The newspapers. The doctor whose car was blown up." Ron rose and went to the window. "I saw it!"

"Dr. Spender was at a deposition when the car blew up," Zangara said.

"You think there's a connection?"

"I know it wasn't a terrorist attack."

"Do you have anything to go on?" Ron said.

"Maybe. What's the status of the malpractice case?"

Ron studied the screen as the information appeared.

"The case is on the trial calendar. The only outstanding discovery is the Examination Before Trial of..." His voice trailed off.

"...Dr. Spender?" Zangara said.

"Yes." Ron tapped a few more keys and waited again. "They claim that the plaintiff, Ruth Santo is dying. That would entitle them to a preference—an immediate trial, as soon as the parties complete the deposition of..."

"...Dr. Aaron Spender?" Jack Zangara said again.

It had happened so many times before when they had worked together, each almost simultaneously reaching the same conclusion. Yes. Zangara had been a perfect partner, despite the difference in their jobs. Judge and Detective had easily moved back into their old roles.

"How much is a case like this worth?" Zangara said.

Ron, again, studied the screen. He scrolled across a document with his mouse. "If a jury finds responsibility? There could be a sustainable verdict of seven to nine million."

"Sustainable?"

"Yes. A jury verdict could go as high as twenty five million. I would reduce it as excessive and then the Appellate Court would reduce it further—but seven to nine million is sustainable."

"That's not chopped liver."

"No, it isn't Jack."

"Could this be a phony case?"

Ron looked at the computer, again. "I don't think so. The lawyer might exaggerate the injuries. I don't know. That's part of the game but if it was a spurious case, the defense lawyers would have blown them out of the water by this time. No. This might be a case where coincidences really have no relationship to each other."

"You're probably right. In fact, I hope you're right because I have other problems."

"Other problems? With my case?"

"No, Ron. With my case. I've compromised an investigation."

"In what way?"

"I've been sleeping with the widow of Dr. DiTucci and she's still a murder suspect. Not that she did it herself, but she might have hired somebody."

"Christ, Jack. That's not like you. Not like you at all. She might be using you."

"Don't I know that! I'm in love with her, Ron. I'm in love with her and I don't know what to do."

Ron nodded sadly. How could he help his old friend when he couldn't even help himself?

"I can't lose her," Zangara said.

"Love is a tough thing," Ron said. "You're not alone."

Zangara paused and then his face brightened with understanding. "Ron, you're in love, too?"

"I thought so but she's been giving me the treatment."

"In what way?"

"You know. Inseparable one day, distant the next."

"That's not my problem," Zangara said. "I think Barbara loves me but it's like the wrong time for us."

"Doesn't seem like the right time for me, either."

"Is she a lawyer?"

"Almost as bad. A real estate broker. I met her through a lawyer, Manny Lentino." Ron paused.

"Lentino?" Zangara knit his brow. "Dollars to donuts he's a lawyer on your Santo case."

"You're starting to make my hair bristle. Colleen called me last week and told me that a classmate had approached her about the kinds of cases I handle. The girl knew that I was a judge and asked Colleen if I was trying a case where one doctor was dead and the other had his car bombed."

"Well, it was in the papers," Zangara said.

"The bombing—not the case!" Ron said. "Colleen didn't even know about my case."

"Come to think of it, how did the girl know that you're a judge?"

"That's when Colleen's antennae went up. She never tells anyone about me."

"Did Colleen tell you her name?"

"Yes. Claudia Penna."

"There's a mob guy with that name," Zangara said. "I'd better check it out." He took out his note pad and jotted down the name.

"They can't be that stupid, can they?"

"Who knows? Is your lady friend Italian?" Zangara asked.

"Her name is Sarah. Sarah Baruch. What difference would that make?"

"Who the hell knows?" Zangara said.

CHAPTER 30

▼

Ron left the courthouse in Brooklyn early, but he knew that he would be late. Traveling north on Eighth Avenue at six in the evening, guaranteed heavy traffic. It was not snowing but its remnants slowed everyone down. Already the grime and dirt of the City discolored the slush.

His occasional glance at pedestrians stumbling on the ridges of snow heaped on the intersections reminded Ron of Sarah's evaluation. Some Winter Wonderland!

And yet, when he finally reached Central Park and Tavern on the Green as if by magic, the dirt was obliterated. The untrammeled earth and the trees, heavy with clean snow, presented a picture of nature undefiled.

It was almost 7:45 when Ron arrived at the restaurant. There was going to be no apologies for lateness this time.

When he reached the table, Sarah put down her martini and presented her cheek to be kissed.

"Hello Sarah," Ron said and sat down opposite her.

"I missed you, Ron."

"Have you?"

The waiter came over and looked at Ron. "May I get you a cocktail?"

"I'll have a diet coke," Ron said.

Sarah, with a wave of her hand, indicated that she wanted a refill. She waited for the man to leave before she spoke.

"Oh? It's going to be that kind of an evening?"

"What did you expect? It seems that with you I have to keep my wits about me—at all times."

"Ron, how many times do I have to tell you that I'm sorry? I am sorry! Damn, I hate apologizing and I hate the way I left you high and dry. I can't help what I am, though. When I see an opportunity, I take it. I've warned you about that before."

"Are you really sorry? I'm not a masochist who enjoys being manipulated—and that's exactly what I think you've been doing."

"That's not true and you'll realize it when you hear the wonderful news." The smile remained fixed on her face.

"About Spain or Mexico?"

"Will you listen!"

"Why not? We're in your Winter Wonderland but you're the one with the goddamned beautiful tan!" Ron looked at her.

Her face was radiant and bronzed by the sun. She wore a wide rainbow colored bandanna, tight about her head, much in the style of a Japanese Samurai. Her navy blue suit and pink blouse enhanced her bold look, as if she did not fear expected combat.

"Wouldn't you like to be a millionaire?" Her voice was now lilting and slightly teasing.

"Sarah, why don't you stop beating around the bush?"

"You stop it Ron! I mean right now!" She looked at the nearby patrons to see if her rising voice had drawn attention to her.

"Tell me why I should?"

"I expected hostility Ron, but not to this extent. I want to tell you things but you won't listen!"

"How come you're staying at the Waldorf? Are they painting your apartment?"

"Very funny, Ron."

"I didn't mean to be funny."

"I told you I'm sorry. I can't do any more." Sarah's voice quivered. She was clearly nervous. She gathered up her gloves and pocketbook and rose to leave. She backed her chair away and extended to him a neatly wrapped package. "Here's your Christmas present," she said petulantly, as if she regretted making a peace offering.

"Sit down. You're not getting off that easy." Ron gazed at her. He took the gift and set it down on the table.

"I love you Ron. I have my faults. Maybe I'm too ambitious. Or greedy. Perhaps both."

"Just tell me, why? Why did you just disappear?"

"I didn't just disappear and I didn't go on vacation."

"You could have called me."

"I was afraid. You don't know the influence you have over me."

"I'm the Svengali in all of this?"

"I was afraid that if I told you about Cancun that you would persuade me not to go. It's such a marvelous opportunity. For the both of us."

"Persuade? You? That's the laugh of the night! You'd drag me around by the nose if I let you. You're such a liar!"

"How have I lied to you?"

"You lied about Spain. You went to Mexico. Or did you?"

"No, I didn't lie. My secretary thought I was in Europe. This was so hush-hush that I didn't give anyone all the details."

Sarah tugged at his arm. "Come on silly. Open your Christmas present, it's a symbol of our future."

Ron opened the gift and held it up.

"It's a ritual calendar. A *Tzolkin*. Sarah said. "The workmanship is amazing."

It was circular and approximately eight inches in diameter with a smaller wheel attached by a central grommet. Ron tested it by turning the inner wheel.

"Look at the ideograms. The outer wheel has 20 named days and the inner wheel has 13 named months. You can align it so that you can, for example, know that today is the day of the alligator in the month of the jaguar."

"13 times 20? That adds up to only 260 days."

"I'm going to have to educate you in Pre-Columbian American. They had several calendars. They had a 'calendar round' that ran for 52 years. Their sacred almanac corresponded more to our year. It was called *Tonalpohualli*. 18 months were divided into 20 days each. That's 360 days my quick calculating friend. The last five days were called *Vazeh*, the days of evil omen."

"Is this authentic?"

"I wish it were. The Conquistadors smelted down much of the art work because it was a more convenient way to ship the gold back to Spain."

"It looks like gold," Ron said. He hefted the object in his hand.

"It's a lead reproduction. It's just painted gold. If it was a sixteenth century antique, I'd be thrown in jail for trying to take it out of Mexico."

"But you have friends in high places. Wouldn't they be able to get you off?"

"Darling, you're showing your jealousy again. Some take it as a compliment, but I don't." She patted his hand. "Be gracious. Just say thank you Sarah. It's a lovely present."

"I wish it was that easy," Ron said. "You have me on an emotional roller coaster. A few minutes ago, I wanted to strangle you."

"I told my partners about you. Your being a Judge. You can be just the right ingredient to make the project fly. Integrity is important in business, too."

"Judicial ethics prohibits me from engaging in any business. You know that."

"It will be well worth your while to leave the bench."

"I was never good at business," Ron said.

"It's a once in a lifetime chance, Ron."

"I'm not really interested."

"You don't have to agree immediately. All I'm asking is that you consider it, meet the principals, view the plans."

"Sarah, let's just slow down."

"Some things won't wait. I can arrange a meeting within the next week or so."

"You'll be at the Waldorf that long?"

"As long as it takes, Ron." Sarah said. "Come on board."

She stroked his arm and Ron felt himself stirring.

"Let's go to your room at the Waldorf," Ron said. He wanted to bite his tongue. It didn't take much, did it, when the brain went south.

"Not this week," Sarah said. "The five evil days of *Vazeh* are upon me."

CHAPTER 31

▼

"What are you? Cowboys?" Joe Pencils said. Whether from caution or fear, he had refused to meet Pete and Eugene at his bar. Instead, he had arranged to meet them at Van Winkle Lanes, a large bowling alley in Staten Island.

"You guys are so hot, I don't want to be seen with you even in public."

"This is private?" Eugene said and raised his arms as if he were first observing the bustling activity.

Joe Pencils looked at Eugene and shook his head.

"Calm down and bowl, Joe. It'll lower your blood pressure and maybe raise your score.

As a concession to the game, Pencils had taken off his suit jacket but he still was an odd sight among the other bowlers. No other bowler was wearing a white shirt and tie. He lifted the ball from the rack, measured the pins, and with less than perfect form, took three steps before throwing the ball. It wobbled down the lane and tapped the seven pin.

"I don't understand you, Joe. We're still going to pop him," Pete said. "It was just a little error in timing. That's all."

"Christ. What ever possessed you guys in this day and age to kill a guy with a bomb?"

"I thought it would throw everyone off the track. And it did. We're not hot. Nobody's looking for us."

"Oh no, Pete. Just the cops, the FBI, the Treasury Department, Interpol and about ten other agencies."

"Interpol?" Eugene said.

"Yeah. They can't decide whether you're a domestic terrorist or an international one! A goddamned simple hit and you make national headlines."

"They're all full of shit. I purposely made it look like a homemade job."

"That's part of the problem," Pencils said.

"What problem? It's been three weeks already and its all quieted down."

"That's what you think. The bomb was so amateurish that they figured it was a Russian hit."

"The Russians from Brighton Beach?" Eugene said.

"Not the Russians from Moscow, dummy." Pete punched Eugene in the arm.

"Hey, that hurt." Eugene rubbed this arm. Pete ignored Eugene.

"They've been complaining to the Falcon about the heat. So now, they're putting pressure on him," Pencils said.

"What kind of pressure?"

"The worst kind of pressure. From the top down. The Feds pressure the cops and the cops pressure us and the Russians. The cops shut down a couple of gambling operations and a bunch of cat-houses. And get this, the Russians are asking for compensation. You know, for the money they lost when their girls were taken out of circulation."

"The Falcon going to pay them?" Eugene said.

"No, you are," Joe Pencils said. "The Falcon figures you screwed up so it's your problem."

"You're full of shit, Joe. Nobody's connecting us with this job."

"You guys really are a comedy team. Do you think everyone is stupid? Where does Dr. Spender live? Coney island? Next to Brighton Beach? These Russians have done their own investigation. They gave the Falcon names, dates and places. They know that Eugene went to a real estate place in the neighborhood. Pretended to be looking for a house." Joe Pencils hitched up his trousers and touched his genitals like a baseball pitcher who had just thrown a strike.

"The Russians are guessing," Pete said.

"Some guess. They see Eugene. They find out this Spender lives in Sea Gate. For Chrissake, your brainy partner practically announced the hit to the world!"

"I'm not worried. The Russkies can suspect all they want but they can't prove a thing."

"They don't have to. It's all too close and the Falcon doesn't like it. The contract is canceled."

"We can still make the hit."

"To kill him now would only complicate things."

"I don't see that at all."

"It's not for you to see, Pete. Do you remember I told you it had to be done quickly?"

"We're not returning the down-payment," Pete said. He knew very well where the conversation was going.

"The Falcon wants ten thousand by next week."

"But we only got five thousand up front," Eugene said.

"The other five is for the Russians," Joe Pencils said. "They have no loyalty, Pete. They'll give you up in a heartbeat."

"Joe, you're really pissing me off," Pete said. "Me? I don't care, but I'm worried about Eugene."

"Hey, come on, Pete. Don't shoot the messenger."

"Tell the Falcon he can go fuck himself," Pete said.

"I'm not going to tell the Falcon that. I'm going to chalk up what you just said to your disappointment."

"You tell him exactly what I said." Pete's eyes were steely and his voice, the sound of sandpaper. "You tell him that he's not getting a dime back and that when I pop Spender, I expect the balance of the payment."

"Christ, Pete. There's some very delicate circumstances here. If you snuff out Spender, you'll ruin everything."

"If he wants to delay the contract, I'll do it but I expect full payment on completion."

"I'll have to get back to you on that, Pete."

"Naturally," Pete said. "We've always been reasonable. I'm just surprised you came down so hard on us."

"Yeah, who wants to shoot the messenger?" Eugene said. "You know what your problem is Pencils?" His narrowed eyes met the narrowing eyes of Joe Pencils.

"I have no problems."

"Sure you do. Your problem is that you bend your arm when you throw the ball. Here, let me show you." Eugene picked up the bowling ball. He raised the ball to his chest and then glided to the foul line. He brought his arm back and then threw the ball 10 feet in the air, high and far down the lane. The force of the sixteen pound ball made visible dents in the wood as it bounced into the pins. The pins tumbled into each other and all ten pins went down. A strike!

"Eugene is right, Pencils," Pete said. "You shouldn't bend your elbow."

CHAPTER 32

▼

"Rules are made to be broken," Andrew 'The Falcon' Peregrino always said. But he would add, "but there better be a good reason."

Joe Pencils, by the urgency of his tone, had convinced Peregrino that something was awry.

"Don't tell me on the phone. Meet me tomorrow in the afternoon. Four o'clock. Usual place," Andrew had said. "I take off for a few days down South and I come home to problems?"

The next day, the sun was already low over the taxpayer buildings that line Eighteenth Avenue when Peregrino arrived. Two feet of snow had fallen the night before and, except for a narrow pathway, the sidewalk still lay un-shoveled.

When he entered the clubhouse, he stamped the snow from his shoes.

There were four card players at the front table.

"When Roman soldiers weren't in battle they built roads! I can't even get you people to shovel the snow," Peregrino said. He smiled broadly as if his observation were not an order.

The four men put down their cards and without finishing the hand, went outside. Within minutes the entire walk, from storefront to roadway was cleaned. By silent agreement, the men did not return to their game.

John and Sonny, the silent soldiers who constantly accompanied Peregrino, took up their positions by the door.

Moments later, Joe Pencils arrived.

"We have a little problem." Joe Pencils waited for the invitation to be seated.

"Come on. Sit down!"

"You look great, Andrew," Pencils said. "What a tan!" Peregrino, although not light skinned, nevertheless had a discernible sunburn that was accentuated by the silver streaks in his otherwise plastered down black hair.

"I hate February. But I can't leave the business for one minute. Why can't you handle this, Joe?"

"They're out of control," Pencils said and then related his conversation with Pete and Eugene.

The Falcon listened. He took out a cigar and bit off an end, but he did not light it.

"So what's the problem? We let the Russians hit them and then deliver them gift wrapped to the cops. Case closed and the heat is off."

"Andrew, the Russians are worse than Pete and Eugene. They're loose cannons, too. They'll mess it up and then we'll end up in a war."

Peregrino looked at Pencils. He had come to rely on Pencils because his analyses of difficult situations had often been accurate.

"Maybe you're right, Joe." Peregrino shrugged his shoulders inviting an opinion.

"I think we need a real pro. Don't forget, we're dealing with two unstable killers. I always said we shouldn't go outside for help—unless we had to."

"You criticizing me?"

"Of course not, Andrew. What I meant was these guys are crazy. It's like you always said, 'killing is only a tool'. But Pete and Eugene enjoy killing."

"A real pro, eh. So you want me to bring in Harry 'O' from Atlantic City?"

"I think he'd be a good choice. He's the only guy I know who could take down Pete and Eugene and make them glad that they're dead."

"Maybe you're right." Peregrino lit his cigar and puffed on it deeply. He exhaled the smoke and blew a large smoke ring.

"I knew you'd figure out something," Pencils said as if it was the Falcon's idea.

"Tell Pete that the hit is not off but only on hold. Tell him it was your fault. You misunderstood."

"I'm going to look terrible, Andrew!"

"Maybe. We'll take care of them in our own time. Meanwhile, just bullshit them."

"We could still use this to our advantage. Pete and Eugene could make a friendly visit to persuade Spender to change his testimony."

"And what if they whack him?" Peregrino said.

"Then how about Vecchio? He could deliver the message."

"No, we need a more subtle hand. A feminine touch." Peregrino laughed. He glanced at his watch.

Joe Pencils rose to leave.

"There's another thing, boss. We have a small problem with Victor."

"Didn't I straighten him out with Six Fingers?" Peregrino said.

"It's not money this time. It's his broad. She's pregnant and threatening to go to his wife."

"What's worse Joe? Ambition without talent or talent without ambition?" He tapped on his cigar and the ash fell to the floor.

What Peregrino did not disclose to Pencils was that Angelina Ferrante's father had already complained to him.

"Well, Victor's not getting it at home. I can hardly blame him," Pencils said.

"That's no excuse. He was sleeping with that Angelina before his wife got sick. And before that there was Serafina Abruzzi. He can't stay away from pussy or the ponies."

"Christ, Andrew. Is there anything you don't know?"

"Yes. I'm not sure of the answer to my own question. I think that maybe Victor Santo is too ambitious for his own good."

"Victor is harmless."

"That's what Caesar thought about Brutus."

"Victor does what he's told. He's totally controllable. Not like Pete and Eugene. They won't wait too long for the money," Pencils said.

"They won't have to." Peregrino sucked on this cigar and savored its strong juice.

"So we don't use them anymore?"

"What do you do when a tool is broken?"

"We fix it?" Pencils' voice was uncertain. It seemed that the Falcon always liked to test him with a question.

"No. We throw it away. We live in a disposable society, Joe."

"That's a good one, boss. We're in the disposing business."

Peregrino winced. He had meant to be instructive, not jocular.

"Meanwhile, you follow up on what's really important, Joe."

"You mean Judge Goodman?"

"Of course. He's key to this whole thing. I don't want any screw up there."

CHAPTER 33

▼

"Victory Dry Cleaners" was constantly busy but the cash register did not reflect its activity. Victor routinely dipped into it.

Any argument over either a stain or a bill was resolved by Angelina Ferrante, his bilingual employee and lover.

Angelina was about twenty five years old and obviously pregnant. Her skin glistened from the steamy heat of the store, and she kept removing the curly strands of her hair away from her face. Her pinched, long nose made her voice shrewish. Her maternity dress seemed more a statement that a sign of her condition because the oversize dress hardly concealed her voluptuous body.

"The stain is permanent," Angelina said in Italian. "I told you that when you brought the suit in. See! I marked it on the ticket!" Her long earrings dangled as she shook her head.

"But you said that you'd try to remove it—not put a hole in the jacket," the man said in Italian.

"Let me talk to Victor. Maybe we can do something."

Angelina took the jacket and walked to the rear. Victor, who had just fired the presser, was working at the steam iron.

"Victor, look at this. How did this happen?"

"I guess I rubbed too hard on the stain." He smiled. He grabbed her and pulled her into a corner, out of sight of the customer. He kissed Angelina and caressed her breasts.

"Victor, he'll see us," Angelina said but she did not resist.

After a moment, she straightened her dress and returned to the front counter.

"Victor said that he'll send it out to the weaver. It'll be like new." She touched her hair to make sure that it was in place.

"How long?"

"Come back in a week or so, Signor."

When the customer left, Victor came to the counter.

"Another problem solved."

"You mean put off. Victor, you can't keep putting things off!" She patted her stomach.

"Angie, baby, love of my life, we have to wait until after the case is over before I can marry you. You know that!" Victor went to the door and peered down the street.

It had snowed again. The Sanitation Department with plows attached to its garbage trucks, had pushed the snow into steep banks, entombing the parked cars on each side of the street. The four lane traffic had been reduced to two lanes.

Victor's cleaning store was located on Eighteenth Avenue not too far from the Falcon's clubhouse and he assumed that Tony Vecchio would be coming from that direction.

"What time is he coming?" Angelina asked.

"Any minute now." Victor looked at his watch. It was three p.m. "He said he had good news, baby."

It was Joe Pencils, however, who drove up. He double parked. Now there was only one lane for moving traffic. Pencils raised his middle finger to the honking cars.

Once inside, he shut the door and the overhead bell tinkled.

"I thought Vecchio was coming?" Victor said.

"Why don't you clean the sidewalk!" The snow hung on Pencils' galoshes and trousers and he knelt to sweep it away. "Why don't you get a kid to shovel the snow."

"Those little bastards want an arm and a leg just to make a pathway."

"Then do it yourself or make Angelina shovel the snow. This way you don't get a heart attack."

"That's very funny, Joe," Angelina said. "And me in a delicate condition."

"This is one blessed event that's not convenient right now," Pencils said.

"We love each other. I don't care if the whole world does know it." She grabbed Victor's arm and cuddled up to him.

"No offense, Angelina, but we need Victor happily married for the trial."

When Tony Vecchio arrived, Victor led him and Pencils to a small room in the rear of the store.

"Angie, watch the counter," Victor said.

"Leave the door open in case I need you," Angelina said.

"Yeah, sure," Victor said. He slammed the door shut.

The room served as a bathroom and supply room. The only window was covered with a gauze curtain and a scissor gate that further obscured the light. A commode with an overhead water tank was set in a corner. Next to it was a small sink. The faucet leaked and made a brown stain on the porcelain.

"Now this is what I call state of the art facilities," Vecchio said.

"It's not the Ritz," Victor said. "But we don't need much here."

"I'd say you could use a little more space," Vecchio said.

Gallons of perc, the dry cleaning fluid, were stacked against a wall. Rolls of thin plastic hangers were heaped on the floor. The only concession to comfort was a cot, which doubled as a sofa.

"This where you do your work, eh," Vecchio said and pointed to the cot as if Angelina were laying there.

"Yeah, who needs the Ritz?" Pencils said.

"You, too?"

"Relax Victor, I think your problems—at least your financial ones, may be over," Vecchio said.

"Firestone got the preference?"

"Yes. He got a doctor's affidavit that your wife is dying."

"That's no joke," Victor said. "I've been worried about that myself. She's been looking worse and worse, every day. They had to rush her to the hospital again."

"What are you worried about? If she dies you can sue for 'wrongful death.' You might be better off. You'll have the money and your problem with Angelina will be solved." Vecchio had intended to be sarcastic but when he saw Pencils' somber face, he realized that he had furnished too much information.

"Who has to go to law school? We have Professor Vecchio here," Pencils said.

"But it's not that simple, is it Tony?" Pencils said. "Now you better explain it to Victor."

"If Ruth should die, her estate sues for the pain and suffering and Victor has a claim for what we call, pecuniary damages. Your kids collect, too, for 'loss of parental care and guidance.' There's only one problem with that," Vecchio said. "If your wife dies before the trial, then the doctor's affidavit will be true but not worth shit."

"What are you saying?" Victor said.

"Firestone would have to start all over again. You'd lose the preference. It's a new cause of action with more pre-trial discovery. And the monies in the 'pain and suffering.' Dead people don't suffer."

"What are we talking about in terms of time?" Pencils said.

"Maybe another year or two."

"Victor, you better keep your wife healthy. The Falcon doesn't like to wait for his money," Pencils said.

"When's the trial?" Victor went to the door and opened it slightly to insure that Angelina was not spying.

"In three to five weeks."

"You going to listen?" Pencils said.

"No theatrics. Don't try to charm the jury with your smile and stick close to your wife in the courtroom. Hold her hand. We want to present a picture of a loving, wounded couple, a marriage destroyed," Vecchio said.

"I know what I have to do."

"Christ, Victor, will you shut up and listen. That's your problem. You hear but you don't listen!" Pencils said.

"Remember the jurors may see you outside the courtroom when you come and leave the courthouse, so be attentive at all times," Vecchio said. "Dress neat. Suit and tie. No casual clothes or work clothes. Tell Ruth not to dress like she's going to a party."

"Fat chance of that," Victor said.

"She can wear frumpy clothes but I don't want her to look poor," Vecchio said.

"That I don't get," Pencils said.

"Juries don't give big money to poor people," Tony Vecchio said.

CHAPTER 34

▼

Ron had adjourned for the day when Zangara called.

"That case we talked about? It's coming up for trial?" asked Zangara.

"Yes. Did you find out anything?"

"Nothing definite. I'm in the Courthouse. You mind if I come up with my partner?"

Within minutes they arrived.

"Tom, this is Judge Goodman," Zangara said.

"It's a pleasure, your Honor."

They shook hands.

"Nice place you have here." Scott glanced around, approvingly. He examined a brass gavel, a Mack Truck Bulldog and other mementos that lay on the end tables.

"I've filled Tom in on everything, Ron," Jack said. "He's been putting in a lot of hours for us that we can't chalk up to overtime."

"Can't catch a nap if you want to catch a crook. It's not a nine to five job." Scott laughed.

"Don't mind him, Ron. My partner thinks I'm not pulling my load on the job."

"And that my friends is the understatement of the year," Scott said.

"We have to work as a team, you know that," Zangara said.

"Oh, we're a team all right. Jack goes in and screws the DiTucci broad and I wait in the car. He leaves and I still wait in the car. That's team work?"

"It wasn't like that at all," Zangara said. "I was going over all those god-damned medical files."

"Will someone explain what's going on?" Ron said.

"I'm watching her for a couple of days. She drops the kid off to school. Jack visits. She goes shopping and returns. Jack visits. She picks up the kid from school. Jack doesn't visit." Scott looked at Zangara and shook his head. "Then one day, lo and behold, a taxi drives up and who steps out but the bombee."

"The bombee?" Ron said.

"Dr. Aaron Spender, your defendant and my victim. I remember him from the time we visited him after his car got blown up," Scott said.

"But he came at 6 o'clock in the evening," Jack said.

"Yeah, the kid was home but Spender stayed for about an hour," Scott said. "More than enough time for hanky panky."

"You couldn't resist that, could you?" Zangara said.

"I'm just reporting facts, Jack. I did *see* the upstairs bedroom light go on and off."

"Did you ask her about it?" Ron said to Zangara.

"How could I? What was I supposed to say? Oh, by the way, I understand that Dr. Spender visited you while my partner was spying on you."

"You're clever enough to broach the subject with her, Jack."

Ron looked at Zangara who had cast down his eyes.

"Why the hell am I staking her out if you discount what I find?" Scott said.

"I'm not discounting anything. I'm just not jumping to conclusions." Zangara glared at Scott.

"I think you ought to confront her, Jack," Ron said. "It's better to know now than later."

"That's easy for you to say. Your lady came up clean as a whistle," Zangara said.

"You followed Sarah?"

"No. I did," Scott said. "While Jack here, was doing his homework at *Chez DiTucci*."

"I thought that it was strange that the same lawyer who introduced you to Sarah Baruch was also involved in a malpractice case that has mob written all over it," Zangara said. "There was no harm in checking it out. She's on the scene just like Barbara DiTucci."

"I told you her name. I didn't give you an invitation to follow me!"

"I tailed her, not you," Scott said.

"Is this man an idiot?" Ron said. His face reddened and he struggled to keep control. "When you followed Sarah, wasn't I with her?"

"Take it easy, Ron. Don't blame Tom. We didn't mean any disrespect. You know better than to take this personally. We're just doing our jobs," Zangara said.

"I thought we were friends, Jack? Putting Sarah into your homicide investigation is the wildest flight of your paranoid, cop mentality imagination!" Ron picked up a pen and threw it on the desk. It bounced off the glass top and fell to the floor.

"Why are you so angry, Judge?" Scott said. "Now you definitely know she's not involved."

"Isn't that wonderful," Ron said. He sat in his judge's chair and rocked back and forth.

"I'm sorry Ron, but I don't think we were out of line." Zangara picked up the pen and placed it on the desk.

"Well, what did you find?"

"She goes from her apartment to the office every day and…" Scott read from his note pad. "…and except for the days she goes to your apartment, she goes straight home. Lunch, inspecting office buildings and so forth. Same habits." Scott snapped his notepad shut.

"What about my daughter and this Claudia Penna?"

"I think that's a dead end," Zangara said. "I found out that she's the kid sister of this Joe Penna. She was probably trying to pump Colleen for some information. I don't make more of it than that."

"You don't?" Ron was incredulous. "Why would a mobster's sister be talking to my daughter about a case?"

"I don't know that yet," Zangara said.

"And neither do I. I spoke with Colleen and she thinks this Claudia Penna is just a spoiled, rich kid with money. Offered her $3,000.00 to take the Economics exam for her. Colleen just laughed at her."

"Maybe you ought to warn your daughter," Scott said.

"I will," Ron said. His voice was cold. He was still shaken by the surveillance. "And what other bright ideas do you have?"

"Tailing isn't enough," Scott said. "If Jack's right, we're dealing with multiple crimes that are connected to Santo. If that's so, there'll be more dead bodies that show up. I think we should tap all the phones!"

"There's not enough evidence. No judge would authorize a wiretap," Ron said.

"Ron. We tap. Get the evidence and then get the wiretap," Zangara said. His voice was patient and parent-like.

"Not in any case that I'm aware of, you won't! From now on, as far as this case is concerned, it's all official business. Any criminal activity, you report it to your superiors, or the District Attorney. Is that understood?"

"Understood," Zangara said.

Ron's stern tone softened so as to appear casual. There was one bit of information that nagged at him.

"Did you follow her during Christmas week?"

"Nah," Scott said. "She went to Mexico with some big shots."

"How do you know that?"

"She breezed through Customs when she came back."

CHAPTER 35

▼

"This is a medical malpractice case," Ron said to the jury. It was composed of several African Americans, an Asian and, what appeared from their names, to be Jews and Italians.

The lawyers, Firestone, Fisher and Lentino jockeyed for a favorable ethnic mix. After all, this *was* Brooklyn. Jurors were perceived to vote their class, their race and their ethnic background.

Middle class was middle class, however, regardless of color or nationality and inclined to parsimony. The African-American teacher, juror number five, although she had insisted that she could be fair, remained on the jury only because Firestone had run out of challenges.

Since this was a civil case, the jury consisted of six persons as mandated in a civil case. Three alternates had been selected. Any doubt that this would be a short trial had been quickly removed. Jury selections had taken five days. The lawyers, in turn, had spoken to prospective jurors. They sought to root out any prejudice on the one hand and hoped to obtain sympathetic jurors on the other.

"*What area of Brooklyn do you live in? How long? How many years of education do you have? Have you ever been sued? Have you ever sued anyone? What do you do for a living? Are you married? What does your spouse do for a living? Have you ever been hospitalized? Have any members of your family ever been hospitalized? Have you ever served on a jury? Are you a shareholder in any insurance company? Is there any reason why you cannot be a fair and impartial juror?*"

Questions often led to other questions and when a juror was excused, either by consent or challenge, the process would be repeated.

Three panels of twenty-five jurors each had been exhausted before a jury had been agreed upon.

Since there was no requirement that Ron preside over jury selection, Ron was seeing them for the first time.

After the jury was sworn, Ron opened his notebook and began to read his preliminary instructions.

The lawyers, with their briefcases and records piled high on their tables, listened in what they hoped was their most attentive manner. Each nodded as Ron formally introduced them to the jury.

"The same principles of law that govern an ordinary negligence case, such as an automobile accident, apply here. Except that in this case, we are dealing with medical negligence and there are several differences. First, a medical malpractice case can only be proved by expert witnesses. So, you will be hearing testimony as to whether there were any deviations or departures from good and accepted standards of medical practice. An expert witness, unlike an ordinary witness, is not amenable to subpoena. In other words, he cannot be compelled to testify and he may be paid to review the records and for his time in court. Also, an ordinary lay witness is usually limited to testifying to what that person saw or heard, but an expert, because of his education and expertise, is allowed to express an opinion for the benefit of the court and jury."

"As far as the order of trial, you've all become educated by television…" Ron smiled. The jury needed a small comment to loosen them up, he thought.

Within days they would be relaxed and attentive. For now, however, they were all sitting stiffly, not knowing exactly what to expect.

The courtroom was crowded with court buffs and lawyers who came to hear the opening statements of the lawyers. Dr. Spender sat quietly in the front row. He stared straight ahead, rigid, except for a slight twitch of his jaw. Ruth and Victor Santo sat together—on the other side of the aisle. Ruth Santo's neat, floral print dress was several sizes too big and accentuated her emaciated look. Occasionally, jurors stole glances toward her as Ron continued his instructions.

"When both sides rest, the lawyers will then sum up. After summations, I will charge you on the law."

Ron ended by reminding the jury not to discuss the evidence until final deliberations and not to speak to any of the persons involved in the case.

Ron used the luncheon recess to confirm his date with Sarah.

"Why don't we have an early dinner at Orlando? The plaintiff's attorney said that he would take all afternoon in his opening statement. So, I'm not sure of the exact time we're going to recess, but 6 o'clock would be perfect. Take a cab. I'll drive you home."

As predicted, Firestone's opening statement lasted for almost two hours. Ron was impressed by its sheer volume and detail. Firestone explained the medicine in the case, first simply and then technically—all without referring to a note. Meanwhile, the two defense lawyers scribbled away on their legal pads and, occasionally tried to break Firestone's rhythm with objections.

"These doctors and their hospitals have destroyed the lives of both Ruth Santo and her husband, Victor." Firestone turned from the jury and pointed to the defendants' lawyers. "She had pain in her stomach—we all have had stomach cramps. All she needed was Maalox. Can you imagine that? Maalox! The doctors ordered tests. Maybe she had an ulcer. Maybe it was her heart. Maybe she had gall stones, they said. She might need her gall bladder removed. Maybe. Perhaps. Then maybe an exploratory. In all, these doctors and their hospitals subjected this poor woman to six surgical procedures and twenty hospitalizations. And all she needed was Maalox!"

"I object, your Honor," Christine Fisher said. "He's not making an opening statement, he's making a summation."

"The objection is sustained, Miss Fisher, but please just object. If I want to know the basis of your objection, I will ask you."

"I wasn't summing up Judge. I'm going to show that all she needed was Maalox, and once they got their hands on her…"

"The objection is sustained, Mr. Firestone. The same rule applies to you as the other lawyers. I don't want any comments. Do you understand?"

Ron did not use a gavel. Usually the tone of his voice was its functional equivalent. A good trial judge established the ground rules immediately. Any lapse would result in endless squabbling between lawyers.

"I will prove—by experts in the field of gastroenterology—that all she needed was Maalox." Firestone smiled. Repetition was good. Adverse rulings were not necessarily bad. "Six operations that have left this 35 year old woman at death's door."

"Objection," said Manny Lentino.

"Sustained." Ron said.

"I will prove she's been in the hospital twenty times, members of the jury, and that she's suffering from hemorrhagic pancreatitis—don't be afraid of those medical terms. You're going to get *some* medical education." Firestone paced slowly before the jurors—his eyes riveted upon them. "You know what that means? Auto-digestion. The digestive juices have eaten away her insides. From a simple diagnostic procedure that shouldn't have been done in the first place, there was a cascade of events that have made Ruth Santo, a hopeless cripple. Today she suffers from diabetes because her pancreas has been eaten away by a gigantic abscess. She has to take insulin everyday—four times a day for the rest of her life. She has massive adhesions and intestinal obstructions, and hardening of the coronary arteries that makes her heart beat irregularly. She now has scar tissue in her heart. The diabetes has made her nearly blind, too. Wait until you hear about T-tubes and the fistula of the colon and the ileostomy—that's when our human waste drains into a colostomy bag on the outside. And guess what, jurors? These lawyers dispute that all this had made Ruth Santo anxious and depressed…"

"Objection!" Both defense lawyers were on their feet.

"Come, Mr. Firestone. You know better than that," Ron said.

"I'm sorry, your Honor."

"I'm sure you are," Ron said.

"As I said, please don't be afraid of the medical terminology. It all started for Ruth Santo because she had stomach pains. Dr. DiTucci, God rest his soul, was the primary care provider. That is, he was her original doctor. Unfortunately, he is deceased, but we do have his records to help us. He referred her to Dr. Spender, a specialist in the stomach and intestines. A Gastroenterologist. Spender performed a diagnostic procedure called an ERCP. That's an Endoscopic Retrograde Cholangio Pancreatography. Those are fancy words for sticking a tube down your throat, into your stomach and looking to see if you have gall stones. And that's when her troubles started." Firestone turned to the audience and pointed at Dr. Spender. "That man put his instrument right through her intestine. He perforated her common bile duct and small bowel. He bungled the operation and then hid it."

"Objection!" Christine Fisher said.

"Not this time Judge! I'm going to prove he concealed his mistake from everyone."

"Mr. Firestone," Ron said. "I'm becoming weary with you. You're doing your client a disservice by your remarks." He turned and shook his head to show his disapproval.

Firestone apologized again. This time, properly chastened, he confined his opening statement to a painstaking reiteration of the medical aspects. He explained words such as "duodenum," "phlegmon," "ventral hernia," and "peristalsis." When he completed his opening statement, it was evident that Roger Firestone—at least in the field of medicine that applied to his client—was as knowledgeable as any medical doctor.

CHAPTER 36

▼

Sarah was waiting for him when he arrived at Orlando's. He was tired, but he knew that seeing Sarah would renew him.

Weeks had passed and their relationship had evolved into a warmth and closeness that Ron did not wish to jeopardize. The Christmas incident, although not forgotten, was pushed from his mind.

March 15th was her birthday and he carried the engagement ring in his pocket, waiting for that day. He was positive that she would accept it now.

"Hi sweetheart," Ron said. He kissed her lightly on her smiling cheek.

"You're late," Sarah said. "And I'm famished."

"And I'm not hungry."

"I came all the way from Manhattan. We could have met there."

"All the way? Brooklyn isn't the end of the world. Besides, Orlando's is our special place. I even outfought you for the check here, once," Ron said.

It's all tax deductible, silly."

"Well, I'm not comfortable with your picking up my tab."

"When you're not paying tuition anymore, you can pick up the tab."

"If I live that long," Ron said.

"You'll live. I don't allow my men to die, sweetheart."

"Men?"

"Just a figure of speech, dear." She blew him a kiss. "But you do look tired. Is this case getting to you already?"

"You don't know how grueling a trial like this can be. The concentration is enormous. Keeping control of the courtroom is a constant chore. These trial lawyers are the best in the business and they'll stretch the rules every chance they get."

"I know darling," Sarah said. She touched his arm that held the martini. "I want to hear all about it."

"I'm not looking forward to this trial, Sarah. There's something going on."

"Like what?"

"I don't know. It's a heavy case. Worth millions. But then that's not unusual for one of my cases. But things have happened." He sipped the martini.

"Like what?" Sarah said. "You're making me sound like a broken record."

"I don't really know." Ron shook his head as if he were disagreeing with himself. "Perhaps it's all unconnected."

"Unconnected or not. Tomorrow is Friday and I'm planning a big weekend together."

"What about tonight?"

"I thought you were tired?" Sarah picked up the menu and opened it.

"I never said I was too tired," Ron smiled and took the menu from her.

"Not tonight, my hero. I want you fresh for the weekend." Sarah took back her menu. "How's the Fettuccini Alfredo?"

"Fattening," Ron said.

CHAPTER 37

▼

Friday began routinely. Except for the litigants and several court buffs, there were few spectators in the courtroom.

When the jury was seated, the defendants' lawyers made their opening statements. When they spoke, Dr. Spender shook or nodded his head in what he thought was a signal of innocence.

Christine Fisher and Manny Lentino employed different strategies than Firestone. Since it was much more difficult to prove a negative, they would both underplay their openings. But plaintiff's lawyer was fair game, and flattery was a weapon.

"Mr. Firestone is one of the leading trial lawyers in this city," Christine Fisher began. "In fact, he is acclaimed nationally." She turned and extended her hand down towards him, palm up, as if in laudatory introduction. "His skills have impressed—deservedly I might add—countless juries."

Firestone sat smiling, his eyes fixed on the jury. How could he object to such praise? The bitch.

"But as talented as he is, Mr. Firestone has a problem. No one denies that his client is seriously ill. No. His problem is that no one did anything wrong. You remember in jury selection that you promised me that merely because a person is sick, does not mean that anyone is at fault. My heart truly goes out to Mrs. Santo, but she was seriously ill long before she ever met Dr. Spender." Christine gestured toward Ruth and Victor.

He was stroking his wife's hand, almost petting her. Christine would reserve some of her cynicism for him—later. Perhaps she might later diminish Ruth

Santo's case by stigmatizing the husband. She tucked that thought in her mind and continued her speech to the jury.

Unlike Firestone, she did not pace back and forth. Instead, she punctuated her remarks to the jury by standing motionless. She waved her pen as if it were a baton and the jurors were the orchestra. Her starched white blouse under her black suit made her look almost nun-like. Her black hair was knotted into a bun and held with a large gold comb. She wore little makeup.

"I'm not going to bore you with all the medical terms. I'm sure that by the end of the case you will be fully acquainted with them," she said. "Hold Mr. Firestone to his promises and his proof. Don't be just another notch on his gun."

Before Firestone could object, Christine Fisher breezed past him and went to her seat.

Ron looked at Manny Lentino, inviting him to proceed.

"Justice Goodman, distinguished colleagues…" Lentino said and nodded to each, "…members of the jury, I'm not as eloquent as Mr. Firestone, either…"

"Judge," Firestone said. He stood up moving his chair nosily so that everyone's eyes were drawn to him. "Enough with all of these compliments. This jury isn't going to be fooled by this false praise about me."

Quick as a shot, Christine rose and said, "you're denying you're eloquent?"

"He's like a magician with words," Lentino stage whispered.

Ron looked at the offending lawyers and showed his annoyance by gesturing for them to sit down. He then motioned for Lentino to continue.

"I'm not going to say much," Lentino began. "…because there is not much that I can say. Beth Torah Hospital is one of the finest hospitals in the City of New York. It is a teaching hospital and it has protocols, that is, rules for its operation. We will show that the only connection we have with this case is that we furnished a place for this patient to be cared for and treated. We did nothing wrong. There is no proof that we allowed improper persons to operate. There's no claim that our equipment or facilities were inadequate. From Mr. Firestone's own proof, we will show that no nurse, intern, resident or house physician participated in any of the procedures that plaintiff claims injured her." Manny Lentino's voice grew soft and reassuring. "I tell you that no one, not Dr. Spender, nor anyone at the hospital, was negligent."

The first witness that Firestone called was Dr. Spender.

"Why is he doing that?" A spectator asked.

"This is a malpractice case. The plaintiff's first witness is usually the defendant doctor," the court buff said. "It's not like criminal trials where the defendant can't be forced to incriminate himself."

"Sure, sure. I know that. But why call him as a witness, now? Everything he says is going to be against the plaintiff. Won't it?"

"Depositions, my friend. Discovery. Firestone knows the case better than the doctor. Watch him!" The court buff said and pointed toward Firestone. "He has the Examination Before Trial in his hand. If that doctor makes one mistake, Firestone will be at his throat."

"Quiet!" the clerk roared.

Firestone waited for Spender to be sworn as a witness. Then when the focus was again on him and not the doctor, he rose.

"Dr. Spender, you're a physician duly licensed to practice medicine in the State of New York?"

"Yes, I obtained my medical degree at Downstate Medical…"

"Your Honor, I move to strike as not responsive," Firestone said.

"Strike it!" Ron said. "Doctor, this is in the nature of cross-examination and you are obliged to answer 'yes' or 'no'. If you cannot answer in that fashion, then state that to the court."

"You're a physician licenced to practice in this State?"

"Yes."

"And you have a specialty."

"Yes."

"But you're not a surgeon."

"Yes, I am not a surgeon," Spender said- and smiled.

Firestone shook his head and gazed at the jury. He waited a long moment before asking his next question. The jury will get the idea, he thought. This bastard is too clever for his own good.

"You don't remove gall bladders, do you, Dr. Spender?"

"No."

"But you do remove gallstones?"

"Yes."

"How do you do that, doctor?" Firestone's voice was firm but not unfriendly.

"You know very well, counselor. It's called an ERCP. You've already explained that to the jury. Quite well, I might add."

"Why thank you for the compliment, doctor. But my explanation was not complete was it? This ERCP. There are two kinds, aren't there? A therapeutic and a diagnostic?"

"Yes."

"The diagnostic is where you look to see if there are any gallstones and a therapeutic is where you try to break up the gallstones with a claw at the end of this tube that you insert down the throat. It goes into the stomach and down into the intestines until you come to the common bile duct."

"That's crudely stated, but not incorrect."

"Thank you, doctor."

Firestone continued in this vein for some time. He asked general questions about the procedure and introduced into evidence diagrams and models of endoscopes that were used in such operations. It was the "Real Evidence," evidence that the jury could touch and feel when they deliberated.

When he was sure that the jury understood, he began to ask questions as to the actual operation.

"When you inserted the endoscope down into Mrs. Santo's throat, what type of anesthesia did you use, if any?"

"We gave her some Valium and a topical spray that anesthetized her esophagus."

"Then you passed the tube down her throat, into her stomach and into her duodenum?"

"That's the procedure."

"And what is the duodenum, doctor?"

"That's the first part of the small intestines."

"That extends from the pylorus to the jejunum?" Firestone pointed to a diagram of the gastrointestinal tract.

"Yes."

"And then you passed this tube very carefully up into the common bile duct, here." He pointed again.

Dr. Spender began to shift in his seat and reached for a glass of water.

"At this time, you weren't performing a therapeutic ERCP, were you?"

"I performed a diagnostic procedure but I did not perforate the common bile duct, but even if I did, it is not an uncommon event."

"Is that so?"

"These procedures are carefully monitored by fluoroscope—they're not three dimensional."

"I see." Firestone turned to the jury and smiled grandly as if to indicate that Dr. Spender had made a major concession.

"What I mean is that, it's a risk of the procedure. Mrs. Santo knew that. She was informed of that prior to the operation…"

"We'll get to that later, doctor. Let's just concentrate on the perforation."

"It's a known complication."

"You've already told us that doctor. Now, if you had caused a perforation, then the bile would back up. Isn't that correct?"

"Yes, of course."

"That would cause an abscess to form in the pancreas and result in hemorrhagic pancreatitis?"

"It might."

"And that causes auto-digestion. That is, that the digestive juices cause the pancreas to eat itself?"

"That's highly inflammatory, counselor!"

"Yes it is, isn't it doctor?"

"I didn't mean it that way," Spender said.

"I object, your Honor. He's badgering the witness," Fisher said.

"No. I think the witness was making an objection. Please answer the questions. The lawyers will do the objecting," Ron said.

"What about this perforation? You monitored the path of the endoscope down the throat."

"Yes."

"You didn't do it yourself, did you?"

"Yes I did."

Firestone stopped. He looked at Spender and then leafed through Spender's deposition.

"Doctor, do you remember giving testimony at an examination before trial under oath, page 8, line 14 'Question: Didn't Doctor Gould, a second year resident, actually insert the endoscope? Answer: Absolutely not!' Do you remember giving that testimony?"

"I was mistaken," Dr. Spender said. "I've thought about it but now I remember. I performed the procedure myself. That Resident probably wasn't watching the monitor. Yes. The Resident was flirting with a nurse. She was very pretty. I had to remind him to pay attention to the path of the probe as I guided it down the esophagus."

Firestone again smiled broadly at the jury and then ostentatiously turned to look at Fisher and Lentino, inviting the jury to look, also, at the crestfallen lawyers.

"If the Resident had been paying attention, then he would have observed the perforation."

"Objection," Lentino said.

"Sustained."

"If no one was watching the monitor, how do you know you didn't cause the perforation?" It was a bad question. Firestone was becoming flustered. He was not used to help from a defendant.

"That's why I can't be sure." Spender said. His eyes closed for a moment as if he were searching for an explanation. He then added, "I would have seen air on the hard plates."

"Doctor, you know perfectly well that there are no hard copies of the x-rays."

"That's not my fault. I wasn't the radiologist."

On the friendly cross-examination, Christine Fisher attempted damage control. Spender was allowed to explain his role in the operation. All was not lost, yet. She still might be able to persuade the jury that her client, too, was an innocent victim.

"I perform hundreds of ERCPs in hospitals all over the City. The treating physician calls me and I go to that particular hospital. I do the procedure, it might take an hour or so, and then I leave. I never see the patient again. I do not treat or care for the patient. I merely do the procedure and report my findings. Mrs. Santo had many problems. Colitis and so forth. And we thought that she might need a cholangiotecomy—that's removal of her gall bladder and that's a job for a surgeon."

"Dr. Spender, let's be frank. In all of those hundreds of ERCP's that you've performed—have you ever perforated a colon?" Christine Fisher asked.

"Sad to say, Ms. Fisher, it has happened several times. I'm never happy about it but I explain very carefully to my patients that it is something that can occur…"

"Objection," Firestone interrupted. "I move to strike!"

"These people are in pain when they come to me…"

"…And you give them more pain," Firestone said.

"What is this a debating society?" Ron shouted. "You all know better but if this doesn't stop I may have the doctor and lawyers enjoy a weekend in the City Jail."

When it was Lentino's turn, he bounded from the chair as if he were going to strike Spender. That bastard had put the hospital right in the middle of the lawsuit!

"Doctor, who was the radiologist?"

"I don't know. I would have to check the hospital chart."

"Isn't it a fact that the radiologist was an attending physician—that is one not employed by the hospital?"

"I don't know that."

"Isn't that the common practice?"

"In some hospitals, yes."

"This Resident. What's his name?" Lentino's face was bright with indignation and his voice was hoarse and accusatory.

"I have to check the chart."

"Go ahead Dr. Spender." He handed Spender the Beth Torah Hospital chart.

Spender went through the hospital chart. He stopped at the operative report and then looked at the progress notes.

"Didn't you read this chart before you testified?"

"Yes, but...the chart is out of order."

"You know very well that there is no Resident listed in the operative report."

"Doctor, isn't it a fact that you were in complete charge of the operation—and no one else?" Lentino advanced toward Spender as if he were a Pit Bull ready to attack.

"I only have two hands. I rely on the hospital to furnish competent residents."

"You're asking this jury to believe that you put a tube down a patient's throat, into her stomach, and probably punctured her intestinal wall, without checking on the fluoroscope? Without taking x-rays? Without leaving any post-operative orders? And just abandoning the patient? Is that what you're saying?"

"That's argumentative, your Honor," Fisher said weakly.

"I am going to sustain the objection," Ron said.

"I withdraw the question," Lentino said. "What I really want to know is what 24-hour copy store gave this doctor a license."

Before the objection could be made, Lentino said, "I withdraw that question, too." He waved his hand in disgust and sat down. He leaned over toward Christine Fisher and whispered, "so much for a united defense, you double-crosser!"

CHAPTER 38

▼

"Nice place you got here," Tom Scott said. He wandered about Ron's living room, weaving between the sofa and the upholstered chairs. He stopped to pick up and examine the bric-a-brac in the open curio cabinet.

"Sit down, Tom," Zangara said. "The judge didn't invite us up here for tea and crumpets."

"Actually, I thought that it might be better to talk here," Ron said. "Rumors acquire a life of their own in the Courthouse. It seems that there are constant rumors that circulate—that the FBI or the police are investigating a corrupt judge."

"You're not alone," Zangara said. "You should hear the stories about cops and Internal Affairs."

"In any event, I want to apologize to you. I was pretty angry about your following Sarah," Ron said.

"No sweat," Zangara said.

"And I have to tell you, I may be embarrassed again. This Santo case is undergoing some odd twists and turns."

"Dr. Spender changed his testimony?" Zangara said.

"Why yes. How did you know that?" Ron said.

"Figure it out, Ron. You think there's something fishy with this trial. Spender almost gets blown up. Dr. DiTucci, I'm now convinced, was murdered and the plaintiff has possible connections with organized crime. Why Spender would throw his own case is in your department, not mine."

"And you're creating a dilemma for me," Ron said. "I'm trying a case while you're investigating a possible homicide or mob connected activity. All we have are suspicions, but nevertheless, I've not reported this to anyone."

"What's to report?" Zangara said. "That I asked you to check out some people on a case?"

"I think we've gone farther than that."

"Who you going to ask and what are you going to tell them? That a couple of dumb cops have involved you in a police investigation? Come on, Ron. I'm your friend not a stranger. In my opinion, you're carrying this ethics question, too far. As you said, all we have are suspicions, nothing else. Besides, you report any of this and you'll blow away our investigation. If it ever develops that you've been compromised, you can deal with it when it happens—if it ever happens."

"And that's your legal opinion?" Ron said. "I'll remember that when they throw me off the bench."

"I have a different opinion but I don't give a shit about any ethics," Scott said. "I think this Barbara DiTucci had her husband killed. Jack, I respect you, dammit, but this woman is too good to be true. We don't have all the answers but things are adding up to it."

"Like what?"

"Like what was Spender doing at her house?"

"That's stupid," Zangara said. "How can anyone make a connection between Barbara DiTucci and Dr. Spender changing his testimony, all based on one visit." He averted his eyes as he sat down.

"One visit, that you know of," Ron said.

"I thought we came here for your benefit," Zangara said.

"Don't be so defensive, Jack. Let me play devil's advocate for a moment," Ron said.

"Go ahead but you're only going to be piling speculation on top of speculation. I'm just pissed off that everyone is enjoying it." Zangara tossed his head in Scott's direction.

"All right. First, Dr. Spender's insurance company is defunct. That means that any verdict against him is uncollectible."

"There are still his personal assets, aren't there?" Zangara tried, without success, to keep the defensiveness from his voice.

"If he has any assets, it's probably pennies."

"That still doesn't connect Barbara to the case." Zangara's face, normally an olive complexion, darkened into burnt amber.

"It does if she's got an old boyfriend named Victor," Scott said.

"You know something, I don't know?" Zangara asked.

"This is getting us nowhere," Ron said. "You people are the detectives. We need more facts!"

"All right, if you want to play devil's advocate. Why don't we start with the others who would profit. How about this guy, Firestone. He's a slimy one," Zangara said.

"I watched Firestone like a hawk," Ron said. "He was stunned by Dr. Spender. Not that he wouldn't take advantage of it. He was prepared to tear the doctor apart and was almost speechless when Spender testified in his favor. His lawyer, Miss Fisher looked like she was standing in front of a firing squad."

"So, who's in on this grand plot?" Zangara said. "If it's not Firestone or Fisher, it must be the other lawyer, what's his name."

"No. Manny Lentino went after Spender as if he were Judas Iscariot. There has to be someone else. And I don't think I'm being paranoid."

"And I say it all comes back to Barbara DiTucci," Scott said to Zangara. "You may think I'm giving you the business, but follow the facts. She spoke with Spender, remember? Two and two, Jack. Two and two."

"What possible connection could there be? Spender is the one who's dumping the case. Life insurance and medical malpractice insurance are two different things!"

"There's a lot of 'what ifs' here. What if Spender helped her murder her husband? What if Spender is her lover?" Scott said. "What if she's black-mailing Spender in order to save her own skin? What if Spender has proof that DiTucci committed suicide? What if she's got Mafia connections and arranged to have her own husband killed? If the mob's involved, then maybe she's involved. And what if she's related to Victor Santo? Maybe, an old flame. Or still has something still cooking. You know that she's not Italian but that doesn't mean she has no ties to the mob."

"She's Jewish," Zangara said. "So what?"

"And what's her maiden name?"

"I don't know."

"Jack, you have no idea how sorry I am. I kept hoping I wouldn't have to tell you." Scott pulled a pad from his jacket and flipped the pages. "Barbara DiTucci's maiden name is Goldberg."

"So what?" Zangara said.

"Guess what Ruth Santo's maiden name is?"

"My God," Ron said. "Goldberg?"

Scott nodded.

"And I still say, what does that have to do with Ron's case?"

"Christ, now you're the thick one. Barbara Goldberg DiTucci has her own husband whacked so that he won't ruin her sister's case! Scott said.

"That's pretty far fetched," Zangara said.

"Maybe," Scott said. "But if I were you I wouldn't fall asleep with her when you sleep with her."

"You're not going to let up, are you, Tom? Zangara said.

A key turned in the door lock and Sarah entered.

Ron was awkward in the introduction. "Sarah, I'd like you to meet Detective Zangara and Scott." He wondered why it bothered him that Zangara and Scott now knew that she had a key to his apartment. Was it because the relationship between these two detectives was unraveling and both knew more than they needed to know?

Both men rose for the introduction.

Sarah pecked Ron on his cheek.

"Is this the legendary Detective Zangara, who Ron always speaks about," Sarah said. She extended her hand to him—straight out—her purse tucked under her other arm. Her smile was wide and her eyes seem to twinkle. Her eyelashes were long and dark. Her crushed maroon velvet dress with its low neckline seemed more suitable for the evening, but then her full length mink coat, which she wore unbuttoned, actually made her appear casual.

"I'm please to meet you, too, Mr. Scott."

"Tom."

Sarah turned to Ron.

"Such handsome men! Ron, isn't Tom the spitting image of Robert Redford—younger of course."

"And a lot heavier," Scott said.

"Yeah, and I must remind you of Robert DiNiro—older, of course." He passed his hand through his sparse hair.

"Nothing like a woman to change the course of a conversation," Ron said.

"We can talk another time," Zangara said.

"Yes, today is Ron's birthday," Sarah said. "You can play at your cloak and dagger stuff on Monday. We have a helicopter to catch."

CHAPTER 39

▼

The stretch limousine was waiting curbside and the tuxedo clad chauffeur held the door open for them.

"What's this about a helicopter?" Ron said.

Zangara and Scott seemed properly impressed when Ron waved goodbye to them. "You definitely know how to make a statement, Sarah."

"You ain't seen nothing yet," she said.

Some snow still lay on the roadside, but there was little traffic. The limo swiftly traversed the streets, entered the Queens Midtown Tunnel, and then the Brooklyn Queens Expressway. With little delay, it pulled into the private area of LaGuardia Airport. Within minutes, they were airborne and on their way to Atlantic City.

"The deal with Mexico came through?"

"No," Sarah said. "Nobody could come up with guarantees."

"Then what's all this for?" Ron looked down as the helicopter banked slightly and passed over Sandy Hook.

It was a bright, clear day and the ocean sparkled in the winter sunlight.

It's your birthday Ron, and I wanted to do something spectacular."

"I don't like you throwing away your money like this," Ron said.

"It's all comped," Sarah said.

Within forty-five minutes they landed on the pad at the Katmandu Casino.

When they alighted from the helicopter over the deafening noise of the whirling blades, Ron heard shouts. He looked up and saw several figures waving to him.

Sarah stayed back and enjoyed the scene as Ron, in turn, embraced his mother and his children, Colleen and Alan.

"Mrs. Baruch arranged it," Alan said. "I flew in from Chicago last night and Colleen came this morning from Boston!"

"And your poor old mother had to suffer with a two and one half hour drive in a limousine," Mrs. Goodman said. She feigned petulance. "I think this is an elaborate scheme to make me gamble away my life savings."

"Nobody's going to get that, Grandma!" Colleen said. "Daddy said you still have the first nickel you hoarded from Grandpa."

"You believe your father? He's a Judge!"

"Judges don't lie," Ron said. He laughed and hugged his mother again.

"Isn't this a great surprise, Dad?" Alan's hug seemed to engulf Ron. His cheeks were ruddy and his eyes were Ron's eyes, deep set and clear.

"He's way taller than you," Sarah said.

"A man is always proud of a son who's bigger and brighter than himself."

"And a daughter?" Colleen insinuated herself close to Ron. Although a twin, she was almost petite. However, there was no mistaking the resemblance. The eyes, the cheeks, the set of her chin- and her smile.

"Putty in your hands," Ron said. "That's all I'll ever be." He caressed her flowing blonde hair that was whipped about by the wind.

Once inside, they made a quick tour of the cavernous casino. The thousands of slot machines and their multi-colored lights blazed and flashed more hypnotically that a snake charmer's flute. The clanging sound of coins, ringing bells, chimes and musical tones made it seem like everyone was a winner.

Ron was further impressed when he saw the suite of rooms. Sarah, anticipating the delicacy of the reunion, had arranged for a separate room for herself. For now, Ron would be away from her and with his family.

"This way you can talk—without tension," she said.

Their suite had a high ceiling and magnificent drapes. There were four large bedrooms off a parlor with a wet bar stocked with expensive liquors. On the counter was an enormous basket of fruit with packets of cheeses and tins of delicacies.

"Wow!" Ron kept repeating as he toured the various bedrooms.

"We have reservations for dinner at 8 o'clock at the Bangalore. That's the gourmet Indian restaurant," Sarah said. "But let's take some of the casino's money first."

They crowded around Sarah at the craps table as she signed for a ten thousand dollar marker.

"I had no idea, Sarah." Conflicting thoughts struck him. Was she a spend-thrift? A gambler? Could he keep up with her on his relatively meager judge's salary? She had seemed to be reluctant to reveal her past and how in one stroke, was she revealing a terrible vice? "I had no idea," he said again.

Sarah gave his mother and the children each a black hundred dollar chip. "Here, cash it and go play the slots."

They looked at Ron and hesitated.

"Go ahead. Take it. It's no fun here if you don't gamble. If you win you can return the money," Sarah said.

Ron nodded. Damn. It would just have to fit in his budget. He could never allow her this generosity.

"Can I play Blackjack?" Colleen said.

"Anything you like," Sarah said. But they did not wait for the response. Instead, they shot off in different directions as if the casino extended to the four corners of the world.

"They give you ten thousand in chips?"

"I have a fifty thousand dollar line," Sarah said.

"I never dreamed…"

"I don't use it. I just have it, silly. I have forty-five days to pay the marker."

"Sarah, you continue to surprise me," Ron said.

"It's only money. I told you I make a lot and I love craps. The way I earn my living, is the way I play."

"I don't understand," Ron said.

"I'll go out on ten deals before I make a hit. You win some, you lose some. It's the same with craps. Life's a gamble, isn't it Ron? Aren't we taking a chance on one another?" She leaned over and kissed him lightly on the cheek. She then proceeded to put a purple five hundred dollar chip on the pass line. The point was *six* and she backed up her bet with two orange, thousand dollar, chips.

"*Place* the *eight* for twelve hundred," she told the dealer and threw down an orange and two black chips.

The shooter at the other end of the table threw the dice.

"*Seven out,*" the stickman said.

"Here, why don't you play," Sarah said and offered chips to him. She seemed unconcerned about having lost thirty-seven hundred dollars in the blink of an eye.

"Not me," Ron said.

Sarah shrugged and repeated the new bet. She seemed to be lost in the transactions. Her face took on a glow that he had not seen before.

"I can't watch this," Ron said. "All this money makes me too nervous. I thought I had nerve! I'm going to find the kids."

Ron walked away. He looked out at the vast expanse of the casino. He systemically walked through the innumerable aisles of slot machines searching for them.

It was people watching time. The waitresses wore skimpy, bunnie type costumes as they cruised between patrons and machines, expertly balancing trays of drinks The players, some elated, most somber, some young, most elderly, wore casual clothes.

He stopped at a dollar machine and took a hundred dollar bill from his wallet. He inserted the bill into the machine and he played. He noted how easy the casino made it for the patrons. One no longer had to pull a lever. Just push a button. The 'one armed bandits' had become 'push button bandits.' Nevertheless, more to kill time than to win, he pulled the lever. There was a certain satisfaction in having the lever snap back into place as each cylinder spun and sequentially came to a halt. Despite his pessimism, there was a moment when his heart pounded and rose as if it were leaving his body. It lasted only for a fraction of a second. Of the three sevens, the third seven almost landed on the line. It stopped, however, in the bowels of the slot machine. The screen showed: "seven", "seven" "blank." No jackpot. And his heart went back to where it belonged. Within what seemed an indecently short time, Ron lost the hundred dollars.

The Bangalore, unlike the other restaurants at the Katmandu was small- and exclusive. The decor as well as the fare was Indian and the waiters with their ornate caftans were dressed as a Maharajah's servants.

The meal was leisurely as was the conversation.

"Is everyone having a good time?" Ron said.

"This place is unreal," Alan said. He gazed at Sarah and touched her arm.

"You approve?" Ron said.

"Most definitely. Sarah, you're wonderful!" Alan said.

"Beautiful and exciting, I might add," Colleen said. "Just like mom."

"Comparisons are never flattering," Ron said. He shifted his eyes in embarrassment.

"I guess that did sound hostile, but I didn't mean it in that way. I plead not guilty," Colleen said to Sarah.

"Of course," Sarah said. "I want us all to be friends."

Ron looked at Sarah who seemed to be forcing a smile.

"Tell Sarah about the time when mom accidentally broke your nose," Colleen said.

"I don't think this is the right time for that."

"Come on, Dad. That's a funny story," Colleen said.

"It's not that funny." Ron shook his head. He'd have to straighten out his daughter. Hostility was one thing but bad manners was inexcusable.

Dinner for five was sumptuous and expensive. Both the steaks and lamb chops were cooked in Indian style with plenty of curry.

The bill came to $725.00. Sarah signed for it and left a $125.00 cash tip. Ron reached to pay it.

"No, no," Sarah said. "You're my guests."

"I lost," Alan said. "But I still have twenty dollars left."

Ron looked at his mother who nodded. "We all lost."

"Not me," Colleen said. "I won $750.00."

Ron looked at his daughter.

"Probabilities, Dad. We study more than Economics at Boston College. Haven't you ever heard of the Gaussian curve?"

"The bell curve?" Sarah said.

"See. Only the men in this family are dumb," Colleen said.

Later, back at the suite and before he sneaked off to Sarah's room, Ron sought Colleen.

"What was that all about," Ron said. "You're turning into a major league bitch!"

"I don't like her, Dad. She's too perfect. Like a mannequin where there's not a hair out of place."

"How can you come to such a quick conclusion, Colleen? Sarah, at great expense, I might add, has flown you and your brother here from school. She wanted us to be together. Thoughtfulness makes you suspicious?"

"And why did she do it? To butter us up or to impress you? She's bad news, Dad. I just feel it. She's like that Claudia Penna you warned me about. Their type think they can buy everything and everyone. You're just a middle-aged sucker to Sarah. God, it galls me that you can't see it!"

"I love her," Ron said. "And I'm going to marry her—if she'll have me." He took the engagement ring from his pocket.

"If she'll have you? My god, Dad, she's chasing you like she were the hound and you were the fox. I tried to talk to her before dinner. Privately, girl talk. All I got from her was banalities. Superficial stuff. Evasions. What do you know about her? Is she divorced? Children? Family?"

"She's divorced."

"How many times, Dad?"

"Colleen, I think your animosity is inappropriate. Do you think that if I get married again, it's a betrayal of your mother?"

"Grandma doesn't like her, either."

"Did she tell you that?"

"She didn't have to. A woman knows another woman, Dad. Chalk it up to feminine instinct, if you want."

"Feminine instinct? Christ, Colleen, you're only twenty years old!"

"That doesn't make me wrong."

"No, and it doesn't make you right, either." He put the engagement ring back in his pocket. "The assessment isn't unanimous. Alan appreciates her."

"You son's a jerk when it comes to women," Colleen said. "The apple doesn't fall from far the tree."

CHAPTER 40

▼

The day Ruth Santo testified, she was again dressed simply, as Firestone had instructed. Ruth's cheeks were sunken and her face was jaundiced. Her gingham dress, ankle length and long sleeved, hung on her.

Her voice was a whisper and she had to be reminded several times to speak up so that everyone could hear her. Despite Firestone's direction that she should look at the jury, her head was bowed and she kept her hands clasped tightly, as if she were holding in her life force.

"How old are you Ruth?" Firestone asked. It was an important question. It would establish a basis for the jury to calculate her life expectancy.

Firestone knew that the jury would have to determine the number of years in the future, that Ruth Santo would endure her pain and suffering.

"I'm thirty-five," Ruth said.

One of the spectators audibly gasped and Ron looked sternly at the offender. Ron noted Ruth's age in his minute book but did take a sidelong glance at her. Not only was she prematurely gray, but her upper lip was wrinkled. Her blue eyes, which were once probably her most attractive feature, were encased in black rings and were set deep into her head. Despite her skeletal face, the skin hung loosely beneath her chin. Thirty-five? She looked fifty-five! Ron compared her with Victor Santo, who was sitting in the courtroom. His somber face did not conceal his robust, healthy appearance.

"How much do you weigh, Ruth?" Firestone said.

"I'm 102 pounds."

"When you first went to Dr. DiTucci, how much did you weigh?"

"That was four years ago. I was 168 pounds."

"How tall are you?"

"I'm 5'5". I guess I was a little chubby then."

"Are you married?"

"Yes."

"And what is your husband's name?"

"Victor Santo."

"How long have you been married?"

"We've been married fourteen years."

"Do you have any children?"

"Amelia is thirteen and Rosario, he's eleven. We call him Ross."

"What do you do for a living?"

"They call it homemaker now, but I'm still a housewife, even though I graduated from Vassar." Ruth managed a wry smile.

"What is your maiden name, Ruth?"

"Goldberg."

Firestone nodded solemnly as if the question was routine and not a blatant call to the blood aimed at the Jewish jurors.

"Tell us, Ruth…" Firestone adopted a folksy voice. "…about the time when you saw Dr. DiTucci. How were you feeling? You weren't in the best of health, were you?"

"When I first went to Dr. DiTucci, I was having severe pain on my side. I was afraid it was my heart because my mother had a heart attack when she was forty-five. Dr. DiTucci said that the electrocardiogram was negative and said it was probably gallstones. So he sent me to Dr. Spender."

"Other than the occasional pain in your chest, how were you feeling?"

"It wasn't occasional, but I had no other complaints. I've always been healthy."

"What happened when you saw Dr. Spender? What did he say to you?"

"He said I might need a gall bladder operation but that he wouldn't know for sure until he performed this ERCP."

"The Endoscopic Retrograde Cholangio Pancreatography?"

Ruth nodded. "He said he would perform it at Beth Torah Hospital and it would be on an out-patient basis."

"Can you describe for the jury what happened then?"

"I was given an intravenous sedative so I can't really tell you much. I was pretty much out of it."

"Was Dr. Spender present at this time?"

"Oh yes!"

"Before they put you to sleep, did you observe other people in the room?"

"Yes. Everybody was watching."

"When you say everybody, who do you mean?"

"There were people from the hospital who set up the equipment and a nurse helped them."

"Objection, your Honor. I move to strike that portion that deals with the witness' conclusion about people from the hospital."

"Sustained," Ron said. "The jury will disregard the witness' statement except that it may consider that there were other persons present at the procedure. Their official capacity may be a question for you to consider during your deliberations."

"Then what happened?"

"When I woke up, Dr. Spender was laughing. He said, congratulations you don't have gallstones anymore."

"He told you he performed a therapeutic procedure?"

"No, he just said that I didn't have gallstones anymore."

"What happened then?"

"About and hour or so later, I started vomiting blood and dark stuff that looked like coffee grounds. I had an IV line in my arm and I started getting hiccups. My stomach burned and became swollen. The pain in my stomach was terrible." Ruth shook her head as if she still felt the pain.

"And they kept you overnight?"

"Overnight? I stayed in the hospital for two months."

"Do you know if a diagnosis was ever made as to the cause of your problems?"

"It took a while but they eventually decided that I had a hole in my intestines and that I had acute pancreatitis. They operated on me and took out most of my pancreas. Then they operated on me again and removed the cotton packing and drains. Then they performed an ileostomy. They placed a bag outside to allow the wound to heal. Then I had another procedure to re-attach my intestines. Then I developed an abscess there, too. It seemed to go on and on. I became an expert learning all the names of the things they did to me."

"Did Dr. Spender explain your condition to you?"

"Mr. Firestone, I never saw Dr. Spender again. At least not during any of my twenty hospitalizations." This time Ruth looked directly at the jury.

There was no artifice in her demeanor as Firestone took her procedure by procedure through every sonogram and C-T scan.

At one point, juror number five, the matronly African-American pulled a handkerchief from her purse and wiped a tear from her eye.

"This jury is going to kill us," Fisher whispered to Lentino.

"Look unconcerned," Lentino said softly. He moved his chair ostentatiously so that the noise drew attention to him instead of the witness. He then jotted a note on his legal pad. Find a way to get rid of juror number 5.

"Can you tell this jury, today, what each day is like for you? What do you have to do? How you feel?"

"Can you ask one question at a time, Mr. Firestone?" Ron said.

"I'm sorry your Honor, I was just trying to move things along."

"You're all heart," Lentino said. It was an opportunity for sarcasm which he could not resist. It was worth the disapproving look he received from Ron. Moving things along? Not likely!

"Tell the jury what a typical day is like for you."

"I have no appetite. I'm constantly depressed. I'm always tired. Ross, my son, Rosario, he doesn't understand. He's only a child. I just can't take care of him properly. I have to take insulin injections four times a day."

"What happens if you don't take the insulin?"

"I'll die." Ruth Santo broke down. She began to sob. It was all the more poignant because she tried to suppress the tears.

Firestone waited for her to recover.

"This might be a good time to take a recess," Ron said.

"Your Honor. I'm all right," Ruth said.

"No, we're taking a short recess." Ron looked up. Jack Zangara and Tom Scott had entered the courtroom. Ruth's testimony had taken up much of the day. There was still cross examination.

When the court reconvened, Firestone asked, as if the prior question had only been moments before, "Ruth, has anything ever happened because you did not take the insulin?"

"A few times, I experimented. I purposely didn't take the insulin. They thought that I was trying to kill myself, but I wasn't."

"And what happened?"

"I woke up in an ambulance."

"How do you feel now?"

"As I said, I'm always tired. The funny thing is I still get the same pains that I had in the first place. Maybe it's my imagination. I don't know. I don't see any of my old friends anymore…"

"I have to ask you this Ruth. How has your relationship with your husband been affected?" Firestone said.

"I'm embarrassed. I can't do the things I used to do and I have no…desire. It's ruining our marriage."

"Thank you, Ruth." Firestone turned to his adversaries. "I have no further questions."

"You say that you're depressed," Christine Fisher said. "Have you ever been treated by a psychiatrist?"

"Yes. After the third or fourth operation. I went to one."

"Didn't you see a psychiatrist well before you met Dr. Spender?"

"Absolutely not!" Ruth Santo said. It was the first time there was any fire in her voice.

Christine Fisher checked her notes. "Didn't you see a Dr. Charles A. Kuffner, Jr. a year before you were married?"

"Dr. Kuffner? Fourteen years ago? Oh yes. But he's a Neurologist, not a Psychiatrist. I had a pinched nerve in my neck and I went to him once or twice." Fisher shook her head as if to show that she had caught Ruth Santo in a lie. Showing that the plaintiff was a hypochondriac or less than healthy prior to Dr. Spender's operation might diminish the damages.

Manny Lentino did not bother with any diminution. He sought exculpation! When it came time for his cross examination, he limited his questioning to Ruth Santo's ignorance.

"Those persons in the operating room, do you know any of their names?"

"No."

"And you don't know what they did during the operation, what their functions were?"

"No."

"But they were all courteous and pleasant?"

"Yes."

When Zangara and Scott left the courtroom, Scott slapped his partner on the back.

"Jack you have to admit it. They could be twins. That broad is the sister of Barbara DiTucci," Scott said. "She looks like shit but they have the same face."

"I don't know about that," Zangara said.

"You're kidding. They're like two peas in a pod. One's just shriveled up, that's all."

CHAPTER 41

▼

Zangara knew that he was making a mistake when he telephoned Barbara DiTucci, but he could not help himself. Worse, he was ambivalent as to the best course of action. Should he play dumb? No, it was better to be blunt. Confront her with the facts. But what were the facts?

Sure, Scott was provoking him. But there was much in what his partner said. Scott only appeared to be bumbling and nonchalant. Maybe Scott was merely trying to protect him in his coarse way.

When Zangara rang her doorbell, he was still unsure of the best approach. All of his detective skills momentarily departed him when he saw her bright, apparently guileless, smile.

"You sounded so serious on the phone," Barbara said. "Are you all right?"

"I'm fine," he said. "Just that a couple of things came up." Zangara glanced at the mantle clock although he was well aware of the time.

"It's one thirty. David won't be home from school for another hour or so."

Barbara nudged him. Expectantly. "Jack, you really need a massage." She gave her teasing smile and looked up toward the bedroom.

Zangara hesitated. Sexual instinct should have prevailed but did not. He led her into the living room and sat her down.

"What's wrong, Jack?"

Zangara looked at her closely. Her cheeks were high and Slavic. The same as Ruth Santo. But it was Barbara's blue eyes, wide and deep set, that were striking and strikingly similar to Ruth Santo. Were they cousins? Or sisters? Was it just a coincidence that Barbara had been the wife of Ruth Santo's doctor?

"Is there something you want to tell me?" Zangara said. He adopted his "questioning of suspects" mode. Sharp and curt.

"About what?"

"Let's start with your maiden name."

"My birth name." She corrected him. She sat on the couch with her arms folded.

"I'm not playing games, Barbara."

"Is this the third degree?" Barbara said.

"Why can't you answer a simple question?"

"Why can't you be honest with me and tell me what this interrogation is all about?"

"I don't like being made a fool, that's why." Zangara spit out the words and regretted it.

"I've never lied to you, Jack!"

"No. You just forgot to tell me things, that's all!"

"Like what?"

"What's your maiden name?"

"Goldberg."

"You never told me that, did you?"

"You never asked!"

"What about Dr. Spender?"

"Dr. Spender? Aaron Spender?"

"That's what I mean. No, you never lied. You just never bothered to tell me the truth."

"Jack. Jack. Jack, why are you doing this?"

Zangara saw her full lips. Lips made for kissing. But for whom? She looked at him in apparent incomprehension, but he was too much a cop to associate it with innocence. "I asked you about Dr. Spender," he said.

"Dr. Spender was my husband's colleague."

"You don't volunteer a thing, do you Barbara? That makes me very suspicious."

"About what?"

"See? You're doing it again. All right, how about this? Dr. Spender is a defendant in a medical malpractice case, along with your husband. He dies. Spender has a bomb put under his car and then changes his testimony. But before he throws the case he visits the sweet widow, Barbara DiTucci. Then I find out that the plaintiff, Ruth Santo's maiden name is Goldberg! And Santo is connected to the mob. Patient and doctor's wife. I don't even want to mention the very large life insurance you're about to collect based on my report. There are too many damned coincidences, Barbara, and they all seem to involve you! What am I supposed to believe?" He leaned over and seized her arms.

"Let go of me," she said. "What are you supposed to believe? You're supposed to believe that I am a decent person, not a manipulator, a good mother, not a murderer, a loving person, not a promiscuous whore. Do you know what love is, Jack? Love is trust! Take all your damned coincidences and get out of here. Right now!"

She rose from the sofa and freed her arms. Barbara met his ferocious look with a rising anger.

"Jack let me tell you something. When I married my husband, I was still in nursing school. Marry a doctor. Wasn't that every nurse's dream? He was a doctor. I was beautiful. I knew it. He liked to show me off wherever we went. Shows, conventions, dinners, whatever. Our marriage wasn't a great romance, but we each adapted. He thought he was light years ahead of me in intelligence, any maybe he was, but he never put me down—and he never distrusted me. The first time I met you, despite that terrible day when my husband was murdered, I felt a warmth and gentleness in you that transcended your policeman's exterior. That does not replace my affection for my husband. No, Jack. I fell in love with you. The fact that it happened so quickly doesn't make it less valid. It was like a union of equals. There was no superiority nonsense. I felt the compassion in you. I sure as hell didn't fall in love with your bald head and pot belly. But you know what? Love is a fragile thing that can be destroyed in a moment—and you've just done that!"

"That's a pretty speech, lady, but no one has ever said your husband was murdered—except you!" He pushed her back onto the sofa.

"Dr. Spender told me." Barbara curled her legs into a fetal position and began to cry.

"Spender?"

"It was right after his car was blown up. Aaron was very upset. No. Upset is not the word. He was terrified. It was the telephone call that did it. At first he thought it was a crank call, because of all the publicity but she convinced him that he was the target. He knew I had Gabe's office records at home. I showed him the piles of records that you had set aside. All the operations that he had performed on the recommendation of my husband, but he knew exactly which record to look for."

"This is pretty far fetched. A mysterious woman calls and the good doctor panics?"

"Do you want to know or not? At this point I could care less."

"It's your story. Go ahead." Zangara's voice was hoarse but now uncertain.

Barbara looked at him crossly. It was sometime before she continued.

"The woman told him that he was to make sure that Ruth Santo won the case against him and the hospital- or else. Aaron told me that she was very specific in the details. She knew that his house in Sea Gate had been damaged in the last hurricane. She told him that it was time for a new car, anyway, and recited his license plate number. His license plate number was not reported in the papers. The bomb was only a warning, she told him. She even knew about his marital problems. She said that they wouldn't kill him as they had my husband. What they would do instead, was murder his ex-wife and frame him so that he would spend the rest of his life in jail. It was like they planned for him a fate worse than death."

"Why didn't you tell me all this?"

"I couldn't. Aaron swore me to secrecy. The woman told him that people would be watching him. You have to know Aaron, he has a great reputation as a physician but a poor one as a human being. Not that I blame him for being frightened."

"Didn't you think this was important enough to tell me? You didn't owe Dr. Spender an oath of silence."

"I gave him my word," Barbara said.

"You know I have to verify all this with Spender."

"Of course. Why should you trust me? After all, I'm the prime suspect!"

"Barbara..." Zangara hesitated. "I have to ask you—for the record. Are you related to Ruth Santo?"

Barbara quickly rose and brushed Zangara aside. She went into the kitchen and returned shortly with a Brooklyn Telephone Directory. She threw the thick book onto the coffee table.

"Here. Let your fingers do the walking through this. Count the number of listings for Goldberg!"

"You haven't answered my question," Zangara said.

"You stupid idiot! Of course, I did!" Barbara said.

CHAPTER 42

▼

"Six Fingers is a client," Pete said. "When he calls, we go."

Pete parked his car on Douglas Street and waited as a 16 wheeler backed into the garage.

"Got to say this for Six Fingers, he has that extra finger in a lot of pies," Eugene said.

"Do me a favor, Eugene, don't ask for a stereo or computer or whatever else is falling off the truck."

"You don't have to worry. This place gives me the creeps. The sooner we're out of here, the better," Eugene said. "It's not the garage, it's the guys he has standing around."

Eugene patted his side to touch the butt of his gun.

"You brought a piece with you? Now, that's really stupid. Six Fingers is going to consider that an unfriendly act. You know we're going to be searched. What if a cop stops us? You invoking the fourth amendment?"

"Which one is that?"

Pete shook his head. "You go down, I go down with you. All because you carry a piece when we're not working."

When they entered the garage and before the pat down, Eugene glanced toward the bodyguards.

"Hand it over," Pete said.

Eugene reached inside his bomber jacket and took out a 9 mm pistol.

"You want the ankle one, too," Eugene said. He gave a short little laugh, bent down to his right trouser leg and removed a pearl handled .25 caliber.

"Go right in, Six Fingers' been waiting for you," a bodyguard said.

"Hey, my man," Six Fingers said. "Good to see you." He reached from behind his metal desk and extended his hand.

Pete slapped his hand in friendship and without waiting for an invitation, sat in the green metal chair. Eugene remained standing.

"Sit. Make yourself comfortable."

"In this dump?" Eugene said. "Christ you could get lead poisoning from the peeling paint in this place."

"Lead poisoning? That's very good, Eugene," Six Fingers said.

Eugene's eyes darted around. Not being armed seemed to increase his vigilance. It was in Eugene's nature to believe that every meeting had a potential for his assassination.

"Relax," Six Fingers said. "Hey Maurice, close the door. Give us some privacy."

The bodyguard closed the door and the three men were alone.

Six Fingers turned up the volume on the stereo. James Brown was singing, "I Feel Good. I Feel Good."

"If this place is tapped, playing loud music won't help," Pete said.

"Yeah, but why should I make it easy for them? What I have to say ain't so incriminating. You remember the guy you met here. Victor Santo. A big, fleshy guy."

"He was at Joe Pencils' bar, too," Pete said.

"You want his lights out?" Eugene said.

"No. No. There's a scam going on and I think we can get in on it. Are you interested?"

Eugene was about to speak when Pete imperceptively kicked him.

"How much?" Pete said.

"Let's make it like the lawyers do. A contingency. I get paid, you get paid," Six Fingers said.

"What's our end?" Pete said.

"Twenty-five percent. You guys are the muscle."

"To do what?" Eugene said.

"Just lean on him when the time comes. I was going to have his legs broke when Pencils tells me that all the money Victor owes me is guaranteed by the Falcon. That's twenty thou and mounting. The chump is a born loser. So I say to myself, the Falcon doesn't go for spit unless…"

"…Santo is coming into money," Pete said.

"Exactly. I check around and I find out that he and his wife have a malpractice case."

"I don't think we should get involved in this," Eugene said. "It ain't healthy to double cross the Falcon."

"Hey, we're not double crossing anybody," Six Fingers said. "I just want some of the crumbs from the table. The Falcon lets everybody eat. I figure once Peregrino takes his cut, we can squeeze a little more out of Santo."

"Even taking the crumbs from Peregrino can be dangerous," Pete said.

"It could be a big score, but you guys decide."

"We'd be working against a good client." Pete shook his head but his meaning was clear.

"All right. We'll make it fifty-fifty," Six Fingers said.

"Is there anything else you can tell us?" Pete said.

"He has a dry cleaning store on Eighteenth Avenue."

"We know that," Eugene said.

After they left the garage, Pete and Eugene drove to Victor's store.

"Why we going there now?" Eugene said.

"Your jacket is dirty."

"You kidding? This is a $450.00 leather jacket. I'm not letting Victor Santo touch it."

"It won't hurt to be a little friendly. I'll buy you ten jackets. Just be careful, you're getting too reckless for this partnership," Pete said. He regretted that he had allowed Eugene to drive because Eugene rarely came to a full stop at stop signs.

"I'm getting reckless?" Eugene said. "I don't care how you slice it but we're moving in on the Falcon."

"I'm talking about you carrying a gun in broad daylight. We don't need it to talk to Santo."

"And I'm saying we might be making an enemy for nothing. If you get my meaning. Fifty percent of nothing is still nothing."

"You're such a dunce. What do we know that Six Fingers don't know?" Pete shoved Eugene but it was gentle.

"What?"

"We hit this Dr. DiTucci, right? We fulfilled the contract. Then we get a contract to hit this Dr. Spender. You can bet your sweet ass that those doctors are the same ones as in the lawsuit with Santo."

"Pete! Damn! I never made the connection."

"That's why I gave you the high sign to shut your mouth. If I'm right then we're talking about big bucks!"

"Yeah, I'm always hearing about the million dollar verdicts in those malpractice cases." Eugene gave out a low whistle. "Those are big cases."

"Big enough to kill two doctors," Pete said.

CHAPTER 43

▼

Jack Zangara seemed to be the only person who did not mind that the Santo case was protracted.

Each day he haunted the trial seeking significance in the most trivial testimony. The billing records of Dr. Spender, hardly an issue in the case, were nevertheless scrutinized as some proof of the plot that had unhinged his relationship with Barbara DiTucci.

Zangara rarely spoke to his partner and shut him out from the DiTucci investigation—an investigation that was now focused on the Santo trial.

Scott appeared to take it all with some grace. Back at the Precinct he mildly complained about having to work alone on the new homicides.

"Jack, I can't do it all alone."

"Sure you can," Zangara said and walked away.

Scott followed him and touched him lightly on the shoulder.

Zangara spun around and grabbed Scott.

"Why did you do it, Tom? Why?"

"Do what?"

"You had to pile it on. It looked bad and you made it look worse. Barbara DiTucci never harmed anyone!"

"Maybe I got carried away," Scott said. "You know how I jump to conclusions."

"Yeah, sure," Zangara said and pushed Scott away.

The trial became tedious as exhibits were introduced into evidence and then used by the expert medical witnesses. Diagrams of the minutest portions of the upper gastrointestinal tract, including the duodenum, along with drawings and models of the pancreas, gall bladder and common bile duct, cluttered the courtroom. More than 50 pages from the hospital charts had been blown up to 30 x 40 inch cardboard placards and stacked against the clerk's desk.

"This courtroom is beginning to look like a warehouse," one of the court officers said.

Zangara, as had become his habit, arrived early and went directly to Ron's chambers.

Ron was uncomfortable in allowing Zangara to discuss a case in which he was presiding.

Zangara, however, eyes bulging and red from lack of sleep, could speak of nothing else.

"Jack, you're prejudicing me with all this talk. I may have to declare a mistrial."

"What are you talking about? I'm just warning you to keep your eyes open. I may be talking about the people in your case, but I'm not talking about your trial."

"You sure you're not an attorney, Jack?" Ron shook his head, as if absurd reasoning was reserved solely for lawyers.

"You declare a mistrial without any basis for it and you'll look like shit."

"But you think I'm being set up?" Ron smiled the smile of the unconvinced.

"Ron, just hear me out. Please…"

"Why don't you go home and get some rest. You look like you've been sleeping in your clothes."

"I've been busy. Real busy, Ron. I've been staking out Santo's dry cleaning store. To tell you the truth, I made myself obvious, figuring that I'd spook Victor Santo. One day I walked into his store when he wasn't there and questioned his clerk. Her name is Angelina and guess what? She's pregnant and she made no secret about who's the father."

"So what? Everyone, including the jury has already figured out that he's a low life."

"It gets better. I've been at the place on weekends and early in the mornings. When court adjourns, I go back."

"No wonder you look so terrible. Your boss lets you get away with all this?"

"I've been using a lot of sick and vacation time," Zangara said.

"I think you're going off the deep end, Jack. You're acting more like a love sick puppy than a first grade detective."

"That's where you're wrong my friend. This case stinks and I'm close to proving it. A couple of days ago, I saw a couple of local hoodlums, Pete and Eugene, visit the dry cleaning store. I figured they were the muscle for the loan-sharks because besides everything else, lover boy Santo is a degenerate gambler. Not more than an hour later, who do I see drive up but this Joe Penna. He was jumping up and down. He's a roly poly little guy and he slapped Santo right out in the open. It was then that I added it all up!"

"I think you're really jumping to conclusions," Ron said.

"Don't you see, Ron? I'm narrowing it down. They're all in on it. Santo, Firestone, that weasel Lentino—and the brains behind it all, Andrew 'the Falcon' Peregrino!"

"That's really narrowing it down." Ron laughed. "Who have you eliminated?"

"Barbara DiTucci," Zangara said. His face looked drawn and thin. "I really messed up with her, Ron." He cast his eyes downward.

"I wish there were something I could do to help. I know how you feel," he said.

"I've been calling her every day but she hangs up on me."

"You'd better be careful, you're in enough trouble," Ron said. "Dr. Spender has made a complaint to the Civilian Complaint Review Board."

"Boy, news travels fast, doesn't it?"

"What did you expect? You've really succeeded in antagonizing him."

"Spender is just a pawn but he knows a lot that he's not telling. I'm sure he lied to Barbara. A mysterious lady, my ass. A little more pressure and I'll crack him like a walnut!"

"You know, Jack. I do have an ethical problem here. This is a medical malpractice case—not a criminal trial. Everything you've uncovered, except for the remote possibility of tampering or even terrorizing witnesses, can't possibly be connected with this trial. What's your theory?" Ron asked. He tucked away in his mind, the mention, again, of Joe Penna. Was his daughter in danger?

Zangara sat back in the sofa by Ron's desk. He smiled as if the question had begged to be asked. He was a detective, again. Sifting and sorting information, discarding the irrelevant and re-arranging the pertinent so as to present an irresistible conclusion. "They found a mark. Someone to milk like a cow. Day after day until the cow dies. Then they eat the cow."

"That is some analogy," Ron said.

"Ron. It's all muscle. It's always been about muscle and money. Only the victims have changed. The mob is more sophisticated now. In the old days, they would extort from little store owners. Then it was restaurants. Then they moved into the stock market. Boiler room tactics—pump and dump. Always a person who could be intimidated." Zangara smiled knowingly as if his logic had defeated mania. "Here's the scenario. A person has a multi-million dollar law suit pending. He's a gambler who needs money and has to go to people who are used to taking it away from him. These leeches—let's not call them the Mafia or the mob—especially today where they might be Chinese or Russian—latch on to Victor Santo, the mark, and become involved with the case. They get him a lawyer, a very good lawyer, and insinuate themselves, for a small percentage. When he finally gets the money, they will bleed him dry, little by little, until they have it all. In the end, they have the money and he can't complain."

"Why would force be needed before there was any money?"

"The hoods are sent to keep Santo in line or cut themselves in for a piece. Why else would Joe Pencils become so excited? The murder and the attempted murder were probably to obtain favorable testimony or keep harmful evidence out of the case."

"Do you realize what you're saying? If you're right, then these people are resorting to murder and intimidation in order for the plaintiff to win."

"They're ruthless people," Zangara said.

"This doesn't absolve Barbara DiTucci, you know."

"There are a few loose ends but Barbara isn't one of them. I've already filed a statement with the insurance company. She's getting the two million dollars for accidental death."

"I thought you told me that Dr. Spender said that Dr. DiTucci was murdered?"

"For insurance purposes, it's the same thing. Murder or accident, the death wasn't natural."

"Are you sure about that?" Ron said. He shook his head. "You fudge the report?"

"Look at it this way, Ron. If Dr. DiTucci's murder was to keep him from testifying, then he wasn't killed for the insurance money and Barbara is not involved."

"Jack? Have you made two different reports?"

"I know Barbara. She's not a killer," Jack Zangara said.

CHAPTER 44

▼

The next day, Tom Scott, as if by appointment, went to the trial.

"You ever coming back to work?"

"What makes you think I haven't been working?" Zangara said.

"All right. So maybe this DiTucci broad isn't involved! Hang me by my thumbs. We still have four new homicides to investigate. I need help."

"Stick around," Zangara said. "You might learn something."

When it was Victor Santo's turn to testify, Firestone led him through the litany of preliminary questions.

"Yes, he was forty two years old. Yes, he was married to Ruth Santo. Been married fourteen years. Was self-employed. Owned a dry cleaning store. No, his wife was a healthy woman before the operation. Yes, she had chest pains. He remembered the day because it happened at his cousin Charlie's wedding. Thought it was the food. Yes. He was the one who took her to Dr. DiTucci. Dr. DiTucci was the one that recommended Spender. Just to take a look. An exploratory. Out in the same day, no more. Except that pretty soon she was vomiting blood and brown stuff—like coffee grounds."

"This puts the icing on the cake," Zangara whispered to Scott when he saw Pete and Eugene enter the courtroom.

"Yeah, I've seen those two hoods around. What the hell are they doing here?"

"Maybe protecting their investment." Zangara pointed to the witness stand. "And take a gander at Santo. He looks like he's just seen a ghost."

"Can you describe for the court and jury, the things you have to do for your wife since her injury?" Firestone said.

"I have to rush home from work, three or four times a day, just to give her the insulin shots. They're painful. If she's not crying from her stomach pains, she's crying from the shots. She's always in pain. Pain…"

"You Honor, I object. This witness can't testify to another person's pain," Lentino said.

"Sustained. Mr. Santo, please limit your testimony to your observations."

"Judge, she's in pain, I swear it!"

"Just tell the jury what you have to do for your wife," Firestone said, unable to hide his annoyance.

"I have young kids. I have to get them off to school every morning. I make them breakfast and lunch. Their mother does dress them, though, but I do the laundry. I go to work but I'm back by noon to give her another shot. She tried to do it herself, but it's too hard." Santo turned to the jury. "It's best in the stomach. Doesn't hurt as much, she says."

"You want me to cross examine him about his little Angelina, or do you want to do it?" Lentino whispered to Christine Fisher.

In the end, however, they decided not to impeach his credibility by mentioning Angelina. Any attack on him might well boomerang. Few juries appreciated being told the obvious.

At the end of the day, Zangara departed from his usual practice of stalking Victor. He and Scott went directly to Ron's chamber.

"We're getting close," Zangara said.

"Jack. You have to stop this insanity! I look out in the audience and you're making faces or talking. You're a distraction in my courtroom."

"All right. All right. It won't happen again. But just listen. I told you I saw hoods at Santo's place. They walked into your courtroom today! They're shooters. They intimidate- and they kill! Tom thinks that they killed Dr. DiTucci."

"That's very interesting," Ron said. "Now what am I supposed to do about it?"

"Ron, you have killers sitting as spectators in your courtroom! Doesn't that bother you?"

"You want me to lock them up?"

"You've changed Ron. The Ron I used to know had a fire in his belly," Zangara said.

"Jack, you're close to being offensive. I'm a judge trying a malpractice case. Our jobs are different. I'm not about to ride shotgun with you so that you can catch the murderers of Dr. DiTucci!"

"So you agree with me!"

"You're irrational, Jack."

"But you agree with me!"

"Go take a look at yourself in the mirror, Jack. The little hair you have left on your bald head is disheveled."

CHAPTER 45

▼

Sixty Sixth Street in Bensonhurst was a street which, architecturally at least, could not make up its mind. Mixed with substantial brick, semi-detached two-family homes were a string of small one-family row houses. The row house owners had solved their parking problems by concreting over their minuscule lawns and, with curb cuts, most of which were illegal, had created their own private parking lots.

It was a neighborhood of Italians and American Jews, all of whom had learned to live together by fastidiously minding their own business. As a consequence, small attention was paid to the man who walked up the front steps of Pete's row house and rang the door bell.

"Answer the damned bell, Eugene," Pete said. "I just got out of the shower."

Eugene looked up to the upstairs landing where Pete, still without clothing, was toweling himself dry.

"Hold your horses," Eugene said. "She's taking her clothes off."

"What?"

"The movie, for chrissake." Eugene cranked the recliner forward and sat up. His gaze remained on the television set as he moved to the door. "It never fails. Right at the good parts!"

When he opened the door, he forgot about the movie.

"Hello, Eugene," Tom Scott said.

"Who is it?" Pete called down.

Eugene turned and looked toward the stairway. "You better put your pants on Pete."

Scott had reached into his pocket and flashed his badge.

"I know who you are, copper. I saw you in court. I made you right away."

He pushed Eugene back and entered. He closed the door behind him. "Hey Pete, come on down but stay where I can see you."

Pete zippered up his trousers and walked down the steps, bare-foot and bare-chested. He gave a sideways glance to Eugene who moved toward his jacket.

"Now, Eugene, I wouldn't do that if I were you. If there's a gun in that jacket, I'm going to take it as a personal affront."

"How do you know my name?" Eugene said.

"A little birdie told me."

"You work for Peregrino?" Eugene said. "Then we're on the same side."

"I don't think so, squirt. I'm here in what you might call my unofficial capacity."

"He's not here to arrest us, stupid," Pete said.

"Look, tell Andrew that we weren't double-crossing him. It was Six Fingers' idea to lean on Santo. We were only going in for a taste," Pete said.

Scott took out a 9 mm pistol and attached a silencer. He pointed at Eugene and motioned for them to go to the kitchen.

"Pete, that ain't no regulation gun," Eugene said. "This guy's not a cop."

"Oh, I'm a cop all right." He nudged them along. "Let's look down your basement."

"Maybe we can straighten this out," Pete said. "We did good work for the Falcon. He can't be that mad at us."

"You kidding? He was ranting and raving. Loose cannons, he called you but I think what really bothered Peregrino was that you went into business for yourself."

When Scott reached the steps leading to the basement, he flicked on the light and followed them down. Additional parts from the bomb made for Spender, were still on the work bench.

"Go down nice and slow. Very slow. Pete, put your hands on Eugene's shoulders and don't take them off. And if you have any ideas, forget it. You ever see the movie, *Viva Villa*? The guy saved bullets by lining five Federales in a row and shooting them all with one bullet."

He directed Pete to a stool and motioned for Eugene to sit at Pete's feet. Scott then surveyed the basement and fingered the pipe filings on the work bench.

"This makes it an open and shut case, doesn't it?" Scott said. "But then there's always illegal search and seizure, isn't there?"

"Can't we work something out?" Pete said. He had half expected to be shot walking down the steps. Maybe Scott only took them down to the basement to gather evidence. Arrest them. Attempted murder. B Felony. 8 and 1/3 to 25 max. He could plea bargain that down and be out in 3.

"What do you suggest?" Scott said.

"Seventy five grand and we disappear."

"Jeez, Pete! That's our whole stash!"

"How much did you get on the DiTucci hit?"

"I can't believe that the Falcon ratted us out!" Eugene said.

"Shut up, Eugene!" Pete said.

"That's no way to talk to your partner. I was going to compliment you on that job. Making it look like an accident or a suicide was very professional but you shouldn't have grabbed the Rolex." Scott pointed to the watch on Pete's wrist.

Pete took the watch off and handed it to Scott.

"It was only a souvenir," Pete said.

"You fellows aren't doing very well, are you? That souvenir made us look closer and then you screwed up with Spender."

Eugene leaned forward and considered tackling Scott from his sitting position. It would be difficult but if he could knock Scott off balance, Pete could do the rest.

Scott, however, anticipated the move and pointed his pistol at Eugene.

"You want your head or your balls blown off?"

"Neither," Pete said. "What about my offer?" Everything could be negotiated.

"How much are you offering?"

"All right, make it a hundred thousand. I don't play games. We can go to the bank right now and get it for you."

"You really insult my intelligence. A man like you doesn't put money in a bank. Me? I play the stock market. Buy Treasury Bonds. Buy a condo. Have deferred income, a pension. But you? I'll bet you have it right here."

Scott followed Eugene's eyes as he looked toward a shoe box on a side shelf.

"Get it," Scott said.

Eugene got to his feet and reached up but Pete stopped him.

"We're going to need a couple of grand to tide us over—right?" Pete said.

"Where you planning to go?"

"Anywhere you say."

"Atlantic City?" Scott said.

"We're not looking to bump heads with anybody. That's Harry O's territory."

"Let me tell you a little secret. Harry O is a big time Casino Host in Atlantic City. He's so law abiding that he's afraid to spit on the boardwalk. That's my alias. What you might call a *nome de guerre.*"

When Eugene raised his arms to retrieve the shoe box, he took a half-step between Pete and Scott.

Pete lunged at Eugene and pushed him into Scott.

Eugene fell on Scott who buckled from the weight of the two men falling on him.

Scott, however, was able to get off a shot. The bullet that went through Eugene's armpit also passed through Pete's eye. Scott fired again and then again—more to push the two of them off him by the force of the bullets.

Blood spurted from Eugene at three places and blinded Scott.

Every shot that struck Eugene also hit Pete.

Pete in his death throe, twisted and his brain matter with bits of his skull splattered over both Eugene and Scott.

"Fuck, fuck," Scott said and shoved them away from him. It took him some time to wipe away the blood and body tissue that had stuck to his face.

The Falcon disposed of the remains of Pete and Eugene to the profit of each. Scott pocketed the hundred thousand dollars but Peregrino still ended up with the greater profit of five hundred and ninety thousand dollars.

Since Pete had no relatives, the Falcon had Tony Vecchio forge Pete's signature to a deed and sold Pete's house. There would be no need to search for heirs, or prove the death. There was no one to complain.

Eugene's parents, used to his unexplained absences, made little inquiry—they knew that it might be both fruitless and dangerous.

Six Fingers noted the disappearance and quickly sought a meeting with the Falcon. Peregrino's assurances only increased the loanshark's fears. The extra fingered man, however, was clever enough to take with him ten thousand dollars.

"Andrew, you wouldn't believe it but that deadbeat, Paul Alongo came up with the money he owed. I never expected it so I want you to take it as a gift from me."

Six Fingers did not have to worry because as the Falcon had often pointed out to Joe Pencils, "you don't whack your money-makers."

CHAPTER 46

▼

Dr. David Samuel Timberman was a graduate of Harvard Medical School. When he had completed his residency at N.Y.U. Medical Center, he had been awarded a fellowship at Columbia. He was board certified in Internal Medicine with a sub-specialty in gastroenterology and was now Chief of Gastroenterology at Sacred Heart Hospital. Timberman also testified that he had published approximately two hundred articles and chapters in medical textbooks in his chosen field. As the plaintiff's expert, he was prepared to render an opinion concerning any departures from good and accepted standards of medical practice in the case, despite the fact that he had never examined Ruth Santo or physically treated her.

"My opinion is based upon a review of the various hospital charts, medical records, depositions of the parties and transcripts of the trial that have been furnished to me." Dr. Timberman adjusted the horn rimmed glasses that seemed to constantly slip from his nose as he looked down at the records that had been placed before him.

"Are you being compensated for your time, Doctor?" Firestone asked.

"Of course."

"And you have examined all of the records before you?"

"Yes. Extensively." Dr. Timberman was nearing fifty and his hair was already completely gray. His hand tailored suit, starched white shirt and crisply made tie, were additional testimony to a successful career. When he spoke, he addressed the jury directly. His resonant voice was both confident and confidential, marking him as an experienced expert witness in his field.

Dr. Timberman's testimony was separated into three categories. Firestone used him to explain the medicine to the jury, then to testify as to the deviations that caused the plaintiff to be injured and finally, the extent of the injuries the plaintiff suffered.

"Dr. Timberman, what is the significance, if any, when a patient regurgitates a substance that resembles coffee grounds? Firestone asked.

"After an ERCP? That's an absolute indication of a perforation."

"Is that life threatening?"

"Beyond all doubt. Steps have to be taken immediately to remedy that condition. Immediately!"

"Now, doctor, have you formed an opinion as to whether there have been any departures from good and accepted medical practice?"

"Yes, I have."

At this point Lentino and Fisher both objected, with little expectation that they would be successful.

"And what is your opinion, Doctor?" Firestone said.

"Dr. Spender perforated the common bile duct during the ERCP." Timberman spoke rapidly, as if he feared that he would be interrupted.

"Were there any other departures, Dr. Timberman?"

"Oh yes. There are no x-rays in the chart. Films should have been taken before and after the procedure. That's a departure. There are no post-operation orders, either."

"Were these departures a substantial factor in causing injury to Mrs. Santo?"

"Absolutely!"

"What about her treatment after the Endoscopic Retrograde Cholangio Pancreatography?" Firestone said.

"As I said, there were no post-op orders. The hospital literally abandoned the patient."

"Objection," Lentino said.

"Sustained."

"Well, there was no one to treat her when she developed the obvious symptoms of a pancreatic abscess. There should have been follow-up x-rays as well as an immediate C-T Scan."

"Wasn't this done?" Firestone said.

"That was done much later in the subsequent hospital, Mount Zion—after she had full blown pancreatitis."

"Was a diagnosis made at Mount Zion?"

"Yes." Dr. Timberman moved his fingers through the Mount Zion chart, and then read, "Hemorrhagic pancreatitis with abscess formation."

"Are you able to form an opinion with a reasonable degree of medical certainty as to whether this medical chain of events was initially caused by the deviations to which you have testified."

"Yes. They were all the result of the perforation and the failure to treat it properly."

"What was the medical management of this patient after her arrival at Mount Zion?"

"She was placed in the intensive care unit. She required intensive fluid and electrolyte management because of the fluid losses into what is called the retro-peritoneum, where the pancreas is located. Several surgical procedures were necessary to evacuate necrotic, that is dead tissue, areas of pus. Eventually, a fistula developed and feculent contents—bowel type contents were draining into the abdomen, and for that reason, Mrs. Santo had to undergo an ileostomy."

"What's that, Doctor?"

"That's a temporary diversion where you drain the bowel contents into an external bag."

Dr. Timberman then went on to testify that as a result of the hemorrhagic pancreatitis, Ruth Santo developed insulin dependent diabetes, which required daily monitoring of her blood sugar level and injections of insulin. Its complications included blurred vision and eventual possible blindness, a hardening of the arteries, an irregular heartbeat, shortness of breath and dizziness. With diabetes, also came vascular difficulties that often led to amputation. It was a terrible, life shortening, painful, prognosis.

Christine Fisher's cross examination, although thorough, was confined to the care rendered by her client, Dr. Spender, because there was no dispute that Ruth Santo was a very sick woman. But first she was going to show that Dr. Timberman was a "hired gun."

"Dr. Timberman, you have testified before, haven't you?"

"Yes."

"How often have you testified in the last three months?"

"I would say about five times."

"Wouldn't it be fair to say then, that you testify twenty times a year?"

"That's fair," Dr. Timberman said.

"And for how many years?"

"Perhaps ten or eleven years."

"So, you have testified as an expert about 200 or 220 times?"

"Approximately."

"Have you ever testified in Buffalo?" Fisher smiled.

"Oh, yes," Timberman said.

"And you've testified in other cities, too?"

"Yes."

"Baltimore, San Diego, Dallas, Detroit…?" Fisher read from a list she had prepared.

"Yes."

"And you even testified last month here in Brooklyn, in this very Courthouse, in the case of *Adler v. Joseph*?"

"Yes."

"That was a psychiatric case, though—wasn't it doctor?"

"Stomach problems often cause mental problems," Timberman said.

"And of all those times, how often have you testified on behalf of a defendant?"

"Half the time."

"Come now, doctor. For medical malpractice cases not other types of cases, how many times have you testified for plaintiffs?"

"Objection," Firestone said.

"Sustained," Ron said. He turned to the jury. "Expert witnesses do not testify for or against anyone. They testify for the benefit of the court and jury." Yes, that was the rule, Ron thought, and I am obliged to state it, but only a blathering idiot would believe it.

"Dr. Timberman, how often have you testified for the benefit of the court and jury in a medical malpractice case and been paid by a defendant?" Fisher said. She looked at Ron and smiled.

Ron was able to keep his poker-face, but he did allow her an almost imperceptible nod, to acknowledge her clever, and unobjectionable, revision of the question.

"Once," Dr. Timberman said.

"And how much are you being paid for your time in court today?"

"Seven thousand dollars."

"And if you return tomorrow?"

"I earn more than that in my practice."

"So, tomorrow you will earn seven thousand dollars, wherever you are," Christine Fisher said. She was smiling but it was a mocking smile.

"In addition to testifying, you also review cases, don't you?

"Yes."

"Would it be fair to say that for every case in which you testify, you review five other cases?"

"If I don't find malpractice, then I tell the lawyer he has no case."

"So the answer is: 'yes'?"

"Yes."

"Now, have you ever testified for Mr. Firestone before?"

"No."

"Did Mr. Firestone ask you to review the case?"

"Yes, he sent me the hospital chart, the bill of particulars and several other records."

"How was it that he did this?"

"I don't know. You'll have to ask him."

"Dr. Timberman, isn't it a fact that you advertise your services in several Bar Association journals?"

"That's true."

"What percentage of your yearly income do you derive from your testifying and review of cases?"

"I would say about 15%."

"And what are you charging for reviewing this case?"

"What I charge everyone. Four hundred and fifty dollars an hour."

"And how many hours have you spent in reviewing the case?"

"About fifteen hours."

"Let's see doctor. If my math is correct, you've earned almost fourteen thousand dollars on this case—provided you don't come back tomorrow."

"I don't keep track. My secretary takes care of the billing."

"Are you telling this jury that you do not know if you've been paid in this case?"

"Yes."

"Didn't Mr. Firestone give you a check this morning—before you testified?"

"I haven't cashed it," Dr. Timberman said.

"Well, let's hope it doesn't bounce," Fisher said.

"It won't!" Firestone said. When no rebuke came, he added, "Can't we get on with this Judge, Miss Fisher is paying her experts, too."

Ron's tactics for control of the courtroom varied. This time he shook his head and clucked his tongue as if to say, "children, children, behave."

"Dr. Timberman, you know that Dr. Spender performed the ERCP but had nothing to do with subsequent treatment, don't you?" Fisher asked.

"Yes."

"And isn't it true that a perforation is a risk of the procedure?"

"It's a known danger."

"A complication? A risk that everyone knows about—yes or no?"

"Yes."

"And it can occur even when there is no malpractice—isn't that true?"

"That's not the point. When there's a perforation, immediate steps have to be taken to treat it."

"Your Honor, I move to strike the answer as not responsive," Fisher said.

"Strike it."

"A perforation can occur even when there is no malpractice, isn't that true?"

"That's why different procedures are used now."

"Just a minute, Dr. Timberman," Fisher said. "You're not saying that Dr. Spender used an outdated procedure, are you?"

"The advances in gastroenterology have been mind-boggling, what with lasers, and all."

"Come on, Doctor." Fisher adopted a blistering tone. "Dr. Spender performed exactly the same operation that you would have performed at that time. Isn't that true?" She stared at Dr. Timberman daring him not to be responsive.

"Yes, that's true."

"And Dr. Spender was not responsible for the care and treatment of Ruth Santo after the ERCP?"

It was one of those rare times when both Firestone and Lentino objected.

Christine Fisher did not wait for the ruling which she knew would be against her.

"I have no further questions," she said.

Manny Lentino's cross examination took a different tack. If he could disassociate Dr. Spender from his client, Beth Torah, or blame others, he could escape unscathed.

"So, Dr. Timberman, it is your testimony that the radiologist should have taken hard plate x-rays at the beginning and end of the procedure." Lentino said. He was smiling as if to ask forgiveness for asking such a simple question.

"It was absolutely essential but there is nothing in the chart to indicate that this was done."

"Isn't it basic radiological practice to do this?"

"Yes."

"Even if there is no record, can't we assume that this is so basic that x-rays were taken?"

"Not at all."

"Did you know that the doctor on call, Dr. Abraham Brownstein, is a world renowned radiologist?"

"Everyone makes mistakes."

"Of course, Dr. Timberman, I imagine that includes you?"

"And lawyers." Timberman smiled.

Lentino looked up at Ron. "Your Honor?"

"Strike it," Ron said.

"The question was stupid, Judge," Timberman said.

"That may be, but leave the objecting to the lawyers."

"So, Dr. Brownstein was negligent for not ordering the x-rays."

"Yes."

"X-rays, generally speaking, show dense material, like bone, unless contrasting material is administered. Isn't that correct?"

"No. It can show other things," Timberman said. "Like air in the abdomen—a classic sign of a perforation."

"You couldn't wait to say that, could you doctor?" Lentino's frozen smile endured through the next question. "Are you aware that Dr. Brownstein is not a defendant is this action?"

"I'm here to give my opinion, not a judgment as to who is being sued."

"Yes, we are all aware of that. What about Dr. Fugatto, the surgeon? Shouldn't he have ordered surgery?"

"Yes."

"And Dr. Chang? Dr. Finestein? Dr. Accetta? They also departed from good and accepted medical practice—isn't that true?"

"According to the hospital chart, they all participated in the care of Mrs. Santo after the ERCP," Timberman said.

"They were also negligent. Isn't that right?"

"I would say so."

"But none of these other physicians are defendants in this action. Isn't that true? Were Drs. Chang, Finestein or Accetta attending physicians at Beth Torah Hospital?" Lentino said.

"I don't know."

"Dr. Timberman, tell the jury what an attending doctor is?" Lentino said.

"He's a physician who is entitled to treat and admit patients to a hospital."

"Treat and admit. We're talking about private patients, aren't we?" Lentino said.

"Yes."

"Doctors not on the hospital staff?"

"Your Honor, I object," Firestone said. His face showed little emotion but his mind was racing. Why had he been so stupid? He should have sued every god-damned name in the hospital chart. It was always the empty chair that got the blame. Why had he listened to Vecchio? He had referred the case to Firestone and had urged a quick trial.

"Sustained," Ron said.

"Your Honor, I was merely speaking generally. Staff physicians are not Attending ones." Lentino pretended to be upset by the ruling.

"Sustained," Ron said. "Please, Mr. Lentino, no speeches."

"In any event, you don't know if Dr. Fugatto, Dr. Chang, Dr. Accetta or any of the other doctors I have mentioned, are employed by Beth Torah Hospital?"

"No, I do not."

"As for Beth Torah Hospital, there is no evidence that Mrs. Santo developed an infection because of any unsanitary conditions. Isn't that so, doctor?" Lentino said. He stepped forward as if he were closing in for the kill.

"The abscess was caused by a perforation," Dr. Timberman said as if he were remembering that he was being paid by Firestone. "and her condition worsened from negligent care."

"Is that a '*no*' doctor?" Lentino said.

"There is no evidence in the chart of any unsanitary conditions."

Lentino looked triumphantly at the jury. "So that we are perfectly clear, Dr. Timberman, Beth Torah did not deviate from good and accepted hospital practice. Correct?"

"Are we talking about nurses?" Dr. Timberman said.

"Nurses, janitors, anyone doctor. There's nothing in the chart, is there?"

"The chart is incomplete Mr. Lentino, how can I answer that?"

"You didn't have any trouble answering Mr. Firestone's questions, did you?" Lentino said.

CHAPTER 47

▼

Ron often felt the effects of a long trial day. The balance required in addressing the disparate interests of the litigants, the lawyers, the witnesses and most important, the jury, created a constant mental pressure that frequently left Ron worn out. It seemed that his colleagues, in proportion to the general population, suffered from a high rate of hypertension and heart disease. Stress and fatigue were a deadly combination.

Anticipation, however, was a tonic for exhaustion. That evening would be a special event. Sarah had insisted upon cooking dinner for him—at his apartment. And he intended to give her the engagement ring.

Ron had settled into any easy relationship with Sarah that had become almost routine. Restaurants after work. Daily and frequent telephone calls. Their romance seemed to be marred only by what he perceived to be her avarice. Her eyes would shine when she spoke about some pie in the sky deal—that never seemed to come to fruition.

And yet her little touches of generosity seemed to compensate for any show of greed.

After the trip to Atlantic City, Sarah had sent a dozen red roses to his mother and a pretty little treasure chest to Colleen.

To Alan, she had sent a copy of Baudelaire's "*Les Fleurs du Mal.*"

"Dad, on one side of a page it's in English. On the other side it's in French."

"That's wonderful but I hope you're keeping up your grades,"

Ron said. It was the obligatory parent comment but he had been pleased by Sarah's gesture.

The sex had been occasional. He worried about that. Fifty Two years old. What if he couldn't satisfy her in a few years?

When he opened the door to his apartment, all fears as well as weariness evaporated.

Sarah in a pinafore apron, white and bordered with starched frills, stood just inside the door. In each hand she held a martini. It was as if the genie had just emerged from the lamp—ready to do his bidding.

"For my master," Sarah said. "Who, tonight, is going to tell me how his wife broke his nose."

"You never forget a thing, do you, Sarah?"

Ron took the drink and clicked his glass with hers.

"Colleen thought it was a funny story," Sarah said.

"She's just a kid who misses her mother."

"And you don't think that will be a problem?"

"What do you think?" Ron said.

After a long pause, Sarah said, "I think that we should both stop thinking. She took their drinks and carefully placed them on the coffee table. She took off his jacket and led him to the bedroom.

Sarah sat him down on the bed and undressed him. Slowly.

The smell and smoke wafted from the kitchen. "Won't the dinner burn?" Ron said.

"Yes."

Later—much later—the choice was either to starve, order Chinese, or go out. They chose to starve.

"I want you to stay the night," Ron said. He caressed her. He brushed her hair away from his lips as he kissed her ear.

She pressed her fingers into each sides of his cheeks.

"I love your dimples," she said.

"You'll stay?"

"No," she said.

"Why not?"

"What will people say? We're not married."

"Then, marry me."

"Marriage destroys romance." Sarah said.

"Time destroys romance. Unfaithfulness destroys romance, but not marriage. I'd want to be with you even if we fought every day." Ron slid off the bed and reached into his night table. He took out a small box and handed it to Sarah.

"No. No." She said. Nevertheless, she opened the box. The diamond ring was small, less than two carets, but sparkled as she held it under the light.

"I've been saving it for the right time."

"It's a beautiful ring." Sarah did not take it from the box.

"I picked it out myself," Ron said just in case she might conclude that the ring belonged to his deceased wife.

"I can't." She shook her head violently and pulled the sheets around her as if a stranger had come into the room.

"Take it. I'm on my knees and naked before you." Ron clasped his hands. "I am asking you to marry me." Only his tone was joking.

"Goddamn it! You're spoiling everything." Sarah threw the ring down. She pushed him aside and gathered up her clothes.

Ron watched as she headed for the bathroom. She slammed the door behind her.

Sarah emerged minutes later, fully clothed. She picked up her briefcase and checked its latch.

"I have a lot of work tomorrow. I have to go."

Ron, still naked, sat on the bed staring at her in disbelief.

"Shall I call a cab?" Sarah said.

"Sarah. What's wrong with you?"

"I'm married. Separated, but still married. The bastard won't give me a divorce. And I don't know if I want one. You men. Marriage makes us possessions. I've had enough of that."

"You're not divorced?" Ron paused as if to catch his breath. "You're still married? Why didn't you tell me this before?"

"I call him my "ex" because it's more convenient."

"We're not living in the dark ages, Sarah. We can work something out."

"I'm sorry Ron. Maybe I am a little crazy." She embraced him but still held on to her briefcase. "Just give me a little time. OK? You're the sweetest man I know. I've had such terrible luck with men." She brushed his cheek with her hand. She had already donned her gloves.

"Sweetest man?" Ron said. "That's really damning me with praise."

"I can prove it." Sarah wriggled her body like a coquette. "You're going to get dressed and take me home."

"You think so?" Ron pulled her toward him and lifted her skirt.

"Be a caveman tomorrow my sweet," Sarah said and removed his hand from her buttock. "I really have to get an early start in the morning."

On the drive to her apartment, she snuggled up to Ron. She clutched his arm as he drove, as if apologizing for her rejection of him.

When they arrived at her apartment building, she did not wait for the doorman to open the door for her. She turned and waved to Ron.

"Call me tomorrow," Sarah said as if nothing had happened.

Ron went several blocks before he noticed that Sarah had left her briefcase in the car. He considered holding it as ransom to guarantee tomorrow's date, but decided that she probably needed her papers.

It was only a short distance. He could leave it with the doorman. He could demonstrate his restraint by not going up to her apartment.

The traffic was light and, instead of going around the block, he made a U-turn. He was about to make a left turn when he saw Sarah's Mercedes speed from the underground garage.

There was a shower of sparks as her tail pipe struck the raised sidewalk, and the car bounced onto the street.

Ron followed, but not too closely. Sarah's license plate, SB-18, made it easy to spot.

The Mercedes zipped around several cars as it sped toward 79th Street and the FDR Drive. Once on the highway, it weaved in and out of the traffic as if it were an ambulance on call.

Ron, however, the old taxi driver, had little trouble keeping up with her. What was going on? It could be perfectly innocent. Perhaps when she arrived home she had found some messages. Perhaps it was the Domestic Violence Hotline. An emergency. Or was there someone else? Ron's mind alternated between understanding and suspicion.

The Mercedes went through the Brooklyn Battery Tunnel on to the Gowanus and the Belt Parkway. Sarah exited at Fourth Avenue and drove down Shore Parkway to Ninety Seventh Street. She circled the block once and then parked by a fire hydrant. She glanced around quickly and then walked into a high rise apartment house that faced the Bay. It then occurred to him that his mother's home was on the next block. Now, that was a coincidence! Or was it a bad omen?

Ron looked at his watch. It was midnight. He parked his car and noted the address. His first impulse was to confront her in the lobby. But he realized that if it all was perfectly innocent, then he, like Jack Zangara, both bulls in a china shop, would be destroying the relationship by distrust.

As the hours past, it became apparent that it was unlikely that there was *any* innocent explanation.

Finally, he turned on the map light and opened the briefcase.

The briefcase contained copies of the Summons, Complaint, Answer and Bill of Particulars in the case of *Ruth Santo and Victor Santo v. Aaron Spender and Beth Torah Hospital.*

CHAPTER 48

▼

"You did the right thing," Jack Zangara said when Ron telephoned him.

"I feel pretty sneaky," Ron said.

"Hey, I'm proud of you. You didn't lose your head."

Despite the hour, Ron had returned to Sarah's apartment and left the briefcase with the Concierge.

"There's no sense in letting her know what we know until I have a chance to check out the place on Shore Road," Zangara said.

The next several days were lost to Ron but there was no discernible difference in his courtroom demeanor. Emotionally, however, he was in a quandary, reassessing every conversation he had ever had with Sarah, now seeing double meanings in statements that once had appeared unambiguous. Despite his hope that there was some innocent explanation, he kept returning to the one conclusion. Sarah had deceived him. *But why?*

Sarah telephoned every day but he managed to either avoid the calls or be noncommittal. "The trial is wearing me down, Sarah. I'm just too tired." And, "I have to research the law tonight." Or worst of all, "I have a blistering headache, I can't talk right now." The excuses were lame yet even now he found it difficult to lie to her. It was as if *he* was cheating on her. Never mind that she was the betrayer. Sarah was a bright woman and she would know by now that something was wrong. Still, he could not confront her—not until he had heard from Zangara.

The trial proceeded, witness after witness. The plaintiff rested his case. Christine Fisher then put on her expert witness who, as expected, contradicted plaintiff's experts.

"The perforation was a risk of the ERCP. Pancreatitis was a risk of the procedure. There were no departures from good and accepted standards of medical or surgical practice." Her defense expert droned on.

There was no need for close attention by Ron and he lost his concentration. Wasn't the jury getting sick and tired of the repetition? The jurors surely understood the medicine by now, as well as who had been injured. Every so often, a juror would glance toward the sad, emaciated plaintiff and her robust husband.

Instead of taking notes in his minute book, Ron doodled on his scratch pad. He found himself stroking the scar on his forehead. A war wound? A reminder of battle? Was he the man on point? A target? He grimaced at the thought. A soldier without a foxhole.

He made lists of facts and tried to determine which were significant. He was introduced to Sarah by Lentino shortly before this trial was to begin. That was a fact. One doctor was dead. Another doctor escaped a car bombing. The plaintiff was obviously ill. There was no faking there. The husband was associated with mobsters. And there was Sarah. What was she doing with a copy of the pleadings in her briefcase? What was she doing on Shore Road?

Ron became aware of the complete silence in the courtroom. He looked up from his scribbling.

The court reporter was looking at him, her hands poised for action. Christine Fisher was standing. Everyone was looking at him expectantly—waiting for his response.

"Yes?"

"I'm sorry your Honor, sometimes I mumble," Fisher said. Nice person. She realized that Ron had been oblivious. "I said, 'Dr. Spender rests'."

"Oh," Ron said. He turned to Manny Lentino. "Mr. Lentino, the case is with you."

"May we approach the bench, your Honor?"

Ron nodded.

They interposed themselves from the jury and spoke in hushed voices.

"Your Honor, I may not put on any witnesses but I need some time," Lentino said.

"Some time?" Lentino was the bastard who had introduced him to Sarah. Was he an enemy?

"I'd like a day to consult with my client. I think the jury is getting tired of all these experts. Whatever I prove, will be cumulative. I think that it's pretty clear the hospital is not involved in this case," Lentino whispered.

"That's absolutely not true," Firestone said.

"I've had enough of your squabbling! All of you!"

"If he rests, we can have motions and the pre-charge conference tomorrow. At this point, another day or two doesn't make any difference to me," Christine Fisher said.

"I'm against any further adjournment," Firestone said.

"Naturally," Lentino said.

"Now, Mr. Lentino, I'm not going to preclude you from presenting witnesses but for scheduling purposes, I would like to know what you intend to do, now."

Lentino turned to the hospital representative who was in the audience and nodded.

"Beth Torah Hospital rests, your Honor."

"All sides rest?" Ron said.

When the lawyers agreed, Ron added, "Pre-charge conference, summations and charge tomorrow."

When he returned to his chambers and before removing his robe, he telephoned the Precinct.

"Jack's not here yet but you guys are coming to my house for linguine and clam sauce," Tom Scott said.

"I don't know if I can make it."

"Sure you can. We're going to compare notes." There was an odd brashness in Scott's voice.

Moments later, Jack Zangara called.

"Meet me at Orlando's," Zangara said. "I'll be there is an hour. Have a martini, you're going to need it."

"What did you find out?"

"You want me to talk about this on the phone?"

"I spoke with Tom Scott. He said we're going to his house for dinner," Ron said.

"That's bull shit. We may go over there but not to eat. Just don't make any plans. Tonight you may ride shotgun with me, like in the old days."

CHAPTER 49

▼

Ron was on his second martini when Jack Zangara entered Orlando's.

"One Bloody Mary coming up," the waiter said. He nodded toward the rear booth where Ron sat.

"Where have you been Jack? It's like you disappeared from the face of the earth."

"You're not undercover if you're conspicuous," Zangara said. He slid into the banquet beside Ron, as if being close increased the confidentiality.

Almost immediately, the waiter delivered the Bloody Mary and Zangara downed it in one gulp. He looked up at the waiter and held up the glass for a refill.

"You're killing me, Jack. What's the connection between Barbara DiTucci and Sarah?"

"None. That's the point. I was led on a wild goose chase. But if we work backwards…"

Jack!" Ron slammed his hand on the table.

"Take it easy. I have a lot to tell you," Zangara said.

"Who lives on Shore Road?" Ron asked.

"Anthony Vecchio, Esquire," Zangara said.

"Vecchio?"

"Yep. The lawyer who referred Ruth and Victor Santo to Firestone."

"But what does Vecchio have to do with Sarah?"

"Ah. That piece of information will have to come from Sarah. Right now, I can only surmise."

"Surmise? I think it's quite evident that they're going to try to intimidate me in some fashion."

"Maybe so, but there's a lot more going on."

"Did you question Vecchio?"

"No. He'd just lie. Don't you remember? I told you that Vecchio does legal work for Andrew 'the Falcon' Peregrino."

"Damn. Damn! Firestone, too?"

"I'm not sure about that. I checked Firestone out. He's not averse to making a buck but he's making too much money legitimately. So I discount him."

"What's with Scott and linguine?"

"That's where this whole thing falls into place. Sarah Baruch has the legal papers, but was never suspected of anything. Why? Because Scott said so! He was the one that checked her out and said that she was clean!"

"You think Scott's involved?"

"Up to his ears. That's why you haven't heard from me. I've been investigating my own partner! Scott always talked about his drinking prowess but never really drank." Zangara imitated the way Scott would wave his drinking glass.

"You do this all the time, Jack. Will you get to the point?"

"Dean Martin didn't drink that heavily but used the booze as a prop. When he was performing, he'd slur his words but he was never drunk. It's the same way with Scott. He gave the appearance of a shiftless, irresponsible gambler and drunkard—that was his persona."

"And you think this was all a front?"

"You tell me. He's a second grade detective who makes a little less than me. About $75,000.00 to $80,000.00 a year. He's divorced with three kids, a girl and two boys. His court ordered child support is $1,200.00 a month. He lives in a big old three story Victorian house on Argyle Road in Brooklyn, right near where you used to live."

"He might have inherited it from his parents."

"Ron, let me be the detective. I'm not finished. He told me he went to Poly Prep, you know the expensive private school near Dyker Beach Golf Course. He said that he graduated from Princeton."

"So he likes to embellish. That's not a crime."

"Come on. Rockefeller's family like the really rich become doctors and bankers. They don't become cops."

"There is nothing wrong with being in law enforcement," Ron said.

"Especially if you can make it pay! Ron. Scott is a dirty cop! In fact, he's a despicable dirty cop. He deliberately threw me off the track with Barbara. He must have really enjoyed playing with my head." Zangara unbuttoned his shirt collar and loosened his tie.

"Let's assume Scott is corrupt. Where's the connection?" Ron said.

"I've been racking my brain about that. I even spoke to Scott's ex-wife. She lives in terror of him. He beat the shit out of her regularly. She took him to Family Court but always withdrew her motion for an Order of Protection."

"This is all very hard to believe."

"It gets better. He's bragged to her about killing people and told her that she's next! I checked the Surrogate Court files and the City Register. Then I checked the Building Department. His parents left him an estate of $150,000.00 which he had to share with his sister. He bought the house on Argyle Road for $700,000.00 last year, all cash, and then gutted it. He put in a new kitchen and bathrooms. His ex thinks that he's really planning to kill her. This way he gets custody and pays no child support- or maintenance."

"Maybe he has a wealthy girlfriend."

"That's the best laugh of all. Scott's taste in women runs to topless dancers and bimbos."

"What's this invitation to dinner all about?"

"He probably found out that I accessed his personal file," Zangara said. "I have friends in the Department but so does he."

"But why was I included in the invitation?"

"Who knows? Maybe he has an urge to confess," Zangara said. He grinned as if he were waiting for approval of his sarcasm.

"Or gloat. If you're right he was the perfect inside man."

"We told him everything and he fed us misinformation. I feel like a chump, Ron."

"Two chumps, you mean." Ron waved the waiter away. They had no need for the menus.

"You'll come with me?"

"I wouldn't miss this for the world," Ron said.

When they left Orlando's, it was almost seven p.m. It would take them another twenty minutes to reach Scott's home. On the way, Zangara slapped his portable, flashing, light to the top of his car, just for the fun of it.

"Did you bring your gun?" Zangara said. "This might be dangerous." He gave a sidelong glance and smiled.

"I haven't carried a gun in years." Ron said.

"You know Scott was up for the promotion. I even recommended him for it. But I have to confess, it was more out of loyalty than belief. I thought he was a foul up, not a crook."

"I hope we're not jumping to conclusions, Jack. Scott might have won big at the track."

"Ron! The man doesn't gamble. Like his drinking, he only pretends."

"Well, I'll tell you one thing," Ron said. "I'm not eating his linguine and clam sauce!"

C H A P T E R 50

▼

When Ron and Jack arrived at Tom Scott's house, they did not have to ring the doorbell because Scott, smiling with a scotch in hand, opened the door to the double door entrance.

He wore a full size apron, which did not fully conceal his shoulder holster. Embossed on the apron, was the word, "Love."

"You guys are late. The sauce is almost ready."

Ron looked around at the wrap around porch with its fluted columns and balusters. The house was freshly painted and it was evident from the gleaming white of the window frames, that they had been newly replaced.

Scott stepped aside and led the men past the foyer into a central hallway. The ceiling was twelve feet high with cross beams that, like all of the woodwork, was varnished in a matte finish. Sofas and chairs heaped with pillows were set opposite to each other and parallel to a huge wood burning fireplace.

As with everything else in the house that looked just right, but was not, the mantel clock chimed eight times. Ron looked at his watch for confirmation. It was not yet 7:30.

"Help yourself to a drink. The bar is over there in the den." Scott pointed to a portable bar that was filled with liquor bottles and crystal.

"Nice place you have here," Ron said. Neither he nor Zangara moved to the bar.

"Not bad for a cop, eh?" Scott said. "Let me show you the kitchen. That's really my pride and joy."

"I didn't know cooking was your hobby," Zangara said.

"There's a lot of things you don't know about me, Jack." He sipped his scotch.

The kitchen had an industrial size stove with a large overhead copper vent. Above the center island were hung, in various sizes, cooking spoons, ladles and spatulas. A large pot of water was steaming on one burner and a large deep pan was set on another.

The smell of oil and garlic filled the room and seemed to increase as Scott stirred parsley into the sauce. He then threw a dozen little neck clams in and covered the pan.

"Wait until you taste this. Learned it from some Italian friends."

"Fuck your sauce and fuck your Italian friends," Zangara said. "Why did you lie to me about Barbara DiTucci?" His normally sallow face glowed with anger.

"That's not good police procedure, Jack. You taught me that you're not supposed to blow your cool."

"I want to know why, Tom? You had to know damned well that Barbara DiTucci was not involved in the lawsuit."

"Jack, she was too young for you."

"That's not an answer, Tom."

"How about this one? The savvy, old detective takes his apprentice under his wing and then gives him every shitty assignment. I have to tell you the truth, Jack. I became very hostile to you. You're an arrogant man. Why don't you both sit down. It's time to put the linguine in the water." He moved his shoulder holster to the side. "It's not easy cooking with a gun." He gave a smirking laugh.

"And Sarah Baruch?" Ron said.

"You know the real secret is that you have to cover the pan, otherwise the clams won't open."

"I'm waiting for you to open up," Zangara said.

"What do you know about Sarah Baruch?" Ron's voice was soft but insistent. He gazed steadily at Scott.

"You don't want to know about her," Scott said.

"I wouldn't believe a word he says," Zangara said.

"Then why did you come here? You're such a great detective I shouldn't have to tell you anything."

"Why did you lie?" Ron said.

"Everybody lies, Judge. We catch the thieves and judges let them go. So, when the occasion permits, there's nothing wrong with turning a profit, is there?" He lowered the flame under the large pot. The boiling water was steaming up the room. "I don't think you fellows are hungry."

"You're telling me that you're on the take?"

"Jack, you're a real asshole. I admit nothing."

"You're living pretty good for a cop," Ron said.

"How I live is my business."

"Maybe—maybe not," Zangara said.

"No maybes about it partner. The fact is that I'm retiring. I have some time in and I'll get a nice little pension. Not that I'll need it. I've a little private security business that I'm developing. That's where the money is Jack. I'd ask you in but you're really not cut out for private enterprise."

"Seems like the business has been very good." Zangara looked around as if he were appraising the value of the house.

"Jack. You never gave me credit for anything. Don't you think I covered myself with the standard of living bull shit? Did you ever hear of 'Yahoo' or 'Dell' or 'Amazon dot com'?"

"What about them?" Ron said.

"I bought 500 shares of Yahoo at $18.00. It went up to $190.00 and split two for one. Then it went up to $200.00 again. You do the math, Judge. On a $9,000.00 investment, I made $190,000.00! Best of all, I got out in time before the dot coms went belly-up. It's all documented, my friend. Of course, I made a few dollars on other enterprises but I won't bore you with the details." Again, Scott laughed.

"Where did you get the money to play the stock market? Or buy this house for that matter? You're late on your maintenance and child support," Zangara said.

"Little acorns, Jack. You start small. Like you always said about investigations. A piece here and a piece there and everything falls into place."

"I still want to know about Sarah Baruch," Ron said.

"I should really let you stew some more but what the hell, I don't want you to be angry with the wrong person. I tailed her and in no time at all, she leads me to this Vecchio. Turns out, she's married to him. Now, I was really curious. Here was this broad making a play for a judge and keeping company with some strange bedfellows—and I do mean bedfellows."

"What else did you find out?" Zangara said.

"I found out that the judge's sweetheart is a very ambitious lady. She's been fucking for everybody. Vecchio, a low life named Joe Pencils, Andrew Peregrino, and probably the whole Mexican government. Still, I couldn't make the connection. What did she have to do with Mr. Justice Goodman?" Scott paused and sipped his Scotch. He smacked his lips to show that he was savoring both the drink and the moment.

"And?" Ron said.

"The next night, I followed her—she goes straight to the home of…" Scott paused, again. "…the home of Mr. and Mrs. Victor Santo! After that, it was easy to move in on your little darling. Turns out that Baruch is her first husband's name and that her maiden name is Goldberg. Your Sarah is Ruth Santo's sister! Now, doesn't that put two and two together?"

"Why didn't you tell us," Ron said. His tone was slow and halting as if he was suspicious of the information.

"It turns out I have other clients who coincidentally have an interest in all this."

"You're on Peregrino's payroll?" Zangara said.

"That's for me to know and for you to find out."

"Why are you telling us this, now?" Ron said.

"Yeah, why this stupid invitation to dinner?" Zangara said.

"I found out you were checking me out," Scott said. "So I figured you'd be coming around and I may as well beat you to the punch. Besides, it's a flaw I have. I couldn't resist the temptation to let both of you know how stupid you were. Great Judge. Great detective, my ass! Baruch was easy but your little paramour was easier. I found out more about Barbara DiTucci in a couple of days than you did in weeks."

"What else?" Zangara kept his hands in his jacket but his fists were clenched.

"For starters, DiTucci was killed. Those two half-witted weasels we saw in the courtroom, bumped him off. The wife didn't know a thing about it. I couldn't resist planting that seed in your mind, though. You did need a comeuppance, Jack."

"I recommended you for First Grade. Didn't you know that? But even without that, arresting those two button men would have insured your promotion."

"Nah, I'm getting the promotion, anyway. A present for early retirement. Besides, there's no proof. I don't have any and neither do you. Pete and Eugene got greedy. Let's leave it at that." Scott looked at their unsmiling faces. "But I'm not greedy, here's a present for you…"

He took the Rolex from his wrist. "It's inscribed, 'Love, Barbara'. Since she won't speak to you, maybe you can mail it to her."

"You're a real piece of shit," Zangara said.

"And what do you think, your Honor? When Sarah Goldberg Vecchio Baruch gets through with you, you'll either be on Peregrino's payroll or you won't be a judge. I have to tell you, Judge, when I confronted your girlfriend, she thought that I was just a cop. So, she tried to bribe me with her feminine charms but I figured that everyone had visited her like the Grand Canyon, so I made her give me a blow job instead. She was terrific!" Scott put his hand on his crotch.

Ron delivered a long overhead, loping sucker punch to Scott's jaw. Scott crashed into the pots and pans that hung over the kitchen's center island.

He fell to the tiled floor and seemed to bounce before he collapsed. He was dazed but nevertheless, reached for the pistol in his shoulder holster.

Before he could complete the draw, Zangara booted Scott's arm. The pistol spun onto the floor and the follow through of Zangara's kick, staved in two of Scott's ribs.

Blood dripped profusely from Scott's mouth and nose. He managed a grunt of pain from a mouth that no longer closed properly. He sat looking at them and the gun just beyond his reach. After a moment, he dove for the weapon.

Zangara, however, kicked the gun away and straddled Scott. He picked up the pot of boiling water and held it over Scott.

"No! No! Don't do it!" Ron yelled.

Zangara's hands burned from the hot metal handles and when he tried to replace the pot on the stove, it slipped from his hands.

The scalding water spilled on to Scott's face and arms and the pot crashed to the floor.

Scott lay screaming and writhing. When he tried to rise, Zangara moved to the side and stomped on his right wrist. The ulna bone popped through the skin.

"Now, you can really apply for a disability pension," Zangara said.

On the way back to the Courthouse, to pick up Ron's car, it was some time before either spoke.

Finally, Zangara said, "Ron, we broke a few laws tonight."

"Including a jaw." Ron said. Damn. I think I broke a couple of bones in my hand." He shook it vigorously.

"Speaking of thinking, you had better do some thinking about Sarah. Do you have any idea what her game is?"

"I have a pretty good idea," Ron said. "A pretty good idea!"

CHAPTER 51

▼

Ron awoke and for a moment, did not know where he was. He looked at his alarm clock. It was almost 7 o'clock. It was not a good day to be late. He had expected a nightmare-filled night but could not recall dreaming of Sarah at all. It was if he had pushed her from his mind so that he could consider his predicament. There was no longer any doubt that he had been deceived and compromised—but to what extent? Who else was involved? Lentino? Firestone? Best of all, what should he do about it? About what? He could surmise, but speculation was different from accusations. No. He would have to continue their game, whoever "they" were.

Ron dressed quickly and was in his chambers by 8:30 a.m. It would be a busy day, and Ron had anticipated the flurry of activity. Pre-charge conference, summations, charge on the law and finally, the long wait during jury deliberations.

Ron's staff would be in early. The written charge as well as the verdict sheet merely needed the final draft. During the course of a trial, he had transmitted notes to his law clerk, Ann Marie, and had discussed with her the elements of the law that he would explain to the jury in his Charge. The verdict sheet was the most important item that would be supplied to the jury. It was the guide that the law require the jury to follow. First, the jury would determine culpability. The jury was obliged to consider each medical deviation and whether it was a substantial factor in her injuries. Then, who, if anyone, was responsible for Ruth Santo's condition? If that was established, then the jury was to consider the extent of the damages, both past and future. Finally, if it had gone that far in its determination, the jury was to decide the amount, if any, that Victor Santo was to receive for his cause of action for "loss of his wife's services."

Ron was not surprised when his secretary announced that Sarah was in his outer office.

"Tell her that I'm too busy to see her now, Joan."

"She says that it's urgent," Joan said.

"All right, show her in but I want you to stay in the room."

Joan escorted Sarah into the room but Sarah blocked her entrance.

"Ron, I have to see you alone. Please trust me this one time."

It was a rainy morning and her raincoat was wrapped tightly about her waist. Incongruously, she was wearing sunglasses. It gave her the appearance of a secret agent.

Ron nodded to Joan and Sarah closed the door behind her.

Without being invited, Sarah sat in the chair in front of Ron's desk.

"You are not to discuss the Santo case, do you understand?"

"Because it's unethical?" She took off her glasses and wiped her cheek. The tears left a streak in her make-up about her left eye.

"So who gave you the black eye?"

"You had to open the briefcase, didn't you?"

"Stop the nonsense, Sarah! What were you doing with my lawsuit in your briefcase?"

"It wasn't my briefcase. It was Tony's."

Ron stared at her. There was a long moment of silence before he spoke.

"Is he the one that worked you over—or was it the Falcon?"

"I made the mistake and I'm paying for it. Ruth Santo is my sister and I love her very dearly. I'll do anything to get her away from her husband and that environment." Sarah cleaned the make-up away from her eye and revealed the full extent of the discoloration.

"What is it that you want me to understand? That you're trying to blackmail me? And when were you going to spring this on me? Or were you going to use the subtle approach and charm me?" His voice was rising and he struggled to lower it. "The hilarious thing about all this is that I think I know what you want me to do—and I probably would have done it without anyone pressuring me. So, what do you want?"

"It's important that you listen."

"I'll listen but it's going to be very hard to believe anything you say."

"You can decide for yourself," Sarah said.

"Fair enough."

"Ruth was terribly ill. Her life was bad enough before she went to the hospital and then the doctors finished the job. She's entitled to be compensated. These cases cost thousands of dollars to try. Where were we going to get the money? I've already spent a small fortune for my sister's private hospitals."

"You always seemed to have plenty of money!"

"Well, I don't. Not the amount they needed. Tony had to go to his friends to bankroll the case. We've already advanced Firestone forty thousand dollars for experts and daily copy of the trial."

"Who advanced the money?"

"That's not important."

"This Andrew, the Falcon?"

"Yes."

"And your ex, pardon me, your husband, Tony Vecchio, paid Firestone the money for his disbursements?" Ron sat back and laughed.

"Firestone wouldn't continue the case until he was paid."

"Is that what Vecchio told you?" Ron said. "Now that's really funny. These medical malpractice lawyers always lay out the disbursements—otherwise their clients would go to others."

"Are you telling me…?" Sarah's voice trailed off.

"Yes. The con man is being conned. This Falcon pays but Vecchio never delivers the cash to Firestone. From your expression, I take it that Vecchio didn't cut you in for a piece of the pie."

"Tony wouldn't deceive *these* friends," Sarah shook her head.

"Oh, I think he has. Tell me, Sarah. What have you planned for me?"

"I'm sure you've figured it out already. I just want you to know that my feelings for you are real and sincere. In a way, I tried to warn you. Didn't I become angry whenever you spoke of marriage—or commitment? Can't you understand how much I hated myself for deceiving you? I went to Tony's apartment that night to tell him that the whole deal was off—that I had fallen in love with you. I can laugh about it now. How silly I was to think that they would let me out of all this. I may not have told you everything but I never lied to you."

"That's probably the biggest lie you've ever told me!"

"It's all gotten out of hand. Spender's insurance company is bankrupt and the only one with money is the hospital. They were afraid that Dr. DiTucci was going to give devastating testimony exonerating the hospital, so they killed him. I swear I had nothing to do with that."

"All this because you love your sister? What makes you think that the mob won't grab every cent that might be awarded to her?"

"That will never happen," Sarah said. "No one is going to get Ruth's money—except Ruth. That I promise you!"

"What is it that you want from me?" Ron was patient now.

"Ron, I love you. We can have a life together. A wonderful life together."

"What do you want from me, Sarah?" Ron's voice was controlled and without inflection.

"Don't let the jury decide. Rule that, as a matter of law, Beth Torah hospital is responsible for Spender and the hospital staff. There's a case, *Hill v. St. Clare's Hospital* that says…"

"…Yes, I know the case," Ron said. Master and servant. *Respondeat Superior*! A hospital, like any business owner might be responsible for its employees actions, and sometimes that included attending physicians. Although this was not one of those cases, it showed that Sarah had been well briefed.

"You still don't understand the danger you're in! You're so damned naive. For a judge, you're so gullible Ron."

"Yes," Ron said. "Honest persons are gullible. Moral persons are gullible. Scrupulous persons are gullible and all for the same reason. They do not connive, cheat or steal. The only fault with a gullible person is that he finds it difficult to believe evil in others."

"Ron, you have no idea to the extent that you've been compromised," Sarah said. "You can't declare a mistrial, because they'll make it look like you were in on the fix and then changed your mind. They're going to hurt you. At the very least, you'll end up removed from the bench and probably disbarred! Worst of all, they'll hurt you personally—ruin your family. These people have a very long reach. Your daughter Colleen's college friend, is ready to charge Colleen with cheating on an examination."

"That's absurd!"

"No, not if they have that friend testify that Colleen took an examination in her place."

"Sarah, you're such a poor excuse for a human being."

"We were good together, Ron."

"No, I was good with the person you pretended to be."

"Don't throw it all away—please!"

"My daughter, Colleen hates you. Did you know that? She saw through you, immediately. Fathers should listen to their children more often."

"Let's not end like this," she said. "They're making me do this."

"Who's making you do this?"

"Ron. You still have the Mayan calendar?"

"Was that another one of your lies—that there was no trip to Mexico?"

"Of course there was! My God, Ron, you are dense. I went with Andrew Peregrino."

"Scott said you were a very ambitious lady."

"I'm going to need that calendar back. It's on loan."

"You mean I'm not to keep the little trinket as a memento?"

"That's not a trinket. It's really worth $25,000.00. The free trip to Atlantic City for your birthday? The plane fare for your children. The comped rooms, the gourmet dinners. They were all paid for by Tony Vecchio. He has the receipts. You know how anxious they are to criticize a judge. The Judicial Commission will probably require your mother and children to testify—even if you admit it. You think it would be in secret? They'll will make sure the story is leaked to the press! And that isn't all. Your rent controlled apartment that you pay $1,875.00 a month? It's real value is $6,300.00 per month. The building is owned by Byrd Realty, Inc. and the sole stockholder is…"

"…Andrew the Falcon." Ron shook his head at his stupidity. Or was it cupidity? Wasn't he at fault? Wasn't it his obligation to check these things out? He could claim innocence but on reflection he was not free from sin. After all, greed was only a matter of degree.

"They've thought of everything, Ron. Just go along. Even if we no longer see each other, it can all still work. I'm not asking you to do anything outrageous. As you said, you would probably have done it, anyway. Please Ron. I don't want to see you hurt."

CHAPTER 52

▼

As his friend, Justice Donovan had often said, "I don't know whether it's better to have appointed or elected judges, but I do know that it's the ones who have come up through the ranks who have the most common sense."

Now, Ron wondered about that evaluation. He had been elected, had engaged in the rough and tumble of clubhouse politics, survived the struggle for power in the District Attorney's office and he had now demonstrated a singular lack of common sense. He had always been on his guard against undue influence and knew that he, like all judges, was constantly being tested. A small Christmas gift, an invitation to a dinner or tickets to a Broadway show. They were all innocuous in themselves but cumulatively susceptible to partiality. Impartiality! Wasn't that why the lady holding the scales of justice was blind-folded?

This attempt at influence, however, was different. Sarah and her cohorts had intentionally, and by stealth, manipulated him. There was no subtle attempt at bribery but rather a blatant assault upon him. They had laid their trap and waited for Sarah to spring it on him. He was caught. What was the proper course? Judicial ethics required him to report the coercion—it was a bribe, after all. And what about Colleen? Wouldn't they ruin her merely to avenge themselves? Hadn't they coerced Dr. Spender by threatening to kill his wife and frame him? Shouldn't he wait until the whole scenario was played out? Then again, Ruth Santo was gravely ill and not a likely conspirator. If there was a wrong, should she be denied compensation because those around her were thieves? There really was little basis for a dismissal against Beth Torah hospital. Dr. Spender had made sure of that when he testified that a Resident, an employee of the hospital, had participated in an operation that had gone bad.

Ron reviewed his trial notes and it was clear that Lentino had conducted a spirited defense for his client but no appellate court would quarrel with his decision if he ruled that the hospital was responsible—as a matter of law. In Ron's mind that did not exclude Lentino as a conspirator. He could not forget that Lentino had introduced him to Sarah.

The day seemed to start as any other Court day. When he took the bench, he stood and gazed at the lawyers as his clerk intoned the proclamation. He departed from his usual custom. He sat down without greeting them. There would be no "good morning" for anyone.

The audience included several persons whom Ron recognized to be the representatives of Beth Torah Hospital. They had attended the trial intermittently, apparently monitoring the course of the trial. Ruth and Victor Santo had not missed a session. Dr. Spender, on the other hand, was now making one of his rare appearances. He could imagine Christine Fisher chastising her client, "you show up or else! It's show-time and the jury is going to think you don't give a damn. Wake up, because when Firestone gets through with you, the only asset you're going to have left is your goddamn stethoscope!"

Now, and out of the presence of the jury, the lawyers sat expectantly waiting for Ron's legal rulings. These decisions could and did on many occasions terminate a trial or change the focus of a trial. There would be no more witnesses.

"All right, counselors. I'm prepared to hear your motions at the conclusion of the evidence."

Christine Fisher rose first. "Your Honor, on behalf of my client, Dr. Aaron Spender, I move to dismiss on the ground that the plaintiffs have failed to make out a *prima facie* case." Her voice was without conviction, as if acknowledging that she was obliged to make a motion that she knew would fail.

"That's denied," Ron said. "The plaintiffs have established that minimum proof necessary to create a question of fact for the jury to determine culpability as to Dr. Spender."

"Your Honor, as to Beth Torah Hospital, I move to dismiss on the ground that there is no proof that Dr. Spender was employed by the hospital or that the hospital was in any way negligent," Lentino said. Plaintiff's experts never established any departures by the hospital. The testimony was all speculative and not binding on Beth Torah." He turned to the hospital representatives in the audience and shrugged so as to indicate that it was a futile motion.

"Would you like to respond, Mr. Firestone?" Ron said. He glanced toward the spectators. The hospital representatives were somber.

Firestone leaped to his feet. "I sure would, your Honor! Even though Mrs. Santo was not admitted through the ER, the hospital treated Spender as an employee. That puts the case squarely in the *Hill v. St. Clare* category. Also, the hospital allowed its personnel to operate the equipment and assist in the operation. Lastly, the post-op treatment and care was horrible. Considering the actions of Doctors Fugatto, Chang and the rest of the staff, it's clear that the hospital is responsible as a matter of law—and I so move."

"I'm inclined toward Mr. Lentino's original characterization that the hospital's role in this was merely analogous to a hotel," Ron said.

Although Ron had no intention of dismissing the case against the hospital, he relished the crestfallen look of Firestone—who also might be a conspirator.

It was at that moment, when Sarah Baruch walked into the courtroom with Anthony Vecchio. She made little stir as she walked in the front aisle and sat down beside Ruth. Victor Santo moved over to make room for Vecchio. Sarah's coat was open and her close fitting red dress afforded a tantalizing glimpse of her well formed body. It was a stark contrast to Ruth. Now that they were side by side, it was evident that they were sisters, except like two roses, only one of which has been watered, one was in full bloom while the other was withered.

Sarah had been in the courtroom before. Now that she sat beside Ruth Santo for the first time, there was no doubt of the brazenness of her threat.

Ron wondered if the jury had made the connection between her and the plaintiff. Had anyone? Lentino, who acknowledged Sarah by nodding, did not seem surprised.

What was most amazing to Ron was the turnaround in his emotions. It had only been days before when he truly believed that he could not live without her. Yes, love *was* blind and so true was the next line, that no one ever quoted…"*and lovers cannot see the pretty follies that themselves commit.*"

Ron shuffled his papers and adjusted his glasses. There was one firm decision that he had made: He was not going to declare a mistrial. If there was any wrong, it would be solely by him—and he hadn't done any wrong—yet. Could he say, "I'm recusing myself because it develops that I've been sleeping with the plaintiff's sister—but I didn't know the relationship until she tried to bribe me? After all, I did try to rectify the situation by breaking a man's jaw." If there was an ethical violation, it could only be in regard to timely disclosure. If he was a victim, so was Ruth Santo. Ron looked at that frail woman. Could she go through this ordeal—again?

"The motion to dismiss against Beth Torah Hospital is denied." Ron said. "I also deny the motion to hold Beth Torah Hospital responsible, as a matter of law. The jury will determine whether or not the hospital, by its agents, servants and employees, was negligent, and if so, to what extent." Ron looked at Lentino.

Lentino sat there with a poker face, as if he was not unhappy with the adverse ruling. Was Lentino also a conspirator? Was he also a paramour ensnared in one of Sarah's traps. Was it corrupted once, blackmailed forever?

Ron's glance went to Lentino and then back to Sarah. He could not resist repeating, "the motion is denied."

Sarah fixed her stare on Ron, as if to notify Ron that he had just condemned himself.

Vecchio rose and whispered to Sarah.

"A jury question?"

"You really fucked up on this one," Vecchio said. "Andrew's not going to like it."

"What are you going to do? Give me another black eye?"

"I'd be worrying about more than a little slap in the face," Vecchio said.

"And I'd be worrying about anyone who double-crossed Andrew by not forwarding disbursements," Sarah said.

"And I can't wait to hear you boyfriend's charge to the jury. If you had wriggled your ass a little better, we would have been home free by now. *That's* what I'm going to tell the Falcon!"

"Maybe we're all getting upset over nothing, Tony. Goodman's not dumb. Even if the jury decides in favor of the hospital, he can always set it aside as against the weight of the evidence."

"That's what I told you. But does he have the balls to do it?"

"As I said, he's not dumb. He didn't let on when I spoke to him but the key is how we set him up. You should have seen the look on his face when I let him know how they were going to ruin his daughter."

CHAPTER 53

▼

"I don't feel well," Ruth Santo said. "You better take me home."

"It won't be much longer," Victor Santo said.

Ruth sat on the bench in the corridor outside the courtroom. Victor, Sarah, Vecchio and Firestone had situated themselves so that the curious, as well as others, were excluded from their group.

"Did you take your medicine today?" Sarah said. She looked down at her sister. Her voice was accusatory, as if Ruth had to be lectured.

"I ran out of it last night."

"Victor, you shit. Why didn't you go to the drugstore?" Sarah said.

"It was closed by the time I got home and we left this morning before the store was open."

Firestone, not used to being a spectator, shifted his head toward them as if he were at a tennis match but he was more interested in their praise.

"What did you think of my summation yesterday?"

"Maybe Victor should go to the drugstore now?" Sarah said.

"You kidding? It's in Bensonhurst." Victor looked at his watch. It was almost two o'clock. "Can't you hold on a little longer, for chrissake."

"I'll be all right," Ruth said.

"Ruth I need you," Firestone said. "I want you there during the Judge's charge. Did you notice how the jury sneaked a look at you every time I described your condition. I have a good feeling."

"That bitch Fisher made some good points. Lentino sounded like he was on our side, though," Victor said.

"Yeah, he did, didn't he?" Vecchio smiled and shook his head. "Victor, you're such a schmuck."

"I thought that Manny Lentino made a choice," Firestone said. "He figured that Spender was dead in the water, so he tried to put all the blame on him. How did you like my sarcasm when I said: 'some hotel. Beth Torah Hospital wasn't the Plaza it was a 'Bowery flea bag'.'"

"How come your summation was shorter than your opening statement?" Victor said. He adopted the tone of an afficionado.

"One trial and he's a critic," Sarah said.

"The jury's had their fill of the medical testimony," Firestone said. "It's coming out of their ears. I wasn't going to drum it into them. I asked for twenty million dollars. Juries usually give half of what you ask for."

"Then you should have asked for forty million." Victor smiled so that no one would mistake his humor.

"Why don't you run to the drugstore," Sarah said. "We don't need you here."

At two o'clock, the court officer unlocked the courtroom door and directed them to enter. The jury was seated and Ron, carrying his charge book, took the bench.

"Members of the jury," Ron said. "We come now to that portion of the trial where I shall instruct you on the law, after which you will retire for your deliberations." He leafed through the pages of his prepared charge, using it more as a reference than actually reading it. The charge would take approximately an hour as he explained the various principles of law regarding false testimony, interested witnesses, the evaluation of expert witnesses, the burden of proof and the need to exclude sympathy in their deliberations.

"Medical malpractice is medical negligence," Ron stressed. *"And negligence is lack of ordinary care. It relates to doing an act that a reasonably prudent person would have done—or failing to act as a reasonably prudent person. For there to be responsibility, there has to be a connection between negligence and an injury. We call this proximate cause. There is proximate cause when the negligence is a substantial factor in causing the injury."* Ron paused and took a sip of water.

"I have prepared a verdict sheet which you will complete. You will note that for every claimed act of negligence, the next question deals with proximate cause. *The standard by which you will judge responsibility as to Dr. Spender and Beth Torah Hospital, will be whether or not there was a departure from good and acceptable medical practice, at the time of the operation, in our community. You will note that a hospital can only be held responsible through its agents, servants and employees, provided those persons were acting within the scope of their authority.*" He then explained apparent agency and imputed negligence.

Ron looked at the jury. He saw that he was starting to lose them in the complexity of his instructions, but there was no other way. Ron reminded them that they could ask for read-back if their recollection of the evidence failed or if they were unsure of his instructions.

When he began to speak of damages, several of the jurors straightened in their seats.

"*Pain and suffering includes mental anguish and distress, as well as the effects of any physical injury. It also includes the loss of enjoyment of life. That is, the loss of the pleasures of life which the plaintiff can no longer enjoy because of her injury.*"

"You will break down your verdict on damages into several parts. First, as to her pain and suffering from the time of the injury to date. Then for the pain and suffering, if any, including the permanent effect of the injury, which she will endure in the future. In this regard, you will calculate her life expectancy. Ruth Santo is 35 years old and, according to the most recent life expectancy tables, can be expected to live for 42.5 more years. This figure is not binding upon you. It is for you to determine from the evidence you have heard as to her health and habits, what her life expectancy is. The law requires that if you make such an award for future damages, that you advise the court of the number of years damages will be sustained. If you find that Ruth Santo is entitled to recover damages, then you will consider the derivative cause of action for Victor Santo. This action is for the loss of services suffered by Victor Santo. This includes not only the loss of sexual relations, but also compensation for all of the normal duties which have now befallen upon Victor Santo, as a result of the incapacity of Ruth Santo. In the verdict sheet, you will see the same breakdown as to past and future damages. If you find both Dr. Spender and Beth Torah Hospital negligent, you will apportion the degree of fault between the two. Since this is a civil action, your verdict need not be unanimous. When five out of six jurors have agreed on any question, you may report your verdict to the Court."

When the jury retired for their deliberations, the clerk leaned toward the bench, and out of earshot said, "Judge, juror number three brought a calculator with him. Should I take it away?"

CHAPTER 54

▼

The jury deliberated for two days before it reached a verdict. During that time, they asked for read-back of Dr. Timberman's and Dr. Spender's testimony. They also requested a clarification of *proximate cause*, as well as a further explanation of *Respondeat Superior*—that is, the obligation of an employer for the acts of its employees.

On the third day, at 4:45 p.m., Ron called his clerk.

"Bob, the jury has had a long day, let's send them home for the night. Have them report tomorrow at 9 a.m."

"Your Honor, they just asked me if they could work a little late. I think they're close to a verdict."

At 6:15, after everyone had been assembled, the jury filed into the courtroom.

"Will the foreperson please rise," Bob said. His normally booming voice was subdued for this solemn moment. He held a copy of the verdict sheet. "Have you reached a verdict?"

Elliott Lieberman, juror number one rose. "We have." He held the original verdict sheet that had been marked as a court exhibit. Lieberman was a slight, middle aged man, bearded and with a yarmulka atop his thinning hair.

"As to Question #1: Did Dr. Spender cause a perforation? Is your answer 'yes' or 'no'," Bob read.

"Yes," Lieberman said.

"Is the verdict unanimous or five out of six?" Bob said.

Lieberman turned to Ron. "All the answers are unanimous, your Honor."

"As to Question #2: Did Dr. Spender depart from good and accepted standards of medical practice in causing the perforation?"

"Yes."

"As to Question #3: Was this departure a substantial factor in causing injury to Ruth Santo?"

"Yes."

There were smiles but no great show of emotion. The finding of other departures were superfluous. Spender had been found culpable but questions still remained—both as to Beth Torah and, of course, the amount of damages.

Bob kept reading the questions and recording the answers.

The courtroom seemed to become disembodied by the silence preceding the answer to Question #8.

"Did Beth Torah Hospital depart from accepted Hospital practice in the care and treatment of Ruth Santo?"

"Yes," Lieberman said.

"As to Question #9: Was this a substantial factor in causing injury to Ruth Santo?"

"Yes," Lieberman said.

Firestone slammed his fist down in triumph and then turned to his clients. Victor had bounded to his feet and hugged Sarah—not Ruth.

Sarah brushed him away. "Get away from me, you son-of-a-bitch."

Ruth's eyes filled with tears. "At last," she cried. "At last."

"Order! Order!" Bob said.

Ron, who had been noting the answers in his minute book, looked up as if he were surprised by the disturbance. "Continue taking the verdict," he said.

"As to Question #10: What is the amount that you award to Ruth Santo for her pain and suffering, up to the date of the verdict?"

"Two million dollars."

"As to Question #11: What is the amount that you award to Ruth Santo for her pain and suffering, and the permanent effects of the injury, if any, to be incurred in the future?"

"Eight million dollars."

In the next answer, Lieberman indicated that the future damages were to be for the life expectancy of Ruth Santo, which the jury estimated to be sixteen years.

Ron made his own calculation. Damned smart jury. The injury has occurred four years ago. Four plus sixteen multiplied by $500,000.00 equaled the ten million award. Ron looked at his clerk who had paused and nodded for him to proceed.

"As to question #12: What is the amount you award to Victor Santo on his derivative cause of action for loss of services up to the date of your verdict?"

"Five thousand dollars." Lieberman, as had the other jurors, turned to stare at Victor.

"What?" Victor said. He again jumped up to his feet. "That's an insult."

"Shut up you idiot," Sarah hissed and grabbed for Victor. "We got ten million!"

In the excitement, they did not notice the pale look of Ruth. She toppled forward and struck her head on the railing.

Ruth clutched her chest. From her throat came the eerie sound of a death rattle.

Benedict Alston, juror number 4, vaulted the jury box and rushed to her side.

"Get back, give us some room," he said. "I'm a firefighter." Alston pushed everyone away and started mouth to mouth resuscitation. Ruth did not respond.

"Bob, call Security! They have a defribulator team!" Ron said.

"Jurors, please take your seats. Everyone stay back!" the court officer said.

"Dr. Spender! You're a doctor. Help her!" Ron said.

Dr. Spender looked at Ruth's inert body. They weren't going to accuse him of injuring her twice. "She's dead and beyond my help," he said. Spender pushed his way past the crowd and left the courtroom.

Court officers responded to the call and the courtroom was soon filled with personnel.

"I want everyone who is not assisting Mrs. Santo out of this courtroom," Ron said. "Bob, clear this place out right now!"

Neither Mr. Alston nor the court emergency team, however, despite their best efforts, were able to revive Ruth Santo.

Victor assumed a worried pose but his mind was racing. All of his problems were being resolved. He had ten million, without interference from his wife. And he could marry the pregnant Angelina—after a decent interval, of course!

The courtroom was cleared and the jury returned to the jury room. Ruth's body was placed on a gurney and taken from the courtroom.

"Counselors, this Court is not yet adjourned," Ron said.

The lawyers returned to their seats. Stiff and uncomfortable. Was anyone ever prepared to be a witness to the awesome event of death?

"Judge. The jury never answered the last question," Bob said.

"It doesn't matter," Ron said.

"Judge, I move for a mistrial." Christine Fisher was the first to return to lawyering.

"Baloney," Firestone shouted. "We have a verdict. I want it recorded. If there's an unanswered question, then let the jury address it."

The Court Clerk shook his head vigorously. "The questions about future damages for Victor Santo were on the last sheet, your Honor. The pages must have stuck together. The answers are blank!"

That's *de minimis* judge," Firestone said. "Victor Santo withdraws his cause of action for loss of services. We don't want the five thousand!"

"That's quick thinking," Lentino said. "But he can't discontinue a case without consent."

"I'm not consenting," Christine Fisher said.

Ron looked at them and shook his head. He had let them ramble on hardly listening to their arguments. Fate had intervened. There was no longer a victim who required justice.

"Mr. Firestone, as a lawyer, you are the agent of your client. Death terminates the agency," Ron said. "This action has not been completed and the action is abated. In addition, the turmoil in this courtroom has so tainted the jury, that even if the action had not abated, I would be constrained to declare a mistrial on the ground of prejudice. Mr. Alston, juror number 4, behaved heroically but it is hard to imagine his being able to continue to deliberate dispassionately, not to mention the effect on the other jurors."

Victor pushed through the rail gate and seized Firestone.

"Does that mean we don't get the money?" Victor said.

CHAPTER 55

▼

Ruth was buried in Green-Wood, the historic Brooklyn cemetery situated on a knoll overlooking New York Harbor. It was the park-like area where George Washington and his rag-tag army had fought the battle of Brooklyn before retreating across to Manhattan and then escaping into the hinterlands of New Jersey.

The cemetery was surrounded by an eight foot, spiked wrought iron fence, erected more to defend against local vandals than the ghosts of Hessian soldiers.

Elaborate mausoleums and huge angelic statues marked the burial sites of the prominent. Traveling the winding cemetery roads was like touring a pastoral necropolis. It was not as awesome as the Valley of the Kings but the old Sycamores, Oak and Maple trees that dotted the slopes and the vast expanses of grass, evoked a majestic serenity.

The final ceremony was held at the grave site, and despite the beautiful weather, it was lightly attended.

The casket was placed over the open grave. Wooden planks bordered the pit and covered with a grass carpet, as if to lessen the shock of seeing raw earth.

Angelina, together with her parents, were there, both as witnesses and reminders for Victor to "do the right thing."

Tony Vecchio held Sarah's arm and appeared suitably solemn. The elder Mr. and Mrs. Santo held the hands of their grandchildren, Amelia and Rosario. Ruth had been a fine daughter-in-law, "almost Italian", Victor's parents had often said.

Victor, dressed in a black suit and tie, appeared nervous rather than distraught. He kept turning around repeatedly as if he expected a knife to his back at any moment.

"What's the matter with you?" Joe Pencils said.

"Joe, I got to see the Falcon. I can't go on like this."

Angelina, her coat now much too small for her belly, stood on the other side of the casket and away from Sarah, who was looking at Angelina, malevolently.

"They aren't going to do anything here," Pencils said.

"It wasn't my fault, I don't care what they say," Victor said.

"Who says it was?"

"There's been talk! Six Fingers told me that a lot of guys are disappearing."

"Victor, let me tell you something. Six Fingers has his own problems—and so do a few others." Pencils nudged Victor and tossed his head in the direction of Sarah and Vecchio.

The funeral director handed long stemmed roses to each of the mourners.

Angelina, followed by several others, placed her flower on Ruth's casket and walked passed Sarah.

"I didn't want it this way," Angelina said.

"I hope your little bastard strangles coming out of your..." Sarah said.

Angelina hesitated for only a moment before she leaped at Sarah and seized her by the throat.

Sarah struck back and snatched Angelina's hair.

Angelina released her grip on Sarah and turned, instinctively, to protect her abdomen. Sarah, however, did not let go and pushed Angelina to the ground.

"Victor, my baby!" Angelina shouted.

Victor looked around but it soon became apparent to him that no one was going to help him.

"What is this, gang-up on Victor, time?" he said.

In a rage, Victor shoved Sarah with such force that they both stumbled over the wooden planks. The planks gave way and Victor and Sarah both tumbled into the grave.

Sarah, deep in the pit, held up her hands, but could neither escape the cascading soil that threatened to bury her nor the edge of a plank that sliced into her face.

Victor almost made it out, but by latching himself onto the casket to boost himself out, he caused the heavy coffin to plunge into the grave at a precipitous angle.

Victor's scream of pain was far louder than Sarah's muffled shriek as the coffin, like a battering ram, struck him. Only Victor, above the din, could hear the crunching sound of his legs breaking.

Accident or providence. Ruth had exacted her final revenge.

Joe Pencils, as the emissary of the Falcon, joined them in the ambulance.

Victor, despite his agony, was laughing hysterically.

"Joe, now I don't have to worry about Six Fingers. I don't have to worry about the Falcon. How many times can they break my legs?"

"What about me, Joe?" Sarah said.

Pencils looked at her lacerated face. The slash was so deep and embedded with dirt that it was obvious that extensive plastic surgery would be required.

"You'll be all right once we get to the hospital," Pencils said and looked away.

"I didn't mean it that way, Joe."

"Andrew wants you and Vecchio to take a trip to Colombia. Has a deal he wants you to work on."

"He holding me responsible for Tony? I want to see him."

"The Falcon was very explicit. You're to do what you're told."

"Tony cheated him. It wasn't me."

"You did screw up, Sarah."

"So he hands out a death sentence for that?"

"Why you talking like that? You been to Mexico. Now you go to Colombia. That's all."

CHAPTER 56

▼

The entranceway to Andrew Peregrino's home in Bay Ridge was elaborate as if to proclaim his importance in his domain. The huge oak door, carved and ornate with its overhead, pseudo—colonial glass window, was sheltered by a portico supported by Doric columns.

Before Zangara could ring the doorbell, the door seemed to magically open.

"Where's the butler?" Zangara said.

"Come on in, flatfoot," the Falcon said. His smile was congenial but nevertheless, he looked both ways. He fixed his eyes on a parked car.

"I'm here alone," Zangara said. "Nobody else from my side. Those two bozos sitting in the Cadillac are yours."

"I never worry about the guys I can see," the Falcon said. He was in shirt-sleeves and his thin striped tie was tightly knotted. He led Zangara past the marbled center hallway into the library.

"When do you have time to read?" Zangara said sarcastically. The room, except for the several busts of ancient Romans, was lined from floor to ceiling with expensively bound books. His desk was cluttered with what appeared to be legal papers.

He gestured to Zangara to sit in one of the armchairs that were situated by the desk, but Zangara remained standing.

"You're very funny, Zangara. I went to Brooklyn Law School for two years before they kicked me out."

"For cheating, of course."

"Why are you disrespecting me?"

"Cut the crap, Peregrino. The next thing you'll be telling me is that we're the same because we're both Italian."

"I invited you to my home. I didn't agree to meet you on the street. I didn't ask you if you're wearing a wire. I showed you respect."

"The only people wearing wires these days are your own people," Zangara said. He laughed and then shrugged.

"What did I ever do to you?"

"It's not only what you did, but who you are."

"I am what I am. You didn't ask for this meet so that you could change me. So tell me what I did that has you so upset. After what you did to my top button man, I should be mad at you. You put him out of business. His face is so scarred, you can spot him a mile away. His right hand is useless and he can't hold a gun, anymore."

Zangara traced his fingers across the neck of the marble bust of Marcus Aurelius. "I'm not finished with Scott, yet."

"As you said, let's cut the crap. I know why you wanted to see me. You're here to beg for the Judge." He sat back in his own high backed judge's chair behind his desk. He took out a cigar and bit off an end. "I have him in my pocket, so why should I let him go? This last case didn't work out but maybe the next case-or cases will be easier. Now that I think of it. I can make it worth both your whiles. You can be the middleman. Maybe line up a few more judges."

"You don't have him in your pocket and you know it. Let's not bull shit each other, ok?"

"You can't blame a guy for trying," Peregrino said. He smiled and fingered his cigar.

"I must say, you were pretty tricky."

"Am I getting signs of appreciation?" Peregrino said.

"Grudgingly. But you were out of your league on this one. I don't know why you even tried."

"Who was it that said, 'you can't cheat an honest man'? But you never know until you try, do you?"

"So this was all a bluff, wasn't it?"

"I wouldn't say that. Your Judge Goodman might be honest but he sure as hell was quick to take bargains!"

"I'm figuring that Judge Goodman doesn't have to be concerned about anyone dropping a dime on him—ever! Am I right?"

"Come on Zangara. I terrorize. That's my modus operandi. I don't rat on anybody. But I should get something for putting the Judge's mind at rest."

"I'll send you a copy of my report."

"You have to be joking," Peregrino said. "What trick you up to now?"

"You can't believe that I came to your home without first advising my boss, do you? You have more agencies watching you than fleas on a junk yard dog. Officially, I'm investigating multiple homicides."

""I hear Pete and Eugene are a part of the new Convention Center," Zangara said.

"Who can stop rumors?" Peregrino said. He raised his arms as if he were beseeching a deity for help.

"Rumors have a way of becoming true," Zangara said.

"Wait a fucking minute! Now I get it! You're not here for Goodman. You're here for Scott! You want me to do your dirty work for you."

"I can't prove it yet, but I've been known to hound people until they're brought to justice. Maybe when I bring down Scott, he'll take you with him."

"You know, sometimes I think we're in the same business," Peregrino said. "I use the same technique. It's called, 'intimidation'."

"Think what you want," Zangara said.

Peregrino returned Zangara's stare with a nod and a smile, as if to acknowledge a stalemate.

Zangara walked toward the door. "I'll let myself out," he said.

"Be careful of the high front step. You might trip."

"Don't worry about me," Zangara said. "You have to worry about tripping yourself up."

"You're some comedian," Peregrino said.

Joe Pencils waited until Zangara had left before opening the library door.

"You heard?" Peregrino said.

"Yeah."

"Zangara is one smart cop. He's just made me sign Scott's death warrant."

"What do you mean?"

"He made Scott a loose end. A broken tool." Peregrino rocked in his high backed chair.

Joe laughed. "Yeah, he is broken, really."

"It's not funny, Pencils. I want you to take care of it personally."

"Christ, Andrew. I haven't hit anyone in years. I'm getting too old for that shit!"

"Do it, goddamn it! And take Victor along with you." Peregrino leaped from his chair as if he were going to vault over his desk. "I'm getting sick and tired of everybody fucking up!"

Joe Pencils recoiled and knocked against the bust of a *Marcus* Aurelius. The statue tilted on its column but Joe caught and steadied it.

"Andrew, I'm not disrespecting you, but Victor is a damned tailor!"

"That's the whole point, Joe. You go to Scott's house with a couple of the boys and it'll end up in a shoot out," Peregrino said calmly, as if his burst of anger had been purely for effect. "You go to Scott's house with Victor and it's a social call. Don't even tell the idiot. Once it's done, we'll have another hold on him."

"Killing a cop is going to bring a lot of heat."

"You took the word right out of my mouth, Joe, *heat*," Peregrino said. He sat back and lit his cigar. "Take Scott to our friend, Pandolfo's Funeral Home for immediate cremation. No body, no crime."

"Andrew, you're a genius."

"Yes, I know," Peregrino said.

CHAPTER 57

▼

The sunlight was sharp and definite as it marked both the brightness of the day and the first days of summer.

"I'm glad you're here, Jack. I have some unfinished business," Ron said.

"I'm supposed to be at Dyker Beach Golf Course right now." Jack Zangara looked at his watch. It was 9:15 in the morning. He paced back and forth in Ron's chambers. "All you have to do is make one lousy phone call."

"Can't do it, Jack," Ron said. "Everyone has to serve on jury duty. Even our Chief Judge has served."

"What lawyer in his right mind would pick a cop?"

"We've had judges in this Courthouse who have served on jury duty. Besides, since when are you playing golf?"

"I needed a hobby." Jack shook his head. "Cold showers weren't doing the trick."

"Still haven't gotten Barbara DiTucci out of your system?"

"No. I don't think I ever will."

"I guess I was lucky. There was little for me to regret," Ron said.

"And everything for me."

"Sit down Jack. You're wearing out the carpet. I want your opinion on this." Ron took a paper from under his desk blotter and handed it to Jack.

Zangara looked at the paper and shook his head. "You're such a Boy Scout! Does everything have to be by the book? Don't you ever give yourself a break?"

The letter was addressed to the State Commission on Judicial Conduct and set forth the details of Ron's involvement in the case of *Santo vs. Spender and Beth Torah Hospital.*

"I can't make accusations against any lawyer because I have no proof but I did accept gifts that compromised me. It doesn't matter that I was innocent. Judicial ethics still requires me to report the bribe—not the taking of one."

"You moving back to Brooklyn, aren't you?"

"Yes, but…"

"…No buts. This is all bull shit. How can you take a bribe when you don't know it's one?" Zangara tore the letter in half and then for emphasis, tore it in half again.

"That was a copy."

"Ron, forget it. You have exactly nothing to worry about. I made some private inquiries and straightened out some crooked people. You don't have to worry about Colleen, Sarah or anyone else.

"What exactly did you do, Jack?" Ron stared at Zangara. "I get the feeling that you're getting me into more hot water."

"That, I would never do! I might have set some things in motion, but that's it. Look, we're rid of some vermin in this town and best of all, I have a new partner. Scott vanished before Internal Affairs could question him about his injuries. Ronnie, you can't lead a perfect life. It can't be done, my friend."

"I'm not as perfect as you think, Jack. I can't help thinking that I profited from someone's death."

"That I don't get," Zangara said.

"Jack, I can't honestly say what I would have done if the jury had found the hospital not responsible. I think that I might have set the verdict aside. I would die for my daughter—and I would lie for her, and that includes violating my oath of office!"

"Now you don't have to do that. So, why create a scandal? I don't care if you call it luck or God's will, you're home free."

Ron looked out the window. Was anything ever as it seemed? The sun was warm and few clouds punctuated the sky. In the street below, he saw a woman with a parasol. Was it elegance or just some mentally disturbed person moving through a chaotic life?

"It's a beautiful day, but you're not playing golf today, Jack!"

"You can do me this one favor, Ron. I deserve at least that." Zangara was annoyed. He was going to break 100 for the first time. He could feel it.

"Not everyone gets what he…" Ron paused for the briefest moment. "…or she, deserves."

"Sometimes they do. How about Victor and Sarah Baruch? Their being thrown into a grave had to be an intentional act of God!"

"I wasn't referring to a physical accident, Jack. I wonder whether our effort to achieve justice is achieved in spite of us."

"I don't know what the hell you're talking about, Ron!"

"I guess what I'm trying to say is, do we only achieve justice by accident?"

"I want to play golf, not discuss morality! But I tell you, Ronnie, one way or another, they'll all get what they deserve—and we don't have to wait for judgment day. Even guys like the Falcon are eventually taken down, either by us or the Feds, then he'll be replaced by someone like that Joe Pencils. And he'll be replaced by a Russian or a Colombian or an Asian. Who knows? But what we do isn't an accident. We just keep the toilets working so that the shit doesn't overwhelm us."

"Now you're talking like a cop, Jack. Being immersed in crime, every day, is not good for your psyche. Spend a few days on jury duty. Watch your fellow jurors and democracy at work. You'll make a terrific juror on a civil trial. You might even be chosen for one of my malpractice cases. You'll find that everyone in the world is not a crook or a faker."

"Just what I need," Zangara said. "A pep talk."

"Jack, I need you here for another reason. I don't have any proof but I'm going to confront Manny Lentino. He's due here any minute."

"He won't talk in front of me," Zangara said.

"No, I just want him to see you. I'm going to make him as uncomfortable as possible. Wait for me in my outer office."

When Lentino arrived, Ron ushered him into his chambers and closed the door behind them.

Ron did not shake Lentino's hand but he did motion him to sit in the chair by his desk.

"Mr. Lentino, I find that despite public opinion, lawyers as a group, are overwhelmingly honest. When they do cheat, it's usually on behalf of their clients. The most despicable act for any lawyer is to betray his client." Ron stared at Lentino.

"You making an accusation against me, Judge," Lentino smiled as if to say, "prove it!"

"You did introduce me to Sarah Baruch."

"That's true," Lentino said.

"Well?"

"Judge, I think you're jumping to conclusions."

"If I'm wrong, tell me."

"I introduced you to Sarah Baruch but she set me up, too. I found out late in the trial that she was Ruth Santo's sister. Meanwhile, I see this great romance going on. What was I supposed to do? I told my people about it and we agreed that if we told you, then you might declare a mistrial. But if we didn't tell you—then at the end of the case, if we lost, we could move to set aside the verdict. It was a win-win situation for us. I must admit, Sarah did approach me. She hinted that your big love affair was going to end with the case and that I was next in line for her favors."

"So you were waiting to see if I was corrupt, weren't you!"

"Judge, they were never going to see a nickel of our money. Face it. Even if Spender was at fault, we were only dragged in because we had the deep pockets."

"I don't like you, Mr. Lentino."

"To tell you the truth, Judge, I don't like you either. I think you're priggish and sanctimonious." He turned to leave and then added, "But then neither of us are in the business to be liked. Are we?" Lentino smiled his big toothy smile.

Zangara watched as Lentino sailed passed him.

"How did it go?" Zangara said. A happy Lentino had to mean an unhappy Ron.

"I'm a world class dummy," Ron said.

"I didn't want to say anything," Zangara said, "but you were naive with Sarah Baruch."

"And you weren't with Barbara DiTucci?"

"The difference was that Barbara was honest. It was my cop mentality that screwed me up. With me, it was warped suspicion not being naive."

"Jack, everyone thinks that a judge is above mistakes. I make them all the time. Christ. I'm not perfect! Never said I was. I'm human and that makes me capable of being foolish. They have a school for law but there's no school for controlling gonads. Sure, I was naive. I *wanted* her to love me. I was a stupid lonely man who happens to be a judge. And I'll tell you something else. It's unethical to manipulate the jury pool. The power to call one for jury duty can sometimes be used as a punishment."

"Big deal. It seems like I'm the one being punished."

"So you want me to add another ethical violation to the list?"

"No. Just help a friend," Zangara said. His tone indicated complete defeat.

"I have," Ron said. "My friend just doesn't know it yet."

Ron picked up his robe and turned his back to Zangara.

"Help me on with my robe."

"This is democracy?" Jack guided Ron's arms into the robe.

"It sure is," Ron said. "I'm going to give you a lift down to the main jury room in the Judges' private elevator." He permitted himself a small laugh.

The Jury Assembly room was a huge room that was fitted with rows of benches designed to accommodate up to 500 prospective jurors.

When Zangara arrived and checked in, all of the seats were already taken and he was obliged to stand.

To the front, and on a small platform, the Jury Clerk announced the procedure for jury selection. Names on small jury cards would be selected from a drum, as in a bingo game and thereafter a juror would report, if it were a criminal trial, to a designated courtroom. They would be interrogated by a Judge and then by lawyers to determine their suitability for a particular case. If the case was a civil case then the juror would report to a small jury empaneling room where the selection process would be conducted by the lawyers alone.

The Jury Clerk with one hand, gripped the microphone while the other reached in and extracted a small jury card.

"Hilda Nieves, report to Jury Room number four." His voice boomed out the loudspeaker. The Clerk was a fat, balding man who spoke with practiced authority. "Nieves?" He waited until a woman raised her hand. He then dipped into the drum, again.

"Kenneth Jorgenson, report to Jury Room number four."

Television sets were mounted on the walls, but during the call for jurors, they were muted. There was nothing to do but listen for your name to be called.

As names were called, seats became vacant. When one was available, Zangara moved down the side aisle to take a seat.

He saw Ron by the entrance door and waved. Ron was going to get him off of jury duty, after all!

Ron, however, ignored Jack Zangara. Instead, he mounted the platform and whispered to the Clerk.

The Clerk nodded and palmed several jury cards.

"Jack Zangara, report to Jury Room number four."

The Clerk glanced at the other card and his voice again boomed over the loud-speaker.

"Barbara DiTucci, report to Jury Room number four."

978-0-595-39636-8
0-595-39636-4

Printed in the United Kingdom
by Lightning Source UK Ltd.
114234UKS00001B/256